LAURA LEE GUHRKE

The Marriage Bed

An Avon Romantic Treasure

AVON BOOKS
An Imprint of HarperCollinsPublishers

AVON BOOKS
An Imprint of HarperCollins*Publishers*
10 East 53rd Street
New York, New York 10022-5299

First Avon Books paperback printing: July 2005

Avon Trademark Reg. U.S. Pat. Off. and in Other Countries, Marca Registrada, Hecho en U.S.A.
HarperCollins® is a registered trademark of HarperCollins Publishers Inc.

Printed in the U.S.A.

10 9 8 7 6 5 4 3 2 1

Chapter 1

London, 1833

When those in society talked about Lord and Lady Hammond, there was one conclusion about the viscount and his wife no one bothered to dispute: They couldn't stand each other.

This dictum was mentioned in drawing room conversations with the same unquestioning certainty given to English rain and Irish trouble. Gossips could only speculate about the reasons that had divided the couple only six months after their wedding, but eight years later, Lady Hammond had not provided her husband with the customary heir, the pair lived thoroughly separate lives, and even the greenest hostess alive knew *never* to invite them to the same dinner party.

Despite the lack of a direct heir to the viscountcy, the marital estrangement of Lord and Lady Hammond showed no signs of being breached by either party. Until the fifteenth of March 1833. That was the day a letter changed everything, at least as far as the viscount was concerned.

The missive came by express, reaching Hammond's London residence about eleven o'clock in the evening. The viscount, however, was not at home. Since it was the midst of the London season, John Hammond, like most men of his social position, was out about town, engaged in the unholy trinity of male excess: drinking, gambling, and skirt-chasing.

His friends, Lord Damon Hewitt and Sir Robert Jamison, were happily assisting him in these endeavors. After several hours at their favorite gaming hell, they arrived at Brooks's just before midnight. Once there, they proceeded to empty their sixth bottle of port as they discussed where to spend the remainder of their night.

"I say, Hammond, at some point during the evening we have to go to Kettering's ball," Sir Robert said. "Just for an hour or two. Lord Damon and I both promised Lady Kettering we would be there, and you know how she is if you don't show. Makes a terrible fuss. We have to make an appearance at least."

"Then I shall be forced to take leave of you before then," John replied and poured himself a glass of port from the decanter on the table. "Viola was invited to Kettering's ball and accepted the invitation. Therefore, I was impelled to decline.

You know my wife and I never appear at the same functions."

"No gentleman appears at the same functions as his own wife, Sir Robert," Lord Damon explained to their younger companion. "Besides, it would be wise if Hammond steered clear. Emma Rawlins will be there, and the fur would surely fly."

John almost wanted to laugh at that. His last mistress was not likely to create any emotion in his wife other than more of the same disdain she had displayed toward him for years. A sad end, given the adoring young woman he'd married. But marriages were seldom happy, and he had long ago given up any stupid notions that his would be one of the few to beat the odds.

"Mrs. Rawlins is a pretty creature," Sir Robert added. "You might see her and regret putting an end to that amour."

John thought of Emma's possessiveness, the smothering possessiveness no mistress had the right to claim, and which had caused him to terminate their arrangement two months before and pay off her contract. "I doubt it. The end was not amicable." He swirled his glass and took a swallow of port. "I believe I am done with women for a while."

"You always say that!" Damon laughed. "It never lasts for long. When it comes to women, you are a Turk, Hammond. You should have a harem."

"One woman at a time is enough, Lord Damon!

My last two mistresses have given me reason enough to be soured on romance."

His mistress prior to Emma, the opera singer Maria Allen, had gotten him shot in a duel two years earlier by her husband. Allen, after years of neglecting his wife, had suddenly decided her affairs with other men bothered him. The two men had each put a bullet into the shoulder of the other and honor had been satisfied. The reconciliation of the Allens had not been happy. He had eventually taken off for America, and she was now Lord Dewhurst's mistress.

Emma Rawlins, however, did not seem inclined to finding herself a new protector. She had been writing to him at weekly intervals from the cottage he had given her in Sussex, letters chiding him, scolding him, and begging him to come back to her. His replies of polite refusal had not satisfied her, however, and she had followed him to London, but he had no intention of seeing her.

In fact, since breaking from Emma, John found himself at loose ends. He was not inclined toward a new mistress, and his reason was difficult to define. A man's relationship with his mistress, to his way of thinking, ought to be simple, straightforward, and purely physical. It so seldom turned out that way, and perhaps that was the reason for his reluctance. He had no desire to become involved in another imbroglio, for he hated emotional scenes. Always had.

John did not express these feelings to his friends, however, and his friends, being gentlemen, did not inquire. If they had, he would have sidestepped their questions with a witty remark or a change of subject.

"No, my friends," he said, shaking his head. "Women are charming, intriguing creatures, but they are also expensive in many different ways. I intend to go without a mistress this year."

"The entire year?" Lord Damon made a sound of disbelief. "And it is only March. This has to be another one of your jokes. You love the ladies too much to do without a mistress for the entire year."

John leaned back in his chair and lifted his glass. "Just because a man doesn't have a mistress, it doesn't mean he isn't loving the ladies."

His companions got a good laugh out of that comment and deemed it worthy of his toast. The three charged their glasses, then decided anything less than several toasts to the loving of ladies was a disservice to the fair sex. Within five minutes the bottle was empty.

"Look you, Hammond," Lord Damon said, his voice suddenly serious, quieting their merriment. "Isn't that footman at the door one of yours?"

John looked up, following his friend's glance. Sure enough, framed in the doorway and scanning the crowded room with an anxious expression was one of his own servants. Catching sight of him, the lad hurried forward and held out a letter. "Come from the north, my lord. It being an express, Mr. Pershing sent me out at once to find you."

Correspondence sent by express almost always conveyed bad news, and John thought at once of Hammond Park, his Northumberland estate. But when he glanced at his own name and direction written on the outside of the folded sheet of paper, he was startled to discover that the handwriting was not that of his steward. It was from Constance, his cousin's wife, and that meant whatever bad news was contained in the letter was a family matter. His apprehension deepened as he broke the seal and unfolded the single sheet.

It contained only four lines, the ink smudged with tears. The news was even more disastrous than he could have imagined. Yet as he stared at the words, reading them again and again, he was unable to quite grasp their meaning. He felt numb, dazed, unable to accept what he read. It simply could not be.

Percy. Oh, God. Percy.

Pain sliced through the numbness. He tried to focus on what this news meant, what he had to do, but all he could think about was that he had let an entire year slip away without seeing his cousin and best friend, and now it was too late.

"Hammond?" Lord Damon's concerned voice broke into his reverie, and John came to his senses. He folded the letter and put it in his pocket. Fighting to keep his countenance neutral, he looked at the footman waiting anxiously by his elbow. "Have my carriage brought 'round at once."

"Yes, my lord."

The footman departed, and his friends continued to study him with concern. Neither asked him what the problem was, but the question hung in the air. John did not enlighten them. He picked up his glass and downed the last of his port, fighting hard to regain the numbness of a moment before.

Later, he told himself, shoving pain aside. He would grieve later. Just now, he had to think of the effect this news would have on his estates. The estates had to come first. They always came first. He shoved back his chair and rose. "Gentlemen, I fear I must leave you. Urgent business calls me away. Forgive me."

Without waiting for either man to reply, John bowed, turned away from the table, and left the room. By the time he reached the street, his carriage was waiting, and he instructed his driver to journey first to his town house in Bloomsbury Square.

Half an hour later his valet, Stephens, was packing his things for the journey to Shropshire, and John was on his way to Kettering's ball. Viola had to be told of this news.

The encounter was likely to be a difficult one. His wife had always been a woman of deep passions, and her strongest passion was her loathing for him. It was a feeling she made abundantly clear at every infrequent encounter they had, her demeanor toward him as frigid as the depths of the sea. Her life would be affected by the news he had just received in a way she was sure to abhor.

He knew that his arrival at Kettering's ball would no doubt cause a stir, for he and Viola did not even bother to pretend their marriage had meaning. It was an empty union, and had been for over eight years. That was all about to change, he vowed as he paused in the doorway of Lord Kettering's ballroom.

Despite the crowd that filled the glittering room and the fact that his wife was a small woman, John caught sight of her easily. She had on a ball gown of deep pink silk, but had she not been wearing her favorite color, he would still have spied her almost at once. Even after so many years of separate beds and separate lives, he could always find Viola in any crowd.

It was her hair, of course. It gleamed in the candlelight of the chandeliers overhead, and as always, its brilliant, golden color made him think of sunlight.

She was turned away from him, and he could not see her face, but that did not matter. He knew every inch of it—the heart shape, the wide hazel eyes and thick brown lashes, the pretty mouth with that tiny mole at the corner, the dimple in her right cheek when she smiled. He didn't know why he should remember that, since it had been many, many years since she had last smiled at him, but he did remember it. Viola had a smile that could make the heavens open. She also had a frown of such scorn, it could send a man straight to hell. John had been to both destinations more than once.

All the guests were engaged in the dancing or in observing of it, and it took a bit of time for his arrival to be noticed. When it was, the quadrille turned into something of a mess, for the dancers became too occupied with staring at him to pay attention to the intricate steps, and after a few moments the musicians gave up playing. Conversation faded to an awkward silence, then murmurs of shocked speculation began to circulate the room. All inevitable reactions, John supposed, for it had been years since Lord and Lady Hammond had appeared at the same social event.

He watched as his wife turned in his direction, and he caught his breath, stunned as always by the sheer beauty of her face and the perfection of her figure. Though it was nearly a year since he had last laid eyes on her, she looked exactly as he remembered.

He watched the delicate color in her cheeks fade to a chalky white at the sight of him, and though schooled in social graces all her life, she was appalled by his arrival and unable to conceal it.

When he started in her direction, however, she had no choice but to recover her poise and play her part as his viscountess in front of all these people. He paused in front of her, and she greeted him with the scrupulous, icy politeness characteristic of their infrequent meetings over the years.

"Hammond," she said with a curtsy.

He bowed in return. "Lady Hammond," he answered, taking the gloved hand she held out. He touched his lips to her knuckles through the fabric, then released her hand and turned so she might take his arm.

She hesitated, but after a moment, placed her hand on his arm. It was the barest touch, but enough. In view of society, she had to play the compliant wife, and both of them knew it, but in private Viola was seldom compliant. One of the privileges of being a duke's sister.

Her brother stood nearby, and John could feel the hostile gaze of the Duke of Tremore on him like the blasting heat of a coal furnace. But when he greeted the other man, his brother-in-law's demeanor was as cold as Viola's had been. No wonder. Tremore viewed his baby sister as an angel. John was in a position to know better. Viola might look as if she should have a halo over her head, but her nature was a very human one indeed.

Tremore, in John's opinion, had been most fortunate in his own choice of wife. Though not the most beautiful of women, the duchess was one of the most placid, tactful ladies of his acquaintance, and her demeanor was far less hostile than her husband's. "Hammond," she said, holding out her hand.

"Duchess." He bowed over her gloved fingers. "You look well," he added as he straightened. "I was gratified to hear your son came into this world healthy and strong."

"Yes, and that was nearly ten months ago," Tremore answered for her through clenched teeth, underlining the fact that since the child's birth, John had never once come to see his nephew. He had not even gone to the christening.

John, being a man possessed of both his common sense and his sanity, never put himself through visits with his brother-in-law if he could help it. "A strong, healthy child is a blessing for any man," he said. "And a son ensures that your estates are secure. Duke, you are a most fortunate man."

John's own lack of an heir was a point not lost on Tremore, who looked away. Feeling Viola's hand tighten on his arm, John allowed her to pull him away from the duke and duchess.

"Why are you here?" she demanded in an angry whisper as they walked arm in arm along one side of the room.

"For a reason that cannot be explained in whispers at a crowded ball. Smile, Viola, or if you cannot manage it, at least be polite. Everyone is staring at us."

"If it bothers you to be stared at, you could just leave," she suggested. "I am sure there are many places in London that would be far more amusing for you. Besides, showing up at Kettering's ball after declining the invitation is the height of bad taste."

They passed a pretty redhead in pale green silk, who gazed at him with imploring eyes. Though John pretended he had not seen her, Viola immediately assumed the worst.

"So Emma Rawlins is your reason for being here?" she said. "The gossips have been speculating for weeks that you ended it with her, but they were obviously wrong. God," she choked, "how you must enjoy humiliating me."

"I live for it," he answered at once, her contempt having its usual affect on him—impelling him to employ his most sarcastic wit. "I pull the wings off of flies, too. Though, I confess, torturing helpless kittens is my favorite. Truly good sport, that."

She let out her breath in an angry huff and started to pull away from his side, but he would not let her. He crossed his arm over his chest, using his free hand to grip hers and hold her to his side. He was keeping tight rein on his own emotions, striving not to think about the letter in his pocket, striving to keep his pain at bay. A quarrel with Viola would send him over the edge.

"Stop trying to pick a fight with me and listen," he murmured. "I have business in the North and need to leave at first light, business I must discuss with you ere I go. I have to speak with you in private."

"Have a private meeting with you? Not a chance of it."

She stared to pull away again, and he tightened his grip. "It is important, Viola. Very important, and it involves you."

She turned her head and studied him for a moment, then gave a reluctant nod. "Very well, but you will have to wait. I am engaged for the next dance. Let go of me."

She pulled against his hold again, and this time he released her. Bowing, John watched her walk away. The rigid set of her shoulders made him appreciate yet again the depth of her animosity for him. He thought of the letter in his pocket and what it meant, and hoped she did not loathe him beyond all amendment. If she did, his life had just become a living hell.

Why had he come? The question kept running through Viola's mind as she moved through the steps of the dance. She felt off balance, baffled, uneasy. It had been years since John had felt the need to discuss anything with her. What was there for them to talk about now? And why tonight?

As she danced with her partner, she kept glancing around the ballroom, her gaze seeking him out in the crowd, unable to quite believe he was really here. Yet his presence was not her imagination. He'd said that important news had brought him here, but as usual, she could discern nothing by his face or demeanor. He stood amid a group of people, talked and smiled and looked as if he hadn't a care in the world, though Viola knew from long and bitter experience that if that were so, he would be anywhere but here. And there had been something tense and hard in his voice, which was uncharacteristic of his usual careless air.

She turned her attention away from her husband and tried to concentrate on simply getting through the steps of the dance. She should know by now that any attempts to understand John or his actions were useless. A hint of the old pain twisted in her heart, and that surprised her, for she thought she had vanquished that long ago.

She fought to regain the icy composure that had served her for so long, the protective shell that shielded her from the pain of his lies and his women, but her uneasiness grew with each passing moment until it became an almost unbearable tension. She could hear the buzzing hum of speculations about his presence all around her and feel the astute gazes of London's greatest gossips glancing back and forth among herself, her husband, and Emma Rawlins. By the time the quadrille ended twenty minutes later, she was a mass of jangled nerves.

She had barely returned to her place beside her

brother Anthony and his wife Daphne before her husband was there to take her arm again. Amid the astonished stares and whispers, Viola and John left the ballroom together.

He took her into Kettering's library and closed the doors behind them. Thankfully, he did not keep her in suspense any longer. The moment the doors were closed, he turned toward her and came to the point. "Percy is dead. So is his son."

Viola sucked in a deep breath of shock. "How? What happened?"

"Scarlet fever. They are having a virulent outbreak of it in Shropshire. I received an express just this evening."

She shook her head, trying to assimilate this bit of news. Percival Hammond, her husband's cousin and best friend, was dead. Without thinking, she reached out and put a hand on his arm. "I am so sorry," she said, and meant it. "I know he was like a brother to you."

John shook off her touch as if it burned and walked past her. She turned to stare at his back, wondering why she had bothered to express her sympathy. She should have known he would never welcome it.

"I have to go to Whitchurch for the funeral," he said over his shoulder.

"Of course. Do you . . . " She paused, dismay filling her at the question she could not quite bring herself to ask. Surely he did not expect her to accompany him. She forced herself to speak. "Are you here to ask me to go with you?"

He turned around to look at her. "God, no!" he replied with such vehemence that she winced, though she had not expected any other answer. He saw her expression and exhaled a sharp sigh. "I did not mean that the way it sounded."

"Did you not?"

"No, damn it. I was actually thinking of your welfare. You've never had scarlet fever. If you accompanied me, you could catch it."

"Oh," she said, feeling awkward all of a sudden. "I thought—"

"I know what you thought," he cut her off. He rubbed four fingers across his forehead, looking suddenly tired. "It doesn't matter, so for once let's not quarrel," he said, and let his hand fall to his side. "I don't expect you to go."

Viola could not help feeling relieved, but she was still uneasy, knowing there was more to come. If his purpose had been to tell her of his cousin's death, he could have dashed off a note to her before departing for Shropshire, especially since she hardly knew Percival Hammond. She studied her husband for a moment, waiting, but he remained silent, staring past her into space.

"Is that the reason you came tonight?" she prompted. "To tell me this news in person?"

He returned his gaze to hers. "His son is dead,

too, Viola. This changes everything. You must realize that."

Those words and their impact hit her with all the force of a blow. Her composure faltered and she stared at him, feeling suddenly sick and unable to hide it. "Why should this change anything?" she asked, hearing a note of shrillness enter her voice. "You have another male cousin. Bertram is a Hammond, and he will be the one to inherit the title and estates instead of Percy."

"Bertie? That useless twit can't even tie his own cravat," John said, making short shrift of her words, justifying the apprehension that was turning her insides to knots. "Because of our estrangement, I was resigned to leaving my estates in Percy's care, for I know he would have managed them as meticulously as I do, and his son would have done the same. Bertie is a different matter altogether. He is a ne'er-do-well and a spendthrift, as worthless as my own father was, and it will be a cold day in hell before he ever gets his greedy hands on Hammond Park or Enderby or any of my other estates."

"Can this discussion not wait until you return?" she asked, desperate to divert the conversation until she had time to think. "Your cousin is dead. Can you not even grieve for him? Do we have to discuss legal matters of inheritance right now?"

His face was suddenly implacable, a rare countenance for a man whose charming, devil-may-care demeanor was well known. It was a look she recognized, one she had seen several times during the first six months of their marriage, one she had never been able to get around. "My first duty is to my estates," he said, refusing to be diverted. "Bertie would be their ruin, frittering away every sovereign in my coffers and undoing nine years of my hard work. I will not let it happen, Viola."

Dread seeped into her bones like the chill of winter as she looked into her husband's brown eyes, watching them take on the hardness of amber.

"When I return from Shropshire," he went on, "the separation between us will end. You will be my wife not only in the legal sense of the word, but the literal and moral sense as well."

"Moral sense?" Fury and desperation choked her, and it took several seconds before she could speak again. "You telling me about moral sense. Is that supposed to be amusing?"

"I know wit is one of my talents," he drawled, "but I simply cannot manage it today. These circumstances warrant a discussion of duty, and alas, that is never amusing."

"What does your duty have to do with me?" she asked, but she knew. Oh, God, she knew.

"I am speaking of your duty as my wife and as my viscountess."

There was a buzzing in her brain, and she felt as if she might faint for the first time in her life.

"Yes," he said, seeming to read her mind as if she were an open book. "I realize how unpalatable my touch is to you, but I need a son, Viola. And I intend to have one."

Chapter 2

He meant it. Heaven help her, he meant it. Viola stared at her husband, appalled, his declaration pounding through her mind like the beat of a drum. He wanted an heir. Now, after all these years, he wanted an heir. After the pain and humiliation she had endured, the social censure and blame heaped upon her for his lack of a son, after all the women he had enjoyed, now he expected to come back into her life, into her bed?

"Not in a thousand years," she said and turned to leave.

He put his hands on her shoulders to stop her. "An heir is crucial, Viola, and you know it. Without Percy, I need a son of my own."

"You already have a son," she reminded him and wrenched free. "Lady Darwin's youngest boy is your son. Everyone knows that."

"I know that is the rumor, but in this particular instance, the rumor is false." When she made a sound of disbelief, he went on, "And even if it were true, it would not signify. I need a legitimate heir."

"Why should I care what you need?"

"Like it or not, you are my wife, I am your husband, and circumstances now force us to do what our positions demand."

"Your circumstance and your position force me to do nothing. I am not your brood mare. Our marriage is a farce and always was. I see no reason to change that now."

"No reason? You are a peeress, the sister of a duke and the wife of a viscount. You know the rules that govern our lives, Viola."

She met his gaze with a determination equal to his, and she could almost hear the clash of their wills like the clang of two sabers. "I may have to be your wife in name, but I do not have to be your wife in deed. Damn the peerage, damn the rules, and damn you."

"Damn me all you like, but we are taking up residence together when I return from the North. Decide whether you would rather stay at our villa in Chiswick or move to my town house in Bloomsbury Square. If you choose the town house, notify Pershing and have your things sent there while I am gone."

"You and I under the same roof? Heaven forbid!"

"The same roof, Viola, the same dinner table." He paused and gave her a heated, knowing look. "The same bed."

"If you think . . . if you really . . . if you believe . . . if—" She broke off, too angry to stop spluttering. The idea of him making love to her after all the other women he had bedded was so galling, so intolerable, she could hardly speak. Taking a deep breath, she fought for self-possession and tried again. "If you think I will ever let you touch me again, you are insane."

"Like it or not, lovemaking is how sons are made. There is nothing insane about it. Married couples do it every day, and from now on so shall we. About damn time we did, if you ask me, since not making love created this whole mess between us in the first place." With that, he bowed, turned away and strode toward the door.

She stared at his broad back as he walked away. "God, how I despise you."

"Thank you for informing me of that fact, darling," he shot back. "I hadn't noticed." He paused at the door with his hand on the knob and turned slightly toward her. His face was in profile, his head lowered, one lock of his brown hair falling over his forehead. After a moment, he looked at her, and to her surprise, no easy, careless smile came to his lips. When he spoke, he made no flippant remark. "I never meant to hurt you, Viola. I wish you could believe that."

If he wasn't such a cad, she might have fancied a hint of regret in his expression and sincerity in his words. But he was a cad, he was a liar, and he had never loved her. Any sign of regret was gone before she could be sure it had ever even been there.

"You cannot really mean to do this. You know how I hate you, yet you expect me to take you to my bed now?"

"A bed is the most comfortable place," he said, "but if you've another suggestion, I am willing enough. I know it has been a long time, but as I recall, adventurous lovemaking was one of our favorite pastimes."

She made a sound of outrage, but before she could express it in words, he was gone.

The arrogance of the man. Seething, she began to pace the library, her animosity toward him so powerful at this moment that she could scarcely believe her feelings for him had once been quite the opposite.

When she had first set eyes on John Hammond nine years ago, it had been like something out of a novel. Across a crowded ballroom, he had looked her way, he had smiled, and her entire life had changed.

Twenty-six, he'd been then, and the handsomest man she had ever seen, with eyes the color of brandy and the body of a man skilled at sport. He had just come into his title the previous year, but had he been a tradesman instead of a viscount, she would not have cared. That night on a ballroom floor, she had fallen helplessly in love with that strong, handsome man, her seventeen-year-old heart captured by his devastating smile.

Loath as she was to admit it, he was even more physically attractive now than he had been then. Unlike most other men in their middle thirties, he hadn't started getting stout or bald. Not John. He still had the body of a Corinthian, and maturity had only made him stronger. Beneath the broadcloth of his evening suit, his chest and shoulders looked wider than ever, his long legs even more muscular. He still had that thick, unruly dark brown hair, the only change a hint of gray at his temples. He still had eyes like cognac, but there were lines around them now. Laugh lines other women had put there.

So many other women.

Viola sank down in a chair, swamped by a bitterness she hadn't felt for years. As baffling as it seemed now, she had loved him, and with a power beyond all reason. She had married him because she thought the sun rose and set each day just to shine on him. What a fool she had been.

He told her he loved her, but that had been a lie. He had married her not for love, but for her money. All her love wasted on a man who did not love her in return, a man whose mind had decided he needed a wife of means, but whose heart had never belonged to her.

Viola stood up. All of that was in the past. She

had long ago accepted his perfidy and her own folly. While he had provided himself with a string of mistresses over the years, she had spent her time building a life of her own. A contented life. A life of charity work and good friends and serenity. A life that did not include him. She had no intention of allowing that to change. Her marital duties and her husband could both go to the devil, where they belonged.

" 'Fear no more the heat o' the sun; nor the furious winter's rages; Thou thy worldly task hast done, home art gone, and ta'en thy wages . . . ' " John's voice suddenly failed him, and he paused for a moment, staring down at the open volume of Shakespeare in his hands. He tried to continue, but couldn't seem to make his mouth form words.

He glanced away and stared at the crumbling gray ruins of Castle Neagh in the distance. He and Percy used to play among those ruins in the summer holidays, acting out sieges and battles. John felt a queer, heavy tightness within his chest, thinking of those days. Thinking of Harrow. And Cambridge. Rowing in the boat races every May Week. And how Percy had always gone along with him, following him through every boyhood scrape and every youthful adventure, every joy and every pain. Even falling for the same girl hadn't broken their friendship.

Your cousin is dead. Can you not even grieve for him?

Viola's words echoed through the silence all around him, penetrating his muddled senses. Grieve? So unfair of her to ask that question. He ached with grief, but to spill it out all over the place in front of people was unthinkable. His emotions were private, hidden by a veneer he had spent his entire life perfecting. Viola was so different; she displayed what she thought and felt openly. He didn't understand that. He never had.

A slight cough brought him back to the task at hand. John drew a deep breath and caught stern hold of himself. Everyone was waiting. With all the discipline he possessed, he found his place in the words from *Cymbeline* and continued, "'Golden lads and girls all must, as chimney sweepers, come to dust.'"

Snapping the book closed with one hand, he bent and reached for a handful of dirt with the other. He held it over the coffin in the grave, listening to the vicar recite from the Book of Common Prayer.

Ashes to ashes. Percy was dead. He held the dirt over the casket, but he could not drop it onto the polished surface. His hand began to shake, and he tightened his fist around the damp soil in his grasp. He turned on his heel and walked away from the silent mourners, breathing deeply of the cold spring air.

When he reached the ruins of Castle Neagh, he

walked around to the other side of the tumble-down turret. Still clenching the dirt in one fist, he tossed the book of Shakespeare aside. Memory guiding him, he placed his free hand on one of the stones, a loose one. Curling his fingers around its crumbling edges, he pulled it out of the castle wall.

Sure enough, it was still there, the niche he and Percy had made behind the stone. Their secret place, where they used to hide things—snuff and pipe tobacco, naughty sketches, things like that. He'd hidden Constance's chemise there once, he remembered, a pretty, lacy thing of delicate muslin with yellow daffodils embroidered on it. He'd stolen the garment off the clothesline at her house one summer day when they were thirteen and hidden it in here. To his amazement, Percy had laid him out with a blow right across the jaw for that. Twelve years later, John had danced at their wedding.

He put the lump of dirt in the niche, crumbling it into a little pile. It seemed right, somehow, to put it there, not drop it over the wooden shell that encased Percy's now lifeless body.

John stared at the niche and the small mound of dirt for a long time, and the burning in his chest deepened, grew thicker and heavier, until he couldn't stand it. He shoved the stone back into place, turned around and leaned against the rough stone wall, sucking in deep breaths of air.

He sank down to the ground and lowered his head into his hands, swamped by grief and a sudden, terrible loneliness.

Percy had always been a brick—a sensible fellow with sound judgment. He would have been good to Hammond Park, and Enderby, and the other estates of the viscountcy. He would have taken care of them, preserved them for the next generation of Hammonds. He'd known Percy would always be there, at his back, ready to take on a responsibility that because of his own disastrous marriage he had not fulfilled.

The security of that knowledge had given him the convenient luxury of avoiding what was truly his responsibility and always had been—providing an heir. Given that he had not been able to stomach the idea of forcing his wife to an act that had become so repugnant to her, John had seen Percy and Percy's son as the only option for the viscountcy. It had never occurred to him that his cousin, his best friend, one of the few people in the world he trusted, would die, that his son would also die. That the next viscount would be Bertram, of all men.

Everything in John rebelled against that thought. He had to have a son of his own or see everything he had spent a decade salvaging go to ruin once again. He and Viola had to find a way to come together and rediscover the spark of desire that had been so explosive between them in the beginning. It didn't have to last long—if it did, they would probably destroy each other—but it had to be long enough to have a son.

"Percy always did like Shakespeare. Thank you."

Constance's soft voice interrupted his thoughts, and John lifted his head an inch, staring at the black bombazine skirt of Percy's widow, the braided trim of black silk at her hem. Mourning clothes. That hot tightness in his chest came rushing back, and he turned his face away, striving for composure.

"They used to call him Owl at school, I remember," he muttered. "He always had his head in a book and had to wear spectacles to read."

"And the other boys teased him mercilessly about it. He told me the story of how three of them took his glasses once and broke them. He said when you found out what they'd done, you went flying after them in a fury. That was the only time he ever saw you lose your temper."

"Percy was right behind me, believe me, and did his fair share to square things up. We beat them to a pulp, and almost got sent down because of it. Afterward, they still called him Owl, but they never broke his spectacles again."

Constance sank down on the grass beside him. "What did they call you, John?"

He turned and looked at the woman he and Percy had both known since childhood, remembering the girl both of them had fallen in love with that summer they were thirteen. Constance had been the first girl John had ever kissed. About her, he had written some of the worst poetry ever conceived. About her, he'd had every erotic fantasy a boy could invent. He had stepped aside when she married Percy that autumn nearly ten years ago, pretending for their sakes that it hadn't hurt. But it had taken a lot of drink, a lot of sleepless nights, and a lot of pretty women to get over Constance.

He looked into the gray eyes and tearstained face of his childhood love and saw his own grief mirrored back at him. Yet he knew it was far worse for her, for she had lost both her husband and her son. He focused his mind on the trivial subject that might keep both of them from shattering. "My nickname was Milton."

"That's right. I had forgotten." She took out her hat pin and pushed back her black straw hat, letting it fall down her back. The sun gleamed on her dark reddish-brown hair, making it look like satin-finished mahogany. "Why Milton?" she asked. "It doesn't suit you at all."

He forced himself back once again to nicknames from Harrow. The mundane seemed comforting just now, comforting and safe. "But it does suit me. Very well, in fact. Didn't Percy ever tell you how I acquired it?"

"Strangely enough, he didn't." She paused, then said, "It's odd, all the things about your spouse's life you don't know. After ten years of marriage, I thought I knew everything there was to know about my husband, but I was wrong. The past few days, so many people have been telling me stories about him. Some of them I knew, of course, but some I had never heard before. So many stories—" Her voice broke and tears glistened on her dark lashes, threatening to spill over.

"Connie, don't cry!" he ordered in a ravaged whisper. "For God's sake, don't cry."

She turned her face away, composing herself for his sake, knowing how much he hated tears. After a moment she turned back around, smiling a wobbly little smile. "So, are you going to tell me how you got your glorious nickname?"

"On my first day at Harrow, I got into trouble—of course—and Master Johnson told me if I kept up that sort of thing, I'd never serve heaven well when I died. I answered that was all right, since I intended to rule in hell."

"You would say something like that," she said, laughing even as she fought back tears. "You've always gone your own way."

The nine years of his marriage flitted across his mind in the space of a few heartbeats. He hadn't ruled his own hell all that well. "I've gone my own way too much, perhaps," he admitted. "So sensible of you to pick Percy instead of me."

"Nothing sensible about it. You were a viscount's son, and would have been a far more sensible match for a girl like me. I was the daughter of a man in trade, a girl who had plenty of money but no connections. No, no. I picked Percy because he loved me so very desperately."

"I loved you," he said with a rueful smile. "It didn't help me."

"Well, he's the one who proposed." Constance smiled back at him right through her tears. "Besides, you never loved me, John. Not really."

He sat back, staring at her, unable to believe what he had just heard. "What are you talking about? If you only knew how it wrecked me to come home from Europe that autumn and find that Percy had stolen your heart away from me. I was in agony at your wedding."

She shook her head. "Nonsense. That was your pride. You never loved me, not in a way that makes for marriage. You always flirted with me, and charmed me, and remembered my birthday. You wrote me letters from school every week, picked my favorite flowers, and gave me the right compliments. You stole kisses from me behind the hedgerows, and said the most torrid things to me, but you never did the one thing that a man does when he is truly in love."

"What's that?"

"You never made a fool of yourself for me."

He blinked, trying to understand what she meant. "Well," he said after a moment, "I did write you some god-awful poetry. Does that count?"

"You did?" she asked in astonishment. "When?"

"Cambridge days. I never showed it to you."

"Exactly my point. If you had read some of it to me, even just once, things might have turned out very differently, for I was madly in love with you."

That startled him. "You were?"

"I was. But I knew you didn't really love me, and when you went to the Continent for your Grand Tour, I got over you."

"With Percy's help." He could say that lightly now, for he felt no bitterness. Many years had passed since then.

"He loved me, John."

"I know." John glanced over his shoulder, looking up at the stone where the niche was hidden, and he thought of the look in Percy's face when he'd found that chemise. "He always loved you, Connie. As I said, you were very sensible to choose him."

She began to laugh. "He blundered his way through the most incoherent marriage proposal you ever heard at the May Day fete, in front of Lord and Lady Moncrieffe, the Miss Dansons, the vicar, and heaven knows how many others. In front of all those people, right on the village green, he got down on his knees, confessed eternal love in the most passionate language you can imagine, and said that if I didn't marry him and end his misery, he would shoot himself and end it for me."

He eyed her with doubt. "Our Percy?"

"Yes, our sensible, straitlaced, calm, reasonable Percy. Given his nature, no woman could have resisted a proposal like that..I couldn't."

John tried to imagine Percy on his knees babbling declarations of love and desperate threats of suicide. He failed utterly. He couldn't make his mind form that picture, not even to win a prize like Constance.

"He made me happy, John. So very happy."

"I am glad of it, Connie," he said, and meant it. "The two of you are the only people in my life who ever gave a damn about me."

"What about your wife?"

The question was soft and cut him like a knife. He did not want to talk about Viola, not with Connie, of all people. Not today, of all days. He opened his mouth to make a flippant remark, but for the life of him, nothing came to mind.

Constance studied him without speaking for what seemed an eternity. Then she laid a hand on his arm. "If there were only one thing I could wish for you, my dear, I would wish you happiness in your marriage. The women, John. The gossip—"

"Isn't worth listening to," he cut her off. "I beg you, do not concern yourself with the wagging tongues of scandalmongers. They talk all the time and say nothing. Amazing, but there it is."

"I am concerned about you."

"No need to be," he said at once. "I am content."

"Contentment is all very well." She let out her breath on a soft sigh. "But John, though marriage is very difficult, it can give so much joy. Mine did." Her voice cracked on a sob. "Oh, God in heaven, what am I going to do without Percy? And my son, my darling son—" She put her face in her hands.

This time he did not admonish her not to cry. He said nothing. There was nothing he could say, no amusing anecdote to make her laugh, no antidote to the pain. For either of them. He closed his eyes, lifted his face to the sun and leaned his weight back on his arms, bearing the sound of her sobs because he had to, feeling her tears flay him with his own grief as if each one were a whip. He envied her that—the ability to cry. He never could.

He was thirty-five years old, and the last time he had cried, he'd been seven. In the nursery at Hammond Park, staring into a glass bowl of trifle that had been brought to him for dessert. He had listened to his nanny as she had broken the news to him about his sister, Kate. He remembered how the tears had rolled down his face, and how the colors of jam and cream and custard had all blurred and swirled together. He loathed trifle to this very day.

He listened to Connie's sobs, and he wanted to do that, too. Lie down, bury his face in the cool grass, and feel the cathartic relief of bawling like a baby. But his eyes were dry, his stomach felt like lead, he wanted to cut his heart out. He curled his fingers into the turf on either side of his hips, set his jaw and did not move.

They sat there for a long time before she finally lifted her head. "What will happen to Hammond Park now?" she asked, wiping at her eyes with the back of her hand. "Bertram will inherit everything after you, won't he?"

"Not if I can help it." He pulled his handkerchief from his pocket and handed it to her. "Besides, if Bertie ever becomes the viscount after my death, he shall rue the day. For I vow to return as a ghost and haunt him."

She almost laughed even as she dabbed at the tears in her eyes. "Is there any possibility you and your wife could reconcile?"

"We already have," he lied. "Viola and I both know our duty. Pray do not burden yourself with concern for Hammond Park. Everything will turn out well."

John spoke with far more assurance than he actually felt, for he knew that as far as Viola was concerned, duty would never be more important than love. And love for him was something Viola hadn't felt for a long, long time.

•

One month later, John discovered just how right he had been about Viola's notions of love and duty. By the time he had finished helping Constance settle Percy's business affairs, the scarlet fever epidemic had subsided, the risk of infection was gone, and he was able to return to London. But when he arrived there, he found that his wife had not moved her things into his town house. Nor was she at Enderby, the villa in Chiswick outside London where she lived most of the year. The servants there did not know her destination, for she had taken only her maid and one footman with her, but John had a pretty fair notion of where she had gone.

When he called at the Duke of Tremore's home in Grosvenor Square, his suspicion was confirmed. She had taken refuge there. He could envision Viola on Tremore's doorstep, asking to be sheltered from her shameful excuse for a husband.

Tremore was as haughty toward him as ever. He came into the drawing room bearing the ducal countenance he reserved for recalcitrant servants, ill-mannered commoners, and John. What his brother-in-law still did not understand about him was that he had never been intimidated by all that hauteur.

Thankfully, Tremore did not try to make polite conversation. He came straight to the point. "I assume you have come to see my sister."

Not in a mood to be clever just now, he met the other man's hard gaze with an equally hard one of his own. "No," he answered, "I have come to fetch *my wife*."

* * *

Viola stared at her brother in dismay. "So Hammond can just drag me off and there is nothing you can do?"

Anthony looked back at her without replying. In his hazel eyes so like her own was a look she recognized, a look of many emotions she had seen before. Rage at Hammond, compassion for her situation, regret that he had allowed the marriage in the first place. But Viola also saw something else—inevitability.

"How can I go with him?" she cried, feeling the chains of her marriage vows tightening around her like a noose around her neck. "After everything that has happened, how can I live with him as his wife again?"

"You are his wife," her brother said, his voice strangled, as if the words choked him. He looked down at the glass of brandy in his hand. "However much I might wish it were otherwise."

Viola turned to give the other woman in the library a pleading glance, a glance that impelled her sister-in-law to speak. "Is there nothing you can do, Anthony?" Daphne asked her husband. "You are a duke, after all, and have enormous influence."

"My influence is useless in this situation, my dear. Hammond has legal right on his side, and even I cannot protect Viola from that."

His glass in his hand, Anthony rose from his

chair and crossed the room to sit beside his sister on the settee. "If I were to gainsay Hammond and prevent him from taking you, he could bring action against me in the House and force your return to him by legal decree. If you wish me to fight him, I will. But I will lose."

It was so tempting to beg him to try anyway, despite the certainty of the outcome. "It would be quite a scandal, wouldn't it?"

"Yes, and you would be the one blamed, Viola, not he. What with his appearance at Kettering's ball the other night and the news of his cousin's death, the gossip is all over London."

"What are people saying?"

Her brother did not answer, but he did not have to.

"No doubt, Hammond is being applauded for finally bringing his recalcitrant wife to heel," she said, fuming at the unfairness of it all.

Anthony did not confirm nor deny her conclusion. Instead, he handed her his glass of brandy. "Here. Drink this. You look as if you need it."

Viola stared down into the fiery liquid that was the exact color of her husband's eyes. After a moment, she set the glass on the table beside her. "I don't need brandy. What I need is a divorce."

"You know that is impossible."

"I know, I know." She leaned forward, resting her elbows on her knees and clasping her hands together. "What am I going to do?" she whispered, feeling almost as if she were saying a prayer. "What am I going to do?"

Anthony muttered an oath and rose. "I'll go down to the drawing room and talk to him again," he said. "God knows, Hammond has taken my money in the past willingly enough. Perhaps I can bribe him to go away."

Her brother left the library, and his wife crossed the room to take his place on the settee.

"Oh, Daphne," Viola mumbled against her clasped hands, "how I wish I could go back and undo the past. What a stupid girl I was."

Daphne, always a good listener and loyal friend, said nothing. Instead, she put a comforting arm around her shoulders. "You have never been stupid."

"Oh, but I was. Anthony tried to warn me all those years ago," she went on. "He told me Hammond was stone broke. He said I was too young, and he wanted me to wait. He tried—in the most delicate terms, of course—to tell me about Hammond's reputation with women. He was just like his father, Anthony said, a scoundrel and a rake. But I was so in love with Hammond, so determined to marry him, I could not see reason. I was relentless, and Anthony gave in. Why did I not listen?"

Daphne's arm around her tightened. "Don't do this. Dearest Viola, do not berate yourself for the past, do not torture yourself with what cannot be undone."

Viola turned and looked into Daphne's violet-blue eyes, the eyes that had so enslaved her brother's heart three years before. In a small way, she had helped to bring Daphne and Anthony together, and she had been delighted to see them fall in love. Yet there were times when she could not help but envy her sister-in-law. To have the honest, true love of one good man must be a wonderful thing indeed. She had always longed for it. She once thought she'd gotten it. How wrong she had been.

She forced herself to smile. "You'd best go down and make certain Anthony doesn't kill Hammond," she advised, and stood up. "They are none too fond, you know."

Daphne hesitated as if unwilling to leave her alone, then nodded. "We will not let him take you against your will," she said and rose to her feet. "We will fight him any way we can if that is what you wish."

Her sister-in-law left the room, and Viola walked to the window. It was a brilliant April afternoon, warm and sunny. Looking down over the square, she could see Hammond's carriage below, and she remembered another spring nine years before. She remembered the countless times she had stood at this very window during that season so long ago, staring down at Grosvenor Square, waiting for the sight of Hammond's carriage, eager and impatient, scared and hopeful, and so, so in love.

God, it hurt to relive those days, to remember how her spirits would soar every time his carriage came into view, how she could barely stand the wait until she heard his voice in the foyer below, how he could twist her heart with sweet, painful pleasure just by looking at her.

Do you love me?

Of course I do. I adore you.

It hurt to remember the innocence with which she had believed him. It hurt to remember her own vulnerability and the blind devotion with which she had entrusted him with her heart, her soul, and her future.

She pressed her forehead to the window glass, remembering the pain of heartbreak, of learning that his words and acts of love had been false, that Anthony had been right all along, and it was her money John loved. It was other women he wanted. She still remembered how he had turned his back on her without even trying to understand her feelings about what he had done, how he had abandoned her and walked into the arms of another woman. Then another. Then another. As she stared down at the carriage below, she felt her frustration settling into the deep rage she thought she had overcome a long time ago. The rage of betrayal.

The liar.

Viola turned her back on that square below and

those memories. She wasn't a girl anymore, she wasn't in love with him anymore, and she most certainly wasn't a fool anymore. There had to be a way out of this mess, and she was going to find it.

Chapter 3

John had always been an amiable sort of person, even-tempered and slow to anger, but when his anger was provoked, when he was pushed beyond his limits, the results could be catastrophic. Most of the time it was easy for him to maintain his good humor, finding from long experience that a clever remark here and there could ease tensions and keep things civil. There were rare occasions, however, when keeping things civil took some serious effort, and those occasions usually involved someone in the Tremore family.

"I am touched by your concern for my finances, my dear duke," he said with deliberate joviality. "Your offer of funds is much appreciated, but I am quite flush nowadays."

He watched a muscle flick in Tremore's jaw, and since he had just been offered a bribe to go away, he could not help taking a certain satisfaction in his brother-in-law's frustration.

"Your lack of interest in my purse astonishes me, Hammond. It fascinated you so much during the days preceding your marriage to my sister."

"If I have been fascinated by your money, how could anyone blame me?" He gestured to the opulent drawing room of turquoise, gold, and white. "You are so superb at waving it about."

"Hammond." A serene voice broke in from the doorway, and both men turned to watch the duchess enter the room. "Thank you for coming to call."

John was glad of her grace's arrival, but he noted that Viola was not with her. In every crisis of her life, Viola always ran to her brother for help, and her brother always gave it to her. John began to steel himself for the inevitable battle that lay ahead. Tremore was a formidable opponent with far more money and power than he, and this situation was bound to become a difficult, wrenching, emotional mess. Viola knew how he hated that sort of thing, but if she thought that would make him abandon his intentions, she was mistaken.

"Duchess," he greeted, with a bow and a kiss on her hand. "What a pleasure to see you again. But then, seeing you is always a pleasure for me."

"I was grieved to hear of your cousin's death. Please accept my condolences."

He stiffened at her words, the wound still too fresh for him to react with conventional poise at a reminder of it. He swallowed hard, and it took him a moment to reply. "Thank you."

He had only met the Duchess of Tremore a few times, but she had always seemed to him to be a sensitive, perceptive woman, and she must have seen something of what he felt. At once, she turned the conversation to trivial topics, and to John's relief, her husband played along.

They sat down in the gilded, petit-point chairs and discussed the weather, the events of the season, and their mutual acquaintance, Dylan Moore—his marriage the previous autumn and the upcoming performance of his new symphony at Covent Garden. But when half an hour went by and Viola still had not joined them, John's patience began to wear thin.

At an opportune moment, he turned the conversation to his wife. "Forgive me," he said to the duchess, "but the viscountess and I must be on our way shortly. I wonder if you might have a footman take her trunks downstairs?"

"I will see if Viola has packed her trunks," she said, and the difference between her words and John's request confirmed his suspicion. He was in for a fight.

The duchess stood up and both men did the same, bowing as she left them. In the wake of her departure, he and the duke moved to opposite sides of the room as if by tacit agreement to keep as far away from each other as possible. Neither sat down again and neither one of them spoke. The tension in the air was thick and heavy, like the hot stillness of an August afternoon just before the storm breaks.

Nearly nine years since he had last been in this room. The windows were still topped with gold silk valances, just as he remembered. The walls were still painted white, with the same gilded moldings and intricate plaster work. Blue and green tapestries hung on the walls and the same blue, gold, and claret Axminster carpet covered the floor. Tremore was a traditional man. He never changed anything. John felt the strange sensation that he had stepped back in time.

He turned to the tall, narrow windows that looked out over Grosvenor Square. He stared through the glass, down to the oval park below, watching the carriages roll along the street that curved around the soft grass and elm trees. Opulent carriages of the ton's most prominent families, their occupants no doubt were on their way home from an afternoon of making calls. He knew it must be nigh on six o'clock.

His own landau, open to the fine spring afternoon, stood directly below, a carriage as luxurious as any that passed it. That had not always been the case. The last time he looked out of these windows, his carriage and his circumstances had been vastly different.

Standing here now, so many years later, he

could still remember the man he'd been then, a man who had inherited not only his father's title and estates, but his father's enormous debts as well, a man showered with the duties of a peer and no means with which to fulfill them.

Before his father's death, he had been like most young gentlemen of his acquaintance—feckless, foolish, and so bloody irresponsible. A man who spent every shilling of his allowance with no thought to where it came from, with no idea that the funds his father sent him were all on credit.

He rested his forehead on the window glass. That London season nine years ago, he'd still been reeling from the shock of discovering that being a peer had responsibilities, ones his parent had so shamelessly ignored. Creditors that needed to be reimbursed. Drains that needed repair to alleviate the typhoid outbreak among his tenants. Animals that had to be fed, crops that had to be planted, and servants who needed to be paid the months of back wages owed them. Looking at his tenants and his servants then, he had known they were taking his measure with cynical eyes, regarding him as not much of an improvement over the previous lord.

He would never forget the desperation in his guts, the desperation that came of having so many people looking at him, being so dependent upon him, when he could see no way to provide for them.

No way but one.

The sound of footsteps approaching caused him to turn away from the window, and he watched as Viola paused in the doorway of the drawing room. The sunlight from the windows shimmered across her upswept hair and her face, crystallizing in his mind more memories of that spring so long ago.

Nine years, yet it might have been yesterday when he had last come calling here. The queer feeling of having stepped back in time grew stronger, for Viola looked as golden and lovely standing in that doorway now as she had then. No wonder she'd had suitors lined up outside her door that season. Time had left only one perceivable difference in her countenance. The face of the girl in the doorway had always lit up like a candle at the sight of him. The face of the woman never did. His fault and hers, he thought.

She entered the room and turned to her brother. "Anthony, I would like to speak with Hammond alone if I may."

"Certainly." Without a glance at John, the duke strode out of the drawing room, and Viola closed the doors behind him.

She did not waste time on preliminaries or polite conversation. "I am not going with you."

The fight, it seemed, was on. "Good thing for me I outweigh you by at least seven stone, then," he answered pleasantly.

"Is it your intent to carry me out of here?" Scorn

came into her face, not surprising since scorn and contempt were the only things she felt about him these days. "Would you really do something so barbaric?"

"In a heartbeat."

"How like a man to use brute force when all other methods fail."

"It does come in handy from time to time," he agreed.

"Anthony would never let you take me against my will."

"Possibly, but if he opposes me, I will petition the House of Lords for your return to my household, and Tremore will have no choice but to hand you over to me. No doubt he has already told you this."

She did not confirm or deny his conclusion. "I could petition the House myself. For a divorce."

"You have no grounds, and after a horrible scandal that would forever ruin you in society, and cast shame on your brother's family as well, you would lose. The only grounds for divorce a woman has are consanguinity and impotence, neither of which are relevant here. We are not related in any way, and as for the other, no one would believe it."

"Not given your reputation!" She made a sound of disgust. "How unfair that if I had lovers, you could claim adultery to divorce me, yet your adultery is well-known and I can use no such grounds."

"You know as well as I the reason why that is so. A man has to know his heir is his own. Women do not have that particular uncertainty."

"Then perhaps I should be like you and have affairs." She lifted her chin, her pose coldly defiant, the queen being led to the Tower. "Would you divorce me if I took a lover?"

That, he could not even pretend to find amusing. His eyes narrowed and he moved toward her. "Don't try it, Viola."

One elegant eyebrow lifted. "Worried, Hammond?"

"The censure heaped on you for taking a lover without having first produced an heir would be unbearable for you."

"I am already criticized for not producing an heir. I might find it worthwhile to endure a bit more of it."

" 'Hell hath no fury,' " he shot back, stung. "Is that it?"

" 'Like a woman scorned,' " she finished the quote. "At least you admit that much culpability." She stepped around him and walked away as if she could no longer bear having him so close to her.

"And a man scorned?" He turned. "What of that, Viola?"

She stopped halfway across the drawing room, and he watched her square her shoulders. She turned her head, and in her profile was all the considerable feminine pride she possessed. He could see it in the tilt of her chin and the determined set of her jaw. He knew there was no way she would ever admit that it was she who had turned away first, she who had given up first, she who had said the first bitter words leading them down this road.

Even as those thoughts ran through his mind, even as he felt a sense of righteous anger surging within him, he knew none of that mattered now. He didn't need to be right, he just needed a truce, one long enough to have a son.

He moved to stand behind her, and he put his hands on her arms. She jumped at the contact, but he tightened his grip to keep her from moving away from him again. Through the moss green silk of her dress, she felt like stone under his fingers. "Divorce is not an option, Viola," he said as gently as he could, "so it serves no purpose to wish for it. Besides, I would not dream of putting us through that. I know you would not, either."

"You seem very certain of what I would and would not do."

"In this case, I am certain. Your love for your brother is stronger than your acrimony toward me. You would never bring that sort of shame down upon him or his wife and son."

"I could still petition for legal separation. After all, we have already been separated for years. It would be nothing more than a formality."

She was running out of ideas. He could hear

desperation creeping into her voice. "I will never consent to such a separation, and without my consent, there it not a chance of it happening. Nearly every peer in the House of Lords is a married man who has no intention of giving his own wife a legal precedent on which to do the same to him."

"Men!" She jerked free and turned to face him. "You have complete control over our lives because of laws you make, including the law that says only men can make the laws! How convenient life is for your sex."

"Well, yes," he agreed. "We men do like things our way."

"Anthony is in the House, and he is very powerful. He would fight for me."

"Even the Duke of Tremore is not powerful enough to change marital law. No doubt he would go through hell and back if you asked him to do so, but in the end he would still be forced to turn you over to me. You are my wife."

She took several steps back. "I could run away. Go to the Continent."

"Hide?" That surprised him. It also concerned him. It was a possibility that had a remote chance of working. Tremore could keep her in funds wherever she decided to go, and he would have to run all over the world chasing her down. If she could succeed at that tactic long enough, she could put herself past the ability to have children, and he would never have a legitimate heir to supplant Bertram.

He knew he could not afford to give her an inkling of his worry at this moment. As impulsive and strong-minded as his wife could be, if he showed any sign of concern over her threat, she'd be off to France within an hour. "I would always find you," he said with far more assurance than he felt, "and if I may say so, hiding is a course of action very unlike you. I never thought you could be a coward, Viola."

That hit a nerve, and she scowled at him. "Having the English Channel between us is a notion I find quite appealing."

"It would be a lonely life for you. To evade me, you would have to conceal yourself in some remote place, change your name, hide your identity. You would have no company. Knowing your love of society, it would kill you by inches to be so isolated, to be without your friends. And never to see Anthony and Daphne again? You could not bear it."

Her shoulders slumped a bit at his words, and when she spoke again, he knew she would not be running off to Europe. "I am surrounded by impossibilities," she whispered, and all of a sudden, she looked so forlorn and lost that if he had not been unjustly judged as a brute and a cad and the entire reason for her present state of misery, he might have felt sorry for her.

"You are making this situation far more difficult that it needs to be," he said.

"Really?" she countered, anger flaring again.

"So you expect me to make it easy? I should just lie back passively and do my duty by my lord and master as other wives do?"

He gave a shout of laughter. "You? I might just as well wish for lightning to strike me dead. The odds are better." He could tell from her outraged expression that she did not share his amusement about that, and he stifled it. "First, since you were never passive when making love, I can't imagine why you would start now. Second, I would like to think you would not only appreciate the necessity of creating an heir, but also remember the pleasure of it."

His words made her blush. Eight years had not destroyed all her memories of their marriage bed, it seemed. John chose to see that as a good sign. "This situation will be as easy or as difficult for you as you choose to make it."

"And if I choose to make it difficult?" she countered. She stiffened and looked at him. Behind the soft, mossy, green-brown of her eyes, he saw something else, the unmistakable glint of Tremore steel. It was a look he knew well. "If I refuse to do my wifely duty? What are you going to do, Hammond? Drag me to bed? Throw me down and force me?"

Of all the women in the world, he had married the most stubborn one of all. "I have never forced a woman in my life," he answered, "and you should know that better than anyone. Many a time, I could have beaten down the door you locked between us."

"Why didn't you?"

"Damned if I know. Perhaps it was that habit you got into of bursting into tears when I touched you."

"Finding out my husband lied to me and deceived me was a good enough reason to weep, I think!"

"Or," he went on as if she had not spoken, "perhaps it was because you started throwing accusations in my face when I tried to kiss you. Or because your fists started hammering me when I tried to take you in my arms. Forgive me, but being made to feel like a cur for touching my own wife took all the pleasure out of it for me."

"You never loved me. How do you think it made me feel when I found that out?"

Christ, have mercy. Were they going to talk about feelings again? He'd lose that battle for certain. He always did. He folded his arms and said nothing.

"How do you think I felt when I learned you'd been keeping a mistress before our marriage? The whole time you were courting me, whenever you kissed me or touched me or told me you loved me . . . " Her voice trailed off, choked by her rage. Her hands balled into fists. "Right up until our wedding day, you were bedding Elsie Gallant. Even after we were married you—"

"*Not* after we were married, Viola. Not after!"

He'd already explained that whole mess about the necklace and paying off Elsie's contract. More than once. He wasn't going to do it again. He gritted his teeth.

"Five mistresses since then, Hammond, and God knows how many other women that I know nothing about."

He would not justify his affairs after being turned out of her bed. A man never had to justify something like that. "Been paying attention, have you?"

"It is hard not to do so when the society papers and the gossipmongers tell me all about them in lurid detail. I had to sit across from Lady Darwin and take tea and pretend to be polite, knowing all the while you were between her sheets. When Lady Pomeroy was your lover, I had to endure her smirking smiles of triumph and her veiled innuendoes of your lovemaking prowess at card parties."

"Viola—"

"I had to listen to people at the theater rave about what a lovely creature Jane Morrow was," she interrupted, her voice cold, her hands balling into fists at her sides, "and how her lack of acting talent didn't matter because she was such a stunning beauty and charming hostess. I heard the compliments at musical recitals about what a lovely singer Maria Allen is, and the bawdy asides of how prettily she sang in your bed until her husband shot you for it! Good for him, I say! And Emma Rawlins is the woman of this season, the one whose beauty and talents and lovemaking prowess I have had to hear about."

"I am not with Emma Rawlins, and have not been with her for three months. Your recount of the gossip is a bit behind the times."

"You care nothing for the humiliation I have endured at your hands."

"I took my pleasure where I could find it after *you* turned me away," he shot back, hating the way she made him into a villain for fulfilling masculine needs that were natural and just when she had been unwilling to do so. "For God's sake, I'm a man, Viola! What did you expect me to do? Come to your bedside and beg? Become a monk for eight years? Wear a hair shirt and flog myself daily because I did what I had to do?"

"What you had to do?" she repeated with disdain. "Marry me for my money, you mean."

"Yes!" he shouted, pushed beyond endurance. "Yes, I married a woman with a dowry and income to save my estates from ruin. I made what I thought was a sensible marriage to a girl I both liked and desired. When that girl turned me out of her bed, trying to manipulate me with tears and guilt, I went elsewhere. In my position, any other man would have done the same."

"Foolish of me, but I once thought you were better than any other man."

"I know you did." He looked at the woman whose face was filled with loathing, and the lovely, vulnerable girl in the doorway flashed through his mind again, a girl with all the lights of the sun in her hair and all the adoration in the world in her eyes. All for him and the pedestal she had put him on. Hating him now because he had fallen off, because he had stopped being a hero and had become a flawed and ordinary man. His flash of anger dissipated as quickly as it had come. "What do you want me to say, Viola?"

"I don't want you to say anything. I just want you to go away. Bertram has two sons. Let him inherit after you."

"I cannot. I will not."

"Then we are back where we started."

Yes, they were, and he was tired of it—tired of the round and round discussions and tit-for-tat accusations, stony silences and separate beds that kept bringing them back to the same problem. No more.

He hardened his resolve. "We started our life together nine years ago, and circumstances now force us to resume that life. The only point open for discussion is which house we shall do it in. Enderby is six miles out of London, which is less convenient, but my house in town is equipped as if for a bachelor and is therefore somewhat spartan, so—"

"I don't even know you anymore." She shook her head, staring at him in horror. "In fact, I never really knew you at all. I cannot live with you as your wife again after all that has happened between us."

"Nothing has been happening between us. I believe that is the material point."

"And you expect me to go along with this?"

He met her appalled and angry gaze. "I do not just expect it, Viola. I demand it. Tomorrow is Sunday, so have your trunks packed and ready on Monday. I will be here to fetch you at two o'clock."

He turned and walked toward the door. He wasn't halfway across the room before she spoke. "Don't you see that this will never work?" she called after him, bringing him to a halt. "Don't you remember what it was like? Living as husband and wife was hell for both of us."

"Was it?" John turned to look at her, his mind calling forth recollections of the times over the years when they had lived together. But it was not the later years, when they spent a few months together during the season for the sake of appearances that he remembered, for during those times, they had never spoken and almost never saw each other.

No, what came to his mind now when he looked

at his wife were the early days. Back then they had scrapped and fought, like any newly wedded pair, probably more than most, in fact, for they both had strong wills and strong opinions. But he didn't remember their life becoming hellish until she turned him out of bed. He slid his gaze down the length of his wife's figure, and for the life of him, the only memories he could bring to mind right now were the early ones. The sweet ones.

Her body, so much smaller than his, was still exquisitely shaped, a figure of delicate bones and soft, full curves. That body might be hidden beneath layers of muslin and silk at this moment, but he still remembered what she looked like without all those clothes. It might have been over eight years since he had seen her nude, but there were some things a man just did not forget.

He remembered the perfect shape of her breasts and the flare of her hips. The deep indent of her navel and the dual dints at the base of her spine. The sound of her laughter, the sight of her smile, the cries of her pleasure. He remembered the places he used to kiss that made her melt like butter—her neck, the backs of her knees, the fiddle-shaped birthmark at the top of her thigh. With those memories, he felt his body begin to burn.

"It wasn't hell all the time," he murmured. "As I recall, there were some heavenly moments here and there."

Before she could say a word of reply, he came to his senses and spoke again. "Monday, Viola. Two o'clock. You have that long to make up your mind about where we're going to live for the remainder of the season." He opened the drawing room door. "Enderby or Bloomsbury Square."

"Neither," she managed to shout just before he stepped through the door and closed it behind him.

Chapter 4

He was delusional. Furious, Viola stared at the closed door, unable to believe what she had just heard. Heavenly moments? After the affairs he'd had, after the hurt she had endured, only John could say something like that, with that knowing look in his eye and that hint of a smile on his face.

Heavenly moments, indeed. She thought of his mistresses and slammed her fist into the palm of her other hand, grinding her teeth with outrage. Heavenly for *him*, maybe. He had been the one having all the fun.

Even during their courtship, he'd been enjoying himself elsewhere. While she had been savoring their moments together at a ball or party and happily contemplating how wonderful and exciting it was to be in love, he'd been amusing himself with Elsie.

Oh, how it had hurt to find out about that woman. Viola stared at the white panels of the door her husband had just closed, but in her mind she was seeing the pale blue walls of Lady Chetney's withdrawing room in Northumberland. She was again smelling the sweet fragrance of wassail that had permeated the Chetney's country house that Christmas. A waltz had been playing in Chetney's ballroom, she remembered, but it hadn't been enough to drown out the chattering voices of Lady Chetney's daughters and their friends.

" . . . pity Hammond's in London. We lack for partners tonight and he dances so divinely."

"Yes, indeed. Waltzing his way across Elsie Gallant's bed at this very moment, I've no doubt. She is a dancer, after all."

"No, no, he gave up the Gallant woman when he married Lady Viola."

"Not a bit of it. He still sees her when he goes to London. Gave her a sapphire necklace when he was in town a few months ago, I heard."

"Paid for the jewels with his wife's income from her brother, no doubt. After all, Hammond has no money of his own . . . "

She had not believed them, of course, and tried to dismiss their words as malicious gossip, but the seed of doubt had been planted. Perhaps if she had not gone searching through the steward's expenditure books, she might never have found the recorded entry for a sapphire and diamond necklace, but she had found it. To this day she could still see the steward's cramped handwriting in the ledger and feel the shattering of her stupid, trusting heart. That was the day the naive, adoring girl grew up and understood just how duplicitous a man could be.

Do you love me?

Of course I do. I adore you.

Upon his return, John had tried to explain it all away. Yes, Elsie had been his mistress, but he had ended their liaison before the wedding. Yes, he'd given Elsie a necklace in September, but only to pay her off and buy out her contract with him, a contract he vowed he'd entered into before he had ever met her. He had flatly denied sleeping with Elsie after marriage, swearing he had been a faithful husband ever since their wedding day. Even if that had been true, it wasn't enough, for he had not denied that he'd been with Elsie right up until the day the marriage vows were spoken.

Galling, even now, to think of his duplicity during their courtship, of how he'd told her again and again how he loved her and adored her and wanted her, yet all the while he'd been keeping that other woman. Broke as was, he had somehow managed to pay for Elsie. Men had their priorities, didn't they?

Her tears and hurt had been met with no understanding, only his biting, sarcastic wit. Her closed bedroom door had not made him realize the error of his ways. There had been no admission of guilt, no words of love, and no apologies. Instead, he waited a month for her to relent, and when she hadn't, he walked out on her without a second thought.

Viola's hands curled into fists at her sides. She'd known most men had mistresses, of course, but until Elsie Gallant, she had never understood that a man could court one woman and sleep with another at the same time. She had never known that mistresses had contracts, and that owing money to a mistress was a debt, like any other debt, and had to be paid, even if a man broke the contract when he got married. Until Elsie, she had never known the sick sense of jealousy or the wrenching pain of heartbreak.

Thanks to John, she knew all about those things now. Thanks to herself, she no longer felt the pain. It had taken a long time to get her imagination to stop forming pictures of him touching Elsie Gallant, only to find that image replaced by each woman who came after Elsie. It had taken years of layering sheets of ice and pride over her heart with each successive mistress he got, until she finally reached the point where she no longer cared what he did or with whom.

Now he wanted to come back. Any why? Not for her, that was certain. No, he wanted to reconcile because he needed something only she could give him. He needed a legitimate son and heir, and she was expected to just forgive and forget.

Her nails were digging into her palms so deeply

it began to hurt, and Viola forced herself to un-clench her fists. She sat down on the settee and with deliberate, focused effort, worked to rid her-self of the hot, smothering outrage that was threat-ening to destroy the delicate state of contentment it had taken her so long to find. She sat there for a long time, taking deep, steady breaths, until the cool, icy pride that had protected her for so long was once again in place. John could bed any woman he wanted, but that woman would never be her. Never again.

On Monday, John arrived back at Grosvenor Square at precisely two o'clock. By then Viola's rage was gone and her heart safely back inside her protective block of ice.

She was in the drawing room, seated at Daphne's writing desk, going over the plans for the annual Fancy Dress charity ball for London hospitals. It was one of the many charities she sponsored, and one of her favorites. She was with her secretary, Miss Tate, going over the menu for the supper that would come after the dancing, when Quimby, An-thony's butler, announced John's arrival.

"Lord Hammond, my lady."

Viola looked up as John entered the drawing room, and a memory sprang to mind of that same sight all those years ago, of John, so dashing and handsome as he would enter Anthony's drawing room, and how that sight used to make her feel so deliriously happy. Looking at him now, she knew he was more dashing, more handsome than ever. But this time around she felt nothing. Numbness was a wonderful thing.

She stood up, giving a perfunctory curtsy to his bow, then sat back down and returned her attention to Miss Tate, who stood beside her chair. It was rude not to give him her attention, but she did not care. She focused on the menu. "These are the courses the duke's chef has suggested?"

"Yes, my lady."

Viola tapped her quill against the rosewood desk with deliberate thoughtfulness, taking a great deal of time to consider the list of dishes before she spoke. "I confess, I am uncertain about the serving of eels, Tate. Lady Snowden is one of our most generous contributors, and she simply cannot abide eels."

"No surprise there," John murmured, and sat down in a nearby chair. "Snails suit that lady so much better."

Beside her, Tate made a choked sound, smothering it when she glanced at Viola. Lady Snowden walked and talked and moved so slowly it was enough to drive one mad, but that was no reason for Tate to reward John by laughing. Viola no longer found her husband's wit amusing, and she did not expect her servants to find it so, either. She maintained a dignified, disinterested air, deciding it was best to pretend he was not even in the room.

"Hmm, I think we shall take eels off the menu and replace them with—"

"Escargot?" he suggested.

She looked up at Tate. "Lobster tornadoes," she said, handed over the menu, and turned her attention to their next item of business.

"Now, as to the guest lists, Tate, I am going to send you to present mine to Lady Deane for her inspection."

"Viola, how cruel you are!" John pronounced. "To send poor Tate to face down that odious Lady Deane on her own?"

She gave him a cold stare. "Is this any concern of yours?"

"Yes. I must object to such cruelty to the servants. And to do it on your behalf. Appalling of you, I say."

"Well, it is not out of cowardice, if that is what you imply," Viola answered even as she reminded herself that she did not have to explain her actions to him. This was none of his affair. "I will not give her the satisfaction she would gain if I called upon her in person. She is a baron's wife, well below me in rank, and I will not give her the social coup of my personal attention. Especially since I cannot stand the woman."

"She'll do something spiteful to you in return. She's like that."

Viola ignored him and returned her attention to her secretary. "Now, Tate, when you present the list, Lady Deane will surely make a fuss about inviting Sir Edward and Lady Fitzhugh. When she does, you must mention as tactfully and apologetically as possible that the Duke and Duchess of Tremore insisted the Fitzhughs be included. That ought to cease any silly squabbles over Sir Edward's rank and low connections and who should be invited to one of these things and who should not. It's a charity ball, in heaven's name. Besides, the Fitzhugh daughters are delightful. Take the very same approach if she objects to inviting the Lawrence girls."

"Yes, my lady," Tate said with a sigh. She was clearly not looking forward to being sent forth with the task of presenting Viola's guest list to the formidable, spiteful Lady Deane.

"Never fear, Tate," John said, and Viola looked up just in time to see him wink at her secretary. The flirt. "Just keep in mind that Lady Deane wears wool underwear and you'll do fine. That's why she's always so out of sorts, you know. Itchy drawers."

Tate began to laugh, but to her credit, she smothered it at once, putting her free hand over her mouth.

Viola gave John a frown of reproof, then began to scan her list one last time. "Lord and Lady Kettering, of course. They always contribute a handy sum to the hospitals. The Countess of Rathmore is fine, too. Hmm . . . Sir George Plowright. That's all right, I suppose—"

"What!"

She glanced up to see John straighten in his chair with an abrupt move.

"You're not really inviting that pompous ass, are you?" he asked, staring at her in dismay.

He did not like it, and that fact was enough to make her want to keep the other man on the list. "Why should I not? He is a wealthy man, and he could make a most generous contribution to the hospitals."

John made a sound of contempt through his teeth and stood up. "I doubt it. He's as cheeseparing as he is arrogant. Except about his clothes, which show all the money in the world cannot make up for horrid taste." He came to stand in front of her desk and went on, "I saw him at Brooks's last night. Mustard yellow trousers and a lurid green waistcoat. Made him look as if he'd had bad fish for dinner."

She would not be diverted to a discussion of Sir George's famously hideous wardrobe. She looked up at her husband and set her jaw. "I fail to see how the guest list for my charity ball is any of your affair."

"Because you are my wife, and since we are reconciling, I am making it my affair."

"We are not reconciling!"

"To invite Sir George is asking for trouble," he said with a breezy, infuriating disregard for her words. "You remember that business last year when he and Dylan got into a fistfight. It could happen again. Or it could be me who goes a few rounds with him this time. That would be worse for you, Viola. I know how it would devastate you if Sir George beat me up."

She smiled. "No fear of that," she said with sickening sweetness. "You are not on the guest list."

"Yes, I am. Add my name, Tate, and take Plowright's name off."

"I am not inviting you! And whether or not I invite Sir George is not your concern. I chose to include him because he is a rich man and the fourth son of a marquess, and hospitals need funds."

"None of that makes him any less of an ass, Viola."

She lifted her hands in a gesture of exasperation and began to grind her teeth. Did the man live to make her crazy? "If ordering me about and interfering in my affairs is how you are going to reconcile with me, it is not working."

He ignored that. "Dylan and I have written a new limerick about Sir George," he said, leaning down to rest his forearms on her desk. "You used to love my limericks. Would you like to hear it?"

"No."

He ignored that, too, of course. "There was a

knight from the Isle of Rum, who's always been too quick with his gun. The demireps say his aim's not astray, he just fires too soon for their fun."

She *would not* laugh. Tate's smothered giggles were making it nearly impossible for her not to, and she pressed her lips tight together. She had to look away from his teasing eyes for a moment before she could get hold of herself. Then she gave him the haughtiest look she could manage. "Stop it, Hammond," she ordered.

Schoolboy innocence was his response, brown eyes widening as he looked at her, his face so close to her own. "Stop what?"

"Making fun. I am working." She shook a handful of papers virtuously and returned her attention to her guest list.

"Deuce take it, Viola. Life is supposed to be fun." He straightened away from her desk and began to laugh. "What is that deliciously wicked line from Jane Austen's novel? You love Austen—you must remember it. Something about how we live for the joy of making sport for our neighbors, and then laughing at them in our turn."

Damn the man. Damn him for remembering how much she liked Austen. Damn his smile and his wit and the ease with which he could find the fun in anything. That had always been one of her greatest weaknesses where he was concerned. How he used to be able to make her laugh at snobbish countesses like Lady Deane and pompous asses like Plowright, how he had made her happy in a world filled with malicious gossip and restrictive rules and closed minds. In the smothering atmosphere of staid drawing rooms and rigid manners, he had been a breath of fresh air to her. He made her feel vibrantly alive.

Only someone who could make her feel like that could have hurt her so much. Never again. Still, he did have a point about Sir George. She looked up at her secretary. "Remove Sir George's name from the list, Tate." She glanced at John, saw his smile. "For Dylan's sake," she added. "I would hate to have fisticuffs break out at a ball and have Dylan get hurt. You may go."

"Yes, my lady." Tate took the sheet of names from Viola's outstretched hand and, being a woman of common sense, she did not ask if she was to add Lord Hammond to the guest list. She dropped a curtsy to her and one to Hammond, then departed, closing the door behind her.

John spoke before she did. "Are your trunks packed? I have a cart here to take them. We can ride in my carriage. Which residence did you choose?"

She sighed. They were going to have another fight, and she did not want it. "Hammond, my trunks are not packed. Before you say a word, let me say a few."

She stood up, facing him across the desk. "We both know that if you wished, you could drag me off. We both know that if I wished, I could run to the Continent or America and you might never find me. Both those options are undesirable. Divorce is not possible."

"You and I in agreement? Things are looking up already."

His voice was still careless and light, but she heard the determination behind it. She used the only recourse she had left. "Before I agree to return to your household, I would like some time to become accustomed to the idea," she said with dignity.

"Accustomed to what idea? Making love with me again?"

No careless lightness in his voice now. He sounded more than just determined. He sounded angry. What did he have to be angry about, in heaven's name? She was the wronged party here. "The situation of living together."

"Stalling, Viola? Hoping if you can stall long enough, I will just walk away?"

Yes, damn you. She looked at him, cool, detached, striving to feel nothing at all. "You always have before," she answered with a shrug.

He sucked in his breath, and she knew her shot had gone home, but she took no satisfaction in that. She just wanted him to leave. Leave and never come back.

"There she is," he said, almost as if to himself as

he stared back at her. "The disdainful, unforgiving goddess who looks down at the sorry, flawed mortals below."

Though it was exactly what she wanted to be when it came to him, his description still stung. Viola's hand tightened around her quill. "And before me is the master of the cutting remark," she answered.

"Forgive me if your contempt from on high always brings out the worst in me."

"Oh, yes, I had forgotten that the sorry state of our marriage is all my fault."

"No, it is not all your fault. Nor is it all mine." He was serious now, and earnest, no sarcastic edge to his voice, no razor-sharp wit attached. He actually sounded sincere, the cad. "I wish you could see that. I have."

"Have you, indeed?"

"Yes."

She watched him lean closer to her, resting his hands on the polished rosewood top of her desk. She looked down at her husband's long, strong fingers and wide palms. She remembered how it felt when those hands had caressed her. She also knew how it felt when she imagined his hands on some other woman's body. Even now, after all he had done, it still hurt to think of it, and that was why she hated him. By all rights it should not hurt anymore. Her icy shell began to crack.

"I am not the one who was unfaithful," she

choked. "I am not the one who lied. But I am the one who has spent eight long years alone."

"Just because a man has a mistress, it doesn't mean he isn't alone, Viola."

Was that supposed to make her feel some sort of empathy for *him*? She stared at his hands, and pride came to her rescue, as it so often had before. She sat down and returned her attention to the papers spread out before her. "Then go find yourself a new mistress. I'll wait to read about how *alone* you are with her in the society papers."

"Here we go again," he muttered with a sigh. He moved around her desk to stand just behind her chair. "This is what always happens when you and I are in the same room for more than ten minutes," he said. "We start finding fault, placing blame, bringing out the worst in each other. Five minutes ago I almost made you laugh, and now we're at each other's throats. How do we manage to do that?"

She bit her lip.

He moved closer. His hip brushed her shoulder. "I do not want us to spend our lives finding endless ways to tear each other apart. It takes too much out of me."

"I do not want that, either," she said quietly. "But nor do I want to live with you again."

"You have made that quite clear over the years, believe me. Saying it yet again is not necessary."

Whatever she said was the wrong thing, it

seemed. "Do you intend to honor my request or not?" she asked as if it were a matter of supreme indifference to her either way.

"You are only postponing the inevitable."

"Perhaps." She turned her head and looked up at him. "Perhaps not."

"I am not going to walk away, Viola. Not this time."

Of course he would walk away. He always did. It was just a matter of time before he left her. Then the pretty face or shapely figure of some woman would draw his attention, catch his desire, and she would have to sit across from that woman at some party. Again.

He saw her thoughts in her countenance. He raked a hand through his hair. "How much time are you asking for?"

The rest of our lives. She thought about how long it would take him to give up and walk away and leave her in peace. "Three months."

"Not a prayer." He walked back around her desk and faced her. "I shall give you three weeks."

"You are not serious."

"Three weeks, Viola. And during those three weeks, we are going to be spending a great deal of time together."

She felt a sinking feeling in her stomach. "That is not possible. We both have commitments, engagements—"

"We shall be forced to rearrange some of them.

We are going to spend time with each other."

Panic swamped her. "Time to do what? We have no mutual friends. Except for Dylan and Grace, of course, and only because they refuse to take sides. We have no shared interests, nothing to talk about, nothing in common."

"We used to find plenty of things to talk about. And plenty of things to do. Remember?"

There was something almost tender in that last word. She ignored it. "We do not even go to the same parties. We move in utterly different circles."

"That is going to change. It won't be long before Lord and Lady Hammond begin receiving the same invitations about town. I shall see to it."

"Oh, heavens," she said, appalled. "I was right. You *do* live to torture me."

"If there is ever going to be a truce between us, it starts with being together, whether we are living in the same house or not."

"I don't want a truce. I don't want to be together."

"But you do want time," he pointed out. "You want those three weeks, you agree to the terms. Otherwise, I will petition the House of Lords right now and you and I will be sharing the same house and the same bed in about two days."

He meant it. When John got that amber-hard look in his eyes, there was no moving him. She had learned that from bitter experience. "Very well," she said, capitulating even as resentment filled her that she had no choice but to do so.

"Three weeks it is. But I warn you, Hammond, I am going to do everything I can to make you see this attempt at reconciliation is futile and that it would be better to abandon it altogether."

"I am warned, then. Be ready Wednesday at two o'clock."

"Where are we going?"

"I'm taking you to my house in Bloomsbury Square."

She eyed him with suspicion and a hint of alarm. "Whatever for?"

"No need to look so distressed, Viola. I'm not kidnapping you. I simply want you to see the place. If you choose that as our London residence when the three weeks are up, you might wish to make some changes to it beforehand."

"I doubt it."

"You may spend whatever you like."

"Thank you so much for your generosity, Hammond, in putting my income from Anthony at my disposal, but—"

"And my income as well," he interrupted. "The estates and investments of the viscountcy are highly profitable, and that is thanks to both of us."

She hated it when he was reasonable. That made her feel some stupid sense of obligation that she had to be the same, and she did not want to be reasonable where he was concerned. "I appreciate your offer to allow me to redecorate your house," she said with complete insincerity, "but to my mind, it is an exercise in futility."

"Your unwillingness to take on this project baffles me," he said. "I fail to understand why you are not overjoyed at the prospect."

"Overjoyed?" She looked up at him, saw a teasing gleam come into his eyes.

"Yes," he answered. "You love to redecorate. You always have. And this provides you with the perfect excuse to go shopping at my expense. Given such an offer, any other man's wife would be jumping up to shower him with grateful kisses."

"You only wish."

"Indeed I do. I live for the day. Of course, when that day arrives, I shall probably be overcome by the shock and expire on the spot. And then you'll be sorry you didn't shower me with kisses long ago."

Don't tease me. Don't. Just go away. She drew in her breath and let it out slowly. "I can never make up my mind which side of your wit I dislike more," she said. "The razor-sharp kind that can cut others to pieces, or the clever, amiable kind that others find so charming."

"There was a time when you loved them both. The irony is that neither of them have ever expressed my deeper nature." With that enigmatic comment, he bowed and walked away.

"I mean it, Hammond," she called after him. "We are not reconciling!"

"The odds of it do look slim," he agreed. "I must place a bet for my side at Brooks's. I shall rake in a substantial sum when I win."

She felt a pang of dismay. "They are betting on our reconciliation at Brooks's?"

He stopped and looked at her with surprise at the question. "Of course. And White's. And Boodles, too, I understand. Will Lady Hammond return to the marriage bed before the season is over? And what will Hammond do if she doesn't?"

She gave a moan of mortification. "God save us poor women from gentlemen and their clubs."

"Buck up, Viola," he advised, grinning. "It is quite a compliment to your stubbornness and strength of will that the odds are currently favoring you by a substantial margin."

"Only because all the men think I am such a shrew you won't be able to stick it," she said dryly.

He laughed, the wretch. Leaning one shoulder on the doorjamb, he folded his arms. "I will not discuss what is said in the clubs. No woman should ever know what men talk about among themselves. Your sex would be so appalled that we should never enjoy the pleasures of your company again."

"A great loss to women everywhere."

"It would be a great loss, for the human race would die out." He turned and disappeared through the doorway, but his voice echoed back to her as he walked down the corridor toward the stairs. "Wednesday, Viola. Two o'clock."

He always managed to have the last word. Hateful man. Spending time with him was the last thing she wanted to do. Still, it was better than living with him, and she did gain a three-week reprieve today. She just hoped waiting him out was a strategy that would work, for she had no other options.

Chapter 5

Two days later John had cause to wonder if his idea to show Viola his town house might have been unwise.

He had begun leasing the London residence for the season two years earlier, when he and Viola stopped pretending for society that they had any kind of a marriage. He was the one to take that final step away, deciding there was no point in keeping up a conventional appearance during the season when everyone in the ton knew they lived separate lives the rest of the year. More than that, he had been unable to tolerate one more tortuous spring of separate bedrooms. It hurt too much, knowing the door to hers was never open for him.

Now, as his carriage took them toward his house, the only sound was the light spring rain that danced on the leather roof. Viola maintained the distant, untouchable demeanor that had become so characteristic of her over the years, the cold goddess he despised. It always flicked him on the raw and brought out the most sarcastic side of his nature, because that demeanor was so uncharacteristic of the laughing, passionate girl he had married. That girl had given him some of the most enjoyable pleasures of his life, but she was little more than a hazy memory to him now. He hated the judgmental creature who had taken her place, especially because he knew he was partly to blame for the transformation.

He studied his wife as the carriage made the slow crawl up New Oxford Street. She was staring out the window, refusing to even look at him, and as he thought about the change in her that time had wrought, he felt no anger this time, just an odd emptiness. He had lost something valuable when that girl vanished eight years ago. Something beautiful and fragile. Something he could never get back.

Her unwillingness to see his side of what had gone wrong was something he did not know if he could ever break down. Charm and wit had worked to win her so long ago, but things were different now, so much damage had been done by both of them, and he did not know if he could ever charm her enough or be witty enough to coax her back.

He knew he had put on a good show the other day, but the blithe confidence he displayed to her was pretense. He wondered as he looked at her smooth, expressionless profile if he could ever make her want him as she once had. Two days ago he'd almost made her laugh. There might have been a tiny hint there of the girl he had married so long ago, but today that hint was gone. She had kept him waiting in Tremore's drawing room for half an hour before coming down, and had not spoken a word to him since then. A truce, a passionate wife, and a son all seemed a long way off.

The carriage pulled into Bloomsbury Square and came to a stop before his door. The footman opened the door and unfolded the steps. John exited first and held out his hand to Viola. She hesitated, looking not at him but at his gloved hand. After a moment, she placed her own hand over it, allowed him to help her down, and they went inside.

Compared to Enderby, their villa in Chiswick, this house was plain. He had only a few servants, for he never entertained here. It had some furnishings, a few carpets and paintings, and plenty of books, but little else.

As he watched her take in her surroundings, he felt compelled to speak. "You see? It is quite sparse. That is why I thought you might wish to purchase some things for it."

She did not reply. She pulled out her hat pin, took off her hat, shook it to release the droplets of rain that clung to the straw, then wove the pin through one side of the crown.

She had always hated wearing hats, he remembered, watching her. That was something he'd always liked about her. When a woman had hair like
sunlight, hiding it under a bonnet was a tragedy.

She studied the limestone floor of the foyer, the
polished walnut staircase, and the butter-colored
walls, then without a word, she started toward
the back of the house, carrying her hat in one
hand.

He gave her a tour of the rooms on the ground
floor, then took her through the kitchens and the
servants' quarters. The entire time, she said nothing.

"We could find a bigger town house next season," he told her as he led her to the drawing
room. "This one is a bit small for entertaining."

She did not even bother to nod, and his pes-
simistic thoughts during the carriage ride began
to deepen into downright gloom. His reference to
next season got no rise out of her, and it ought to
have. When he could spark her feisty side, when
she was quarreling with him, he knew what he
was dealing with, knew she felt something. This
cold silence was what he loathed, and though he
wanted to break it, he did not know how.

"The drawing room is here," he told her as he
gestured to a set of open doors on the first floor.

She started into the room, then stopped so
abruptly he almost ran into her from behind.
"Heavens above, I don't believe it," she mur-

mured, the first words she had spoken in the hour and a half they had been together. She took several steps into the room and made a slow turn, staring about her in complete surprise.

John watched her, tense, wondering if she would notice the first thing that had struck him about this room.

"Pink wallpaper," she murmured, confirming that she had, indeed, noticed. She looked at him in disbelief. "You leased a house with pink wall-paper."

"It is crimson, Viola," he said, contradicting her, "not pink."

"Crimson?" she cried, shaking her head. "Oh, no, no, Hammond, that won't do. It is pink. Rose-pink." To his utter astonishment, she smiled. It was like the sun coming out from behind a cloud. Even more astonishing, she began to laugh, a low chuckle deep in her throat. "John Hammond, of all men, with a pink drawing room. Who would have thought it?"

He stared at her, feeling rooted to the floor as he listened to her laughter. It was something he had not heard in years, yet it was so familiar. No woman laughed like Viola, low and throaty like that. So wicked, and so erotic, and from a woman who looked like an angel, that laugh had always been able to arouse him in the space of a heartbeat. It still did. He felt desire flaring up inside him with sudden, unexpected force.

"Hammond, whatever is the matter?" she asked as he continued to stare at her while arousal coursed through his body, thick and and warm.

"I remember that sound," he murmured. "I always loved the way you laugh."

Her laughter stopped. Her smile faded. The grandfather clock began to chime, and she looked away. "Four o'clock already?" she said, and started toward the door. "You had best show me the rest quickly. Lady Fitzhugh's dinner party begins at eight, and I must return to Grosvenor Square and change."

He forced down the lust that had flared up so suddenly, but could not stop hearing that low, throaty chuckle in his mind as they started up to the second floor. Viola's erotic laugh. How could he ever have forgotten the sound of it and what it did to him?

At the second floor, he turned left and led her down a short corridor. "Our suite of rooms is here," he said, opening a door about halfway down the corridor. "This one will be yours. Mine adjoins it."

Viola hesitated a moment, then stepped into the bedchamber. She glanced around at the grayish-blue walls, darker blue draperies and walnut furnishings, but expressed no opinion of the room.

"Repaint if you like," he said, following her through the doorway and moving to stand beside her. "I know you do not care for blue walls," he went on, glancing at her as he spoke, "so—"

He broke off, watching her as she stared straight ahead, saw the sudden hardness in her face and the way her brows drew together. He heard the rustle of straw and looked down to see that she was clenching the brim of her hat so tightly the straw was crumpling in her gloved hand.

Following her gaze across the room, he realized she was looking through the doorway into his bedchamber. He returned his attention to her as she stared at the bed itself, a wide comfortable affair with thick feather mattresses, fat down pillows, and maroon velvet coverlet. There was no mistaking the pain in her face.

He felt impelled to speak. "Since I have lived here, no woman has slept in these rooms, Viola."

She turned away without replying and walked to the walnut armoire. Her back to him, she opened it and began to examine the empty interior as if it were a matter of vast importance.

He wished he could think of something to say that would make her laugh again. He wished she would say something—talk about the furnishings, mention she liked the Gainsborough on the wall, say that yes, she would repaint this room—anything. When she did speak, her question caught him completely off guard.

"What is your intention, Hammond?" she asked

without turning around. "When the three weeks are over, and if I do not fight you in the House, and if we resume a life together, are you going to begin imposing your husbandly rights immediately?"

He blinked. "What?"

"It's a straightforward question." She faced him, but lowered her chin at once. She stared at the carpet beneath her feet, tapping the hat in her hand against her thigh. When he did not reply, she looked at him. "Are you?"

Christ. John let out his breath in a slow sigh. The brutal truth that had kept them apart—that making love with him would be as distasteful to her now as it had been throughout most of their marriage—was one he kept shoving out of his mind. Even the other day, when she'd asked for time to get used to the idea of living with him again, he hadn't wanted to think about that. But now, standing in the bedchamber that would be hers, faced with a question like that, asked like that, it was something he could no longer shove aside to think about later.

He'd known resuming a life together was going to be awkward and difficult, but to have her looking at him as if she were actually afraid, and asking when he intended to start imposing his husbandly rights . . . how the hell was any man supposed to answer a question like that?

John rubbed a hand over his face, utterly at a

loss. Viola, timid about making love? He couldn't believe it.

He thought again of the early days of their marriage, and though it had been a long time, the uninhibited way Viola had once made love with him was something he had never forgotten, something that made her contempt for him so much harder to bear. Looking at her now, he felt dismay hit him like a kick in the stomach. What if he could never make her feel that way again? What sort of life would they have?

"God, Viola," he said, forcing the words out past the sudden sick fear that clenched his guts, "is it all gone? All of it?"

She frowned in perplexity at the question. "What do you mean?"

"There was a time when all I had to do was look at you, or you would look at me, and we were racing for the nearest bed."

She winced and glanced away. "Don't."

"There used to be sparks between us," he went on. "And fire. I remember how you used to love it when I touched you. God knows, I loved it when you touched me." As he spoke, he could feel desire rising up again, the desire that had been burning deep within him like banked coals when he'd heard her laugh again. "It was good with us once. Remember?"

Her face suffused with color, her chin quivered. She did not look at him.

He pushed, knowing he had to make her remember what it had been like back then. "Hot and wild and good. I can't believe you've forgotten how it felt when we made love. The ache, the burn, the bliss—"

"Stop it!" she cried, and threw her hat at him.

The bonnet swirled into his chest, bounced off, and fell to the floor in a flutter of straw, silk, and feathers. He stepped over it, his thoughts, words, and memories setting his body on fire. "Are we now reduced to talking about the way we make love as something I will impose on you? Is there none of that magic left between us? Do not tell me we destroyed it all."

"I didn't destroy anything!" she burst out. "You did."

John didn't give a damn right now who was to blame or for what. She could still arouse him as quick as lighting a match, and he had to find out if he could still do the same to her. If he couldn't, there was no hope. As he took another step closer, she took one back, hitting the open armoire behind her.

"You said the other day that our life together was hell," he went on, pulling up long-buried memories as he spoke. "But when I look back, I don't think of it that way. I remember how much fun it was. I remember you always liked making love in the mornings best, and how we used to eat breakfast in bed. Blackberry jam was always your favorite."

She turned as if to flee, but he was in front of her before she could. Enough running away for both of them. He brought his arms up on either side of hers, trapping her, gripping the shelf of the armoire behind her. He leaned down closer to her, inhaling a soft, delicate fragrance he needed no time to recognize. Violets. She still smelled like violets.

He thought of the mornings so long ago when he'd wakened to that scent and her warmth filling his senses. He closed his eyes, breathing in, images of the past flashing through his mind—their wedding journey into Scotland and three months at a secluded cottage there, making love and more love, with her tawny hair falling across his face like golden sunlight. Autumn in Northumberland and the massive mahogany bed at Hammond Park, snowy muslin sheets, the scent of violets and Viola all around him. Lust coursed through his body as he thought of all those mornings when he'd kissed blackberry jam off her lips for breakfast. Perhaps she was right about their life together being hell, because right now his body was getting hotter than hellfire. But it was a lovely way to burn.

"I remember how bad you are at chess," he went on, his eyes closed, saying anything he could think of about those early days. "I remember racing horses on the downs with you, and how you'd tear off your hat and toss it up in the air, laughing.

And how much I always liked the way you laugh." He opened his eyes and looked at her. "Even though you look like an angel, you've got a laugh lustier than any courtesan could ever have."

"You should know."

He ignored that. "I remember cat and dog fights and making up afterward." He fixed his gaze on her pretty pink mouth with its full lower lip and that tiny mole at the corner. "Making up was the best part."

Her remembrances of their early married life did not seem as delicious as his, for her mouth thinned to a tight line. She folded her arms and her eyes narrowed. She was giving him that look—the withering glare of the disdainful goddess about to strike him dead with a lightning bolt. "Your memory is flawed, Hammond."

"I don't think so." He bent closer to her and tilted his head to the side. "Come on, Viola," he murmured and pressed his lips to her neck. "Let's make up."

He felt her shiver, and he smiled against her skin, a rush of relief surging through him. "You still like it when I do that, don't you?"

"No, I don't," she snapped. "I don't like anything about you. Not anymore." She unfolded her arms, flattened her palms against his chest and pushed at him.

He pulled back and looked into her face. The goddess was nowhere to be seen, and in her place, by God, was a woman. True, she was a woman whose face was filled with outrage, hurt, confusion, desperate panic, even hate. But John also saw something else there, something he had not seen for eight long, cold years. A hint of desire.

"Haven't we been at war long enough?" he murmured, bringing his mouth closer to hers. "Can we not call a truce?"

Her palm came up under his chin, pushing his face away. "I want your word, Hammond."

"My word?" he asked against her gloved fingers. He lowered his chin to kiss her palm, and she jerked her hand away.

"Before I even consider living with you again, I want your word of honor as a gentleman that you will never impose your husbandly rights on me by force."

John froze, those words stopping him more effectively than anything else she could have said or done. He straightened and tilted his head back, expelling his breath in a sigh as he looked at the ceiling. Life would be so much simpler, he thought wryly, if God had blessed him with a compliant wife. A biddable wife. A wife who would just do what she was told and like it. But he didn't have that kind of wife. Instead, he had Viola—who was beautiful, spoiled, and imperious. Viola, who still hated him after eight years, but could still make him rock-hard with one tiny laugh. With a supreme effort, he banked the fires inside himself once again and returned his gaze to hers. "You long ago branded me a liar and a faithless husband and a cad. Why is my word worth anything to you now?"

"It's the only card I have to play. And . . . " She paused to take a deep breath, staring into his ruffled shirtfront. "I am hoping that your word of honor as a gentleman actually means something to you."

"And so you can fling my promise and my honor in my face at moments like this."

She did not affirm or deny it, but that did not matter. He would never use force with her, and she knew it damn well. She was afraid, but not of him. She was afraid of herself. Now he understood that timidity she'd displayed earlier. Both of them were aware of that fine line where a man and a woman could stop lovemaking or they could complete the act, and she was afraid she would soften, afraid that with time, she would let him take her to that fine line, maybe even over its edge. She wanted a way out, a way to still resent him and make him the villain at any point she liked, even the morning after. She was afraid there might be a morning after. He grinned.

"Why are you smiling?"

He wiped the grin off his face. "I will not force you, Viola. I never have, and I never will. Since you seem to need my word of honor as a gentleman, you have it."

He saw a flash of satisfaction in those big, expressive hazel eyes.

"Think you've won a victory, do you?" he asked lightly.

"Yes."

"Think my promise gives you all the control, do you?"

Her jaw set. "Yes."

"You're right. It does. And I don't mind in the least. I always enjoyed letting you be on top." He ducked his head, kissed the side of her neck once more, and stepped back.

"I had best return you to Grosvenor Square or we shall both be late for our engagements." He turned away, leaving her spluttering. "Well, come on, Viola," he urged over his shoulder. "You did say Lady Fitzhugh's dinner party was at eight. And you know it always takes you hours to get ready for a party."

"Where are you going tonight?" she demanded, following him out of the room. "Temple Bar?"

John paused and looked at her. He grinned again. "Do you have a better suggestion of how I should spend my evening?"

She halted beside him and lifted her chin a notch, every inch the duke's sister. "Go to all the brothels you please," she said, looking at him with haughty dignity. "It doesn't interest me in the least where you go or what you do or what woman you do it with."

"That relieves my mind," he said, and started down the stairs. "I should hate for you to ruin your evening fuming and fretting about it."

Right behind him, she fired back, "Don't worry, I won't!"

During the ride back, she did not say a word, but now John didn't mind her silence. He said little himself, too astonished by what had just happened to come up with conversation.

He was jubilant and pleased and completely stunned. All the coldness with which she had kept him at bay for so long was a sham. Deep down, underneath her hurting heart and wounded pride, she still felt desire for him. She might still hate him, she might still want to slap his face or tell him to go to the devil, but something had changed between them today. She had softened. Just a little, only for a moment, but she had softened.

It was amazing. He and Viola had been combustible as flint and powder during their courtship and those early months of marriage, loving and fighting with equal abandon. But after everything had fallen apart, they had never been together, except a few short weeks at the height of the season.

Even when forced to be under the same roof, they had seldom seen one another, nodding politely as they passed each other in the corridors like ships in the night. She had shown him in every possible way she couldn't bear even the sight of him, and he had believed it.

They had become strangers. He even reached the point where it no longer bothered him to know how the girl who once adored him had become the woman who despised him. He'd been sure nothing but a miracle could bring back the fire they'd had.

But today, in a single instant, everything had changed. Some of the old, scorching desire had returned, and there was no going back.

Viola knew it, too. Knew he was as determined to have his way as she was to have hers, knew that she had only two weapons with which to fight him—his promise and her pride.

Formidable weapons, both of them, but they were not going to win her the war. He intended to have a son, and that meant regaining the willing, passionate wife he'd had in the beginning. Passion was something Viola still possessed in abundance. Willingness was another story. To succeed in this, he had to keep fanning the spark of desire that he now knew was still inside of her, fanning it until it was burning out of control.

It would not be easy. Viola was just as passionate in her rage as she was in her desire, just as stubborn in hate as she had been in love. Seducing her would require all the ingenuity he possessed.

He had to make it fun. That was what they'd had once and lost—the fun. The laughter and desire and the sheer pleasure of the other's company. He had to find a way to bring all of that back.

When they reached Tremore House, he walked with her into the foyer, where they paused just inside the door and a maid took Viola's damp pelisse and bonnet. "Good day, Hammond," she said, and started to turn away.

"Viola?" When she stopped and looked at him, he added, "I will see you again on Friday. We are going on an outing."

"An outing? Where?"

He smiled. "You'll see. Be ready at two o'clock."

Being Viola, she could not just go along without some sort of objection. "Why do you get to choose where we go on these outings?"

"Because I am the husband and you vowed to obey me?" When she did not look suitably impressed by that, he added, "Because I have a particular plan in mind."

"I was afraid of that."

"We're going on a picnic."

"A picnic?" She looked at him as if he'd gone mad.

"You always loved picnics. It used to be one of our favorite things. And two o'clock is the perfect time to go. You always get hungry around three."

"Do I not have any say in this?"

"No, but you can choose where we go next time. And yes, there is going to be a next time. And another next time, and—"

"Oh, very well," she said crossly. "When you get something in your head, there is just no reasoning with you."

"And you said we have nothing in common anymore."

She turned away with a sound of exasperation and started up the elegant, wrought-iron staircase. He watched her go, and when he saw her touch her fingers to the side of her neck, he wanted to laugh with exultation. Viola still got all shivery when he kissed her neck. Damned if that wasn't some kind of miracle.

Chapter 6

On Friday, Viola prayed for rain.

Since John had said they would go on a picnic, she hoped for inclement weather. God, however, seemed as indifferent to her wishes as her husband had been. Unlike the day they'd gone to his house in Bloomsbury Square, this particular day was bright and beautiful, the April afternoon warm and pleasant. It was the perfect day for a picnic.

Going on such an outing with him filled her with dismay. Picnics had been one of their favorite activities years ago, and there were too many memories associated with them, memories of when their life together had been good. She never went on picnics anymore. And when he told her where he planned for them to have this picnic, her reluctance to go multiplied tenfold.

She froze, hand poised to take her gloves from the maid who stood beside her in the foyer, and she stared at her husband, horrified. "Where?"

He gave a shout of laughter, his amusement inexplicable to her under the circumstances. There was nothing amusing about this as far as she was concerned.

"You needn't look as if I've asked you to run naked along the Mall," he said.

"Hammond, really!" she admonished him, and shot a pointed, sideways glance toward the maid and footmen who stood by the front door.

"We are only going to Hyde Park," he said, still laughing.

"That means a carriage ride on the Row." She was appalled, and showed it. "Together."

"I fail to see what you find so distressing."

"You and I out riding together in an open landau?" She began to feel sick. "On a day such as this, half the ton will be there," she pointed out. "*Everyone* will see us together."

"We are married, Viola. It isn't as if we need a chaperone."

Unimpressed, she glared at him as she took her gloves from the maid and yanked them on. "You are the reason chaperones were invented. You always were."

He grinned at that, looking so pleased by her words that she wanted to take them back at once. "I did think of all sorts of ingenious ways to get you out from under your brother's eye, didn't I?"

"I do not want to go out on the Row with you."

"Why not? Afraid people will see me kissing your neck?"

That was exactly what she was afraid of. Viola felt her neck begin to tingle. "Hammond, stop saying things like that," she ordered with another, even more pointed glance at the servants nearby. "It is not decorous. Besides, that doesn't concern me in the slightest."

"No?"

"No. Because I'm not going."

"What's wrong, Viola? You don't want to show all our acquaintances we have reconciled?"

"We have not reconciled! And I am not going to go gallivanting around Hyde Park with you, giving people the impression that we have."

"Since we are not living together yet, that is hardly a concern."

"If you meant what you said about making certain we receive the same invitations, the gossip will spread fast enough, I daresay. I have no desire to fuel it in this manner. I am not going."

"If you do not come with me . . ." He paused and glanced at the servants, then leaned close to her ear and murmured in a voice too low for anyone but her to hear, "If you do not come with me, I will drag you out and put you in the carriage myself. Any of the duke's neighbors walking in the square will see me do so, and since I can only assume you will fight me every step of the way, they will know our reconciliation is not going well. Does that suit you better?"

"You gave me your word you would not use force," she reminded him in a fierce whisper.

"No, I gave my word I will not use force to get you into bed," he murmured in reply. "To my mind, anywhere else is fair game."

"I am now able to add brute to my list of descriptions for you."

"Yes, well, as I told you before, brute strength does come in handy from time to time."

Viola had no doubt he would follow through on his threat, and she reminded herself that waiting him out was her strategy. After a while he would tire of this game and go away.

"Let's be on our way, then," she said, and turned to the door. When a footman opened it, she stepped outside, adding, "The sooner we go, the sooner it will be over."

"There's the Viola I remember," he said, following her out the front door. "Spirited, adventurous, ready to try anything."

His landau was standing at the curb. He assisted her into the open carriage, then followed her, settling himself beside her on the seat of roll and tuck red leather. On the floor at their feet were a picnic basket and a leather sack.

They used to picnic all the time in their courting days. Chaperones present, of course, but as he had reminded her earlier, he had always managed to steal her away for a quick, passionate kiss or two, fueling her awakening desire for him with those precious, stolen moments. It had worked like a charm, and he thought it would work again.

He was attempting to bring back their courting days, hoping it would renew her affections for him, but with the added luxury of being able to touch her and kiss her without having to spirit her away from watching eyes. They were married. He could be as bold as he liked, and he knew it.

Just as she had predicted, Hyde Park was crowded. Carriages and people on horseback crowded Rotten Row, and the slow traffic made their journey into the park seem excruciatingly slow to Viola. She could see people leaning closer together, whispering, no doubt speculating about the sight of Lord and Lady Hammond out together side by side.

She hated being the subject of talk, and she had endured more than her share of stares, whispers, and rumors over the years. There was some scrutiny that came with being the sister of a duke, but it was Hammond's mistresses and exploits that had made her one of society's favorite targets. She knew there were many who viewed her as responsible for his lack of an heir. Through years of quiet, restrained living and impeccable, decorous behavior in response to the gossip, she had finally succeeded in becoming such a dull topic to society that they had ceased to discuss her, much to her relief. Now, thanks to John's absurd desire to reconcile, her name was once again being spread all over the scandal sheets.

Both of them nodded greetings to their acquaintances as they passed them, for politeness demanded that sort of acknowledgment, but John did not stop the carriage at any point, much to her relief. It was not until they reached a less crowded part of the park that he had his driver pull the carriage over and come to a stop.

The pair of footmen who had accompanied them carried the picnic items and followed behind as John led her to a grassy, shaded spot beside a small pond. "Will this do?" he asked her.

They did not have any real privacy, for there were still many people strolling by, and any who knew them would stare and whisper, but it was as quiet as any spot in the park was likely to be on a day like this. It would do well enough.

When she nodded, the pair of footmen laid out the blanket for them. She sat down, her ivory-white silk skirt billowing out around her. She tucked it in a bit to make room for John, and he sat down on the blanket opposite her as the servants laid out plates, silver, and linen.

Viola stared down at her hands and took a great deal of time pulling off her gloves as these picnic preparations were made.

"Viola?"

She forced her gaze up. "Hmm?"

"It doesn't matter what people think."

"It does matter."

"Well, it doesn't do to show it."

She took another look around. "By tomorrow, the odds at the clubs will no doubt be in your favor. And everyone will applaud you," she added, galled by the notion, "for finally making your shrewish, disobedient wife do her duty."

"If that's what they'll be saying, then they don't know you very well, do they?"

"Because I'm going to win our little war?"

"No. Because you're not a shrew." He began to laugh. "Disobedient is a whole other story."

Damn him and his self-deprecating charm. He could say anything, do anything, and yet there were times when he could make her want to smile. She looked away and did not reply.

After the footmen had placed the picnic basket and the leather sack beside John, he waved them away, and they stepped back a respectful distance, far enough to be out of earshot but still close enough to respond promptly should they be needed for anything.

John untied the drawstrings on the leather pouch and pulled out a bottle of wine, a bottle dripping with water from the melting ice in which it had been packed.

"Champagne?" She raised an eyebrow. "Laying it on a bit thick for me, aren't you, Hammond?"

"Very," he agreed as he pulled a champagne

glass from the basket. He popped the cork on the bottle and poured some of the sparkling liquid into the tall crystal flute.

"What else did you bring?" she asked as he handed the glass to her, too curious about the contents of the basket to pretend she wasn't. "Oysters, perhaps?" she guessed. "Or, since we have champagne, did you bring chocolate-dipped strawberries?"

He shook his head and set the champagne aside. "No, no, something much better, something you love more than either of those. Scones." He reached into the basket and pulled out a bowl of the round, golden brown pastries and set them on the blanket. He then brought out a small pot of jam.

She adored scones and jam. Another of her favorite things. John seemed to remember so much about her, and she realized that was his biggest advantage. There were too many things about her he knew—how hungry she always got at this time of day, what foods she loved, how delightful it used to be when he kissed her neck.

"I have no doubt," she murmured with a sigh, "that the jam you brought is blackberry?"

He opened the tiny pot, peered inside with a thoughtful glance, then looked back at her, a smile curving one corner of his mouth. "You know, I believe it is blackberry," he said, trying to act surprised by the discovery. "Your favorite kind. What a coincidence."

"This is a blatant ploy to soften me," she accused. "To make me like you again."

To make me fall in love with you again.

"True," he agreed lightly as he set aside the jam and poured champagne for himself. He leaned back opposite her, his weight resting on one arm, his legs stretched out beside her own, his pose one of complete indifference to the fact that she found him utterly transparent. "Is it working yet?"

"Yet?" She frowned at him and took a sip of champagne. "You are assuming that your victory is only a matter of time? Awfully cocky of you to think I can be won over with such ease, especially when you employ such shallow tactics as picnics and champagne."

He paused, giving her a look of pretended bewilderment. "Does that mean you don't want any scones?"

She pressed her lips together, head tilted to one side, pride wavering as she glanced at the pastries in the basket. "Did you bring the cream?"

"Of course." He set aside his glass and produced another jar.

She capitulated. "Pass me a scone," she said, and set her glass of champagne on one of the plates beside her lap.

He sliced the round pastry lengthwise for her and handed her both halves along with a spoon. "I knew bribery would win out."

"On the contrary," she said as she used the

spoon to slather clotted cream onto the pastry in her palm. "I am not fooled. The scones, the jam. The champagne." She took a hefty bite of her scone. "None of it will do you a bit of good."

"Viola, take pity on me," he said as he prepared a scone for himself. "Look at what I am forcing myself to endure in order to win you over."

She couldn't help it. She smiled as she watched him take half his scone in one bite, a scone piled high with both cream and jam. "You poor man. You look as if you are suffering terribly."

He nodded agreement with that as he swallowed the bite in his mouth. "I am suffering. You know I prefer apricot over blackberry." He wiped a dab of jam and cream from one corner of his mouth with his thumb, then licked it off, then looked at her. "But blackberry does have its advantages."

She saw what was in his eyes, and her mind and her body and her heart all recognized it. That heated, knowing look. She tensed as she watched him set the uneaten half of his scone aside, but she could not seem to move away as he began easing his body forward on the blanket, moving closer to her. His hip grazed hers. "You have jam all over your mouth."

"You're making that up," she accused, her mouth full. She touched her fingertips to her mouth, verifying for herself that he was teasing as she swallowed her bite of scone. "I do not have jam on my face."

John reached back behind him, his forearm brushing her ankles as he scooped a dab of jam from the pot onto his finger. He then turned toward her and touched the corner of her mouth. "Yes, you do."

This was a game, their game, the one they used to play years ago. During those picnics, if no one was looking, he would dab jam on her mouth, then kiss it off. When they were married, it had become part of their morning ritual. Breakfast in bed and blackberry jam and making love. He had spoken of it yesterday, and today, he was reminding her again, making her remember how she had once felt about him, dredging up things she had forced herself to forget.

You always liked making love in the mornings best.

He leaned forward, bringing his mouth close to hers, that knowing look still in his eyes, and it suddenly seemed as if her attempts to be cold and frozen were futile. Something in the brandy brown depths of his eyes could still make her feel languid and warm, something tender in that smile could still spread heat through her body and soften her like butter in the afternoon sun. He leaned closer.

She hated him. She did.

He paused, his mouth only a few inches from hers. "I wouldn't want you to spend the whole afternoon with purple jam on your face. I mean, what would people say? I could kiss it off for you."

She fought to come to her senses. "What a noble and gentlemanly offer, but this is a public place."

"That doesn't matter if two people are married."

"It didn't matter to you when we *weren't* married."

He laughed low in his throat, bringing his lips another inch closer, and she began to panic. She brought her palm up between them, pressing it flat against his chest to stop him before he could kiss her. "Am I not safe from your advances even in public?"

"You are not safe from my advances anywhere."

She froze. So did he. Both of them remained motionless, suspended by her hand and her hesitance. His chest was a hard, muscular wall beneath her palm, and she imagined that she could feel his heart pounding as hard as hers. A fancy of her imagination, perhaps, for his white linen shirt and coffee-colored waistcoat made it impossible to be certain if that were true, but there was no mistaking the desire in his eyes. So long since he had looked at her that way, so long since she had wanted him to.

She didn't want him. Not anymore.

"This is not proper." She frowned at him, striving to be that icy goddess she knew he despised. "Hammond, you forget yourself."

"Viola, you are not really going to make me mind my manners, are you?" he asked. "Not when you have blackberry jam all over your mouth."

"I am." She lifted her fingers from his chest to her lips and wiped at the sticky jam he'd placed there before he could take this game any further.

"You just made it worse," he told her, his voice grave, his mouth smiling. "You've smeared it, and now you have a big purple streak on your face." He lifted his hand and his fingers traced a line just beneath her cheekbone. "Right there."

She drew in a sharp breath. How long had it been since John had touched her like this, tender and wanting? Over eight years, and yet it still made a thrill run though her, as if no time had passed at all. "People are watching us," she whispered, desperate.

His fingers caressed her cheek. His lashes lowered as he looked at her mouth. "If they are watching us, then let's give them something worth staring at." His voice sounded thick, heavy, echoing the way she felt.

He was a cad. He was.

He touched her lips with his, and a weightless sensation dipped inside her. For a brief instant she felt as if she were falling.

So, so long. She had forgotten all of this: how he used to dab blackberry jam on her mouth just to kiss it off. Forgotten what his kisses tasted like, what his touch felt like. He was making her remember things she did not want to remember, things that had given her so much joy.

Hadn't she learned a thing? None of this was

real. He was manipulating her to get what he wanted, just as he had done during their courtship. John had taught her the bitterest lesson a woman could learn about men. That his love and his desire were not the same thing. She would not be fooled this time around.

With that vow, she came to her senses. She jerked back, shoving his hand aside as she scooted back on the blanket, giving herself the breathing room she needed. She took a frantic glance around, and it confirmed her worst fear. "People are talking about us right now."

"Saying horrible things, of course." He did not pursue her, but instead leaned back, resting his weight on his elbows, seeming much more at ease than she. "Kissing one's own wife, especially in public, is the height of bad taste. My friends will never let me hear the end of it. I'll try to keep my wits about me next time you have jam on your face."

"I don't suppose you could simply refrain from putting it there?"

"But Viola, that wouldn't be any fun."

"I know life is always fun for you."

"God, I hope so. Should it not be?"

It had been fun for her once, too, when she'd been with him, but her life wasn't like that anymore. Contented, yes. Busy, yes. Satisfying, yes. With some moments of happiness and moments of sadness. But not fun, not exhilarating, not heady and exciting. Not like with John.

She dipped one corner of her serviette in her champagne glass to moisten it, then rubbed the linen vigorously against her cheek. After a moment she looked at him. "Is it gone? And don't lie to me."

"It's gone. But you rubbed so hard, you have a rash."

Balling the serviette, she threw it at him. She was tempted to take another glance around to see if she could identify some of the faces of those watching them, but she refrained. She would hear the gossip soon enough, and so would everyone else. By tomorrow morning everyone in his circle of acquaintance and hers would know Hammond had been seen kissing his wife in public, and they would know Lady Hammond hadn't been fighting very hard to stop him. And they would say it was about time she took her husband back into her bed and learned to be a proper wife.

Viola, however, had no intention of doing either.

Chapter 7

Covent Garden Opera House was once again popular after several years of turmoil, and many peers of consequence had renewed their subscriptions for boxes there. Because Dylan Moore was England's most famous composer, because he had recently published a new symphony, and because he was conducting his new symphony himself, the theater was filled to the rafters for his concert on Tuesday night.

Hammond had a box, but it was Viola who most often used it. Seated with her this evening were the two daughters of Sir Edward Fitzhugh and three of the Lawrence sisters. Viola had made these arrangements on purpose, for John had sent her a note on Saturday, stating his intent to sit with her for Dylan's concert. She had sent a reply back at once, informing him she had already filled the seats and he would have to sit elsewhere. Then, of course, she'd gone on a frantic search for the extra person or two she needed to keep him away.

"This is so exciting," Amanda Lawrence, Dylan's sister-in-law, murmured to her over the squeaky sounds of the orchestra as they tuned their instruments. "My sister told me Dylan has not conducted in years."

"I am excited to see it, too," Viola confessed. "I have only seen him conduct once myself, and that was years and years ago. I was at school in France, and my brother came to visit me. Dylan was on a tour of Europe at that time, and Anthony took me to the concert."

Amanda glanced at her program. "His symphony comes after the intermission. Do you know anything about this other composer, Antoine Renet? He is presenting a violin concerto."

"I have not heard much of his music," she answered as bells began to ring, the call for people to take their seats. A few minutes later ushers dimmed the lamps, and the first part of the concert began.

Viola gave it only the most superficial attention, her mind preoccupied. She was fully aware of the discreet stares directed her way from behind opera glasses. It had been four days since her picnic with John, and by now everyone in London society was discussing the amazing reconciliation of Lord and Lady Hammond.

At intermission, the Fitzhugh and Lawrence

girls went to get ices, but Viola remained in her seat. When her companions returned, Amanda was not with them, and her youngest sister, Jane, explained to Viola, "I saw her being introduced to a pair of very handsome men by your sister-in-law, the Duchess of Tremore. One of them looked quite entranced with her." She laughed. "We didn't want to spoil things by interrupting."

The bells rang again, announcing that the second half of the concert was about to begin, but Amanda still had not returned. Viola leaned forward over the rail and glanced sideways toward Anthony's box, thinking perhaps Daphne had invited Amanda to sit with them after intermission.

"Looking for me?"

The unmistakable sound of her husband's voice had her turning in her chair, and she watched in dismay as John sat down in Amanda's vacant seat. "What are you doing?"

"Joining you, of course." He leaned back in the chair and smoothed his perfectly tied cravat, smiling at her. There was such a complacent expression on his face, she wanted to bash him with her fan. He was as handsome as ever, looking quite the dashing man about town in his dark blue evening suit, silver silk waistcoat, and white linen shirt, but his good looks and heart-stopping smile didn't negate the fact that he was her greatest irritant.

"You cannot sit with us, Hammond."

"Of course I can. This is my box, after all."

She ignored that truthful, ghastly fact. "I told you, I filled the seats. You have to leave."

"Leave? I couldn't possibly, my dear. Dylan is a friend of mine, too, you know, and I wouldn't miss the chance to see him conduct for all the world. He's nervous as a cat on hot bricks, by the way. I saw him backstage a short while ago. He said to give you his regards."

"What happened to Amanda?"

"Who?"

"Grace Moore's sister," she said, and jabbed her fan in his direction. "The young lady who was sitting here before you usurped her seat. Miss Amanda Lawrence."

"Ah, yes, Miss Lawrence." He pointed to their left and up one tier. "She has moved into Hewitt's box."

"What?" Viola groaned and pressed her fingers to her forehead, feeling a headache coming on at yet another reminder of what her life was going to be like until she got this absurd reconciliation idea out of her husband's head. He was going to be the proverbial bad penny, turning up no matter how she arranged things to prevent it. He seemed to live for the purpose of making her life a mess, for it had been a mess ever since she had danced with him on a ballroom floor and fallen in love.

"The Duchess of Tremore was kind enough to

make me acquainted with Miss Lawrence during intermission," John explained, "and I introduced her to Lord Damon. He took one look at her and invited her to sit with his family. His father, aunt, and two sisters seemed to favor the idea, for they did have an empty seat. Wasn't that a coincidence?"

She lifted her head but did not look at him. "A most amazing coincidence, one arranged by you, no doubt."

"Not a bit of it. Lady H has a cold. Even I, as calculating and devious a fellow as I am, and as determined as I am to have the pleasure of your company—even I cannot give a marchioness the sniffles. As to the rest, Damon took one look at Miss Lawrence, saw that blond hair and those hazel eyes, and he was lost, poor fellow. Had an expression on his face rather like a stunned sheep. I've never seen him look like that before, but since I've always had rather a passion for a certain hazel-eyed blonde myself, I can't blame him for losing his head to one almost as pretty."

She refrained from pointing out that his preferences hadn't stopped him from enjoying the company of quite a few redheads and brunettes over the years. "Lord Damon is a wild and undisciplined fellow of the worst description!" she said instead. "He carouses around with *you*."

"That is a most despicable offense, I grant you,

but Lord Damon is also the eldest son of a marquess. Think what a coup such a marriage would be for the sister of a country squire from Cornwall like Miss Lawrence. Very sensible match, I'd say."

"Sensibility being the most important thing in a marriage," she shot back, remembering his words about why he had chosen her. "Love, of course, has nothing to do with it."

"I wouldn't say that. Damon looked like a man in love to me," he said, ignoring the barbed reference to himself and his marriage choice. "Besides, you seem to have taken on the project of launching Grace's sisters into good society, and I am helping you help them. How can you complain when I've just introduced one of them to a future marquess?"

"I promised Dylan last autumn that I would introduce his wife's sisters into good society, but they do not need suitors like Lord Damon. As a future marquess, he might be a marriage coup, but he is a disaster for happiness. Amanda is a sweet girl."

"Just what Damon needs to steady him."

"Really?" she countered smoothly. "That didn't work for you."

"I didn't marry a sweet girl."

"Thank you so much. If you are trying to win me over with compliments like that one, save your breath."

The lamps were dimmed once again. Relieved

by the distraction, Viola leaned over the rail, watching as Dylan Moore stepped into the orchestra pit, took his place at the podium, bowed to the audience, then turned to face the orchestra. If Dylan was nervous, it didn't show.

John moved forward in his chair and leaned closer to her, resting his forearms on the rail. His shoulder touched hers. "I didn't marry a sweet girl," he repeated in a murmur beside her, "because I didn't want a sweet girl. I wanted a passionate one."

"You wanted a rich one, you mean."

"No, I *needed* a rich one." He didn't sound the least bit ashamed of himself. "I wanted a passionate one. And that was what I had, until she forgot what passion was all about."

"How cruel you are!" she cried. But her words were spoken just as the music began, and that was a blessing, for with the deep opening notes of the symphony played by a one hundred piece orchestra, no one else could have heard her words. She leaned even closer to her husband, but kept her gaze on the concert below. "If I forgot passion," she told him in a harsh whisper, "that is your fault."

"Yes, it is."

The quiet admission startled her, and she turned her head to look at him. He was so close her lips almost touched his, but she couldn't seem to move away. "John, that is the first time I have ever heard you admit any culpability for our mess of a marriage."

"Yes, well, it's awfully hard for a man to admit he's wrong about anything. It's due to lack of practice, of course. Because we're almost never wrong."

She pressed her lips together.

"Ah," he murmured, "I almost got a smile there, didn't I?"

"No." She turned away. "You're imagining things again."

"Am I?" His knuckles brushed her cheek, and she almost jumped in her chair. She clenched her carved ivory fan tight in one hand and curled the fingers of her other hand around the carved railing in front of her, tense and wary, acutely aware of the stares they were getting as he moved his hand to the back of her neck. His fingertips traced feather-light circles at her nape. His lips brushed her ear.

"Don't. People are watching us."

Being John, he ignored that. "If you have forgotten all about passion, and it is my fault, then I need to rectify my mistake, don't you think?"

"John—" She broke off, forgetting whatever she'd been about to say as he kissed her ear and his thumb began to caress the line of her jaw.

"I could think of all sorts of ways to remind you," he went on. "If you let me."

She closed her eyes. Why was he doing this to

her? She had forgotten passion, it was true, but it was all coming back to her now with a vengeance. She was over him now, and she did not want to remember that passion she'd once had for him. She did not want to remember making love in the mornings with him, and racing horses with him, and how he could make her smile and laugh just by being near. She did not want to feel that sort of dizzying happiness ever again. It was too painful when it ended.

She opened her eyes and deliberately turned her head in his direction, but she did not look at him. Instead, her gaze sought out one particular box among the many that ringed the second tier of Covent Garden. Sure enough, Lady Pomeroy was there, and the sight of the dark, striking beauty was enough to dampen any passion John might being trying to evoke in her now. How many times during that woman's amour with John had some clueless hostess forced Viola to sit across from Anne Pomerey at tea or cards? Viola's safe, icy shell, a familiar friend that had protected her for so long, wrapped itself around her now. "You know far more about the passions and pleasures of lovemaking than I, Hammond," she said. "You've had so much more practice."

Though she was not looking at him, she knew both her words and the direction of her gaze had hit their mark. Beside her ear, she heard his sharp, indrawn breath. His hand slid away from her cheek and he leaned back in his chair without a word.

Safely numb again, she leaned back in her seat as well, letting go of the rail and loosening the tight, tense grip she had on her fan. Her gaze moved to the stage below and she tried to concentrate on that. But as much as she hoped for the success of Dylan's performance, as sure as she was that it would be a triumph, she could not have judged any of that for herself, since the only thing she could seem to hear was John's voice promising passion when she knew passion was not enough.

When the symphony ended with a final, rollicking flourish of strings, horns, and cymbals, the crowd was on its feet at once, roaring with approval. Viola stood up as well, only then coming out of her reverie. Applauding along with everyone else, she watched as Dylan turned and bowed to the audience, and she was so happy for her friend that for a moment she forgot her own troubles.

Until John reminded her. Amid the curtain calls, he leaned close to her again. "No matter what I have to do, I will make you remember how passion felt, Viola. The passion we once had. More than that, I will make you feel it again. I swear it. I shall see you on Thursday. Two o'clock. It's your turn to decide where we go this time."

He was gone before she had the chance to reply. She stared down at the milling crowds below and had a sinking feeling her husband would succeed. That was exactly what she was afraid of.

On Thursday, John found himself regretting the fact that he had allowed Viola to choose their outing this time. He groaned. "You're not serious."

"Oh, but I am." She gave him a smile of triumph as she stepped up into his carriage. "I want to spend the afternoon at Anthony's museum. I heard him mention this morning that he would be there all day." Her smiled widened. "He can give us a tour himself. Won't that be nice?"

It was going to be hell. He settled himself beside her on the carriage seat, trying to find a way out of this. "Viola, history bores you to tears."

"It used to bore me. I have broadened my interests."

"To include Roman antiquities?"

"Yes." She looked at him, cool, composed, and oh-so-pleased with herself. "This may come as a shock to you, but I have managed to make quite a full and satisfying life for myself without you. I have developed interests in many things."

That might very well be true, but he didn't believe for a second that she had chosen Tremore's museum because she had developed a fascination for Romano-British pottery shards. No, she had selected the museum because her brother was sure to be there and would watch his every move like a hawk, haughty and hostile, and making it impossible for him to do any serious wooing of his wife. And she knew it, too.

As they rode to the museum, he studied her profile in the sunlight of the open carriage. She had just thrown down a challenge to his wits, and that made him vow that before they left that museum today, he was going to steal at least one kiss from her. With her brother hovering about, it was going to take a bit of ingenuity on his part to get her alone, but he used to be quite ingenious about that sort of thing during their courtship. He began to form some plans of his own.

As it turned out, Tremore was at the museum that day, but he was giving a tour to a contingent of Venetian antiquarians when they arrived, and would be unavailable for at least the next two hours, possibly longer.

It was John's turn to smile. "Well, now," he murmured, glancing at his wife as they stood in the enormous foyer of the museum, "Tremore cannot join us. Isn't that a shame?"

She wasn't looking quite so pleased with herself now, he noticed. "We'll come back later," she said.

"No, no," he said, trying not to laugh. "We are here, after all. Besides, you have developed such a passion for antiquities, you should be able to give me quite a tour of the place."

He was the one issuing a challenge now, and she knew it. Her chin rose a little higher. "Very well," she said with dignity. "Where do you want to start?"

"I don't know yet." He glanced around at the high, domed ceiling overhead, at the walls and floors of travertine and marble, and at the corridors that branched off in all directions. It was a magnificent building. He had to admit that when Tremore did a thing, he did it well.

He took a printed map from the young man standing nearby and opened it. A quick scan told him everything he needed to know about the design of the place. "They have a new wing, I see."

"Yes," she answered as she loosened the ribbons under her chin. She pushed her hat back and it fell behind her, to hang between her shoulder blades. "There isn't much in it as yet. A few rooms of arms and weapons. I've only been in that part of the building once before."

"Excellent place to begin, don't you think?" He handed her the map. "Lead the way."

The museum was full of people, especially in the new wing, and they spent the next hour weaving their way amid the crowds gathered around displays of bronze shields and iron spears.

John was surprised to note that she proved more interested in the antiquities than he would have thought. "When did you start liking history?" he asked as they leaned over a glass cabinet that displayed jeweled knives.

"Daphne and Anthony's enthusiasm is infectious, I think. They talk about it so much that one can't help being enthusiastic along with them." She gestured to the knives. "Besides, jewels have always fascinated me."

"That I remember." He decided it was time to make his first move, and he glanced toward a doorway across the room. Remembering the map, he knew that was the way he wanted to go, and he began maneuvering Viola in that direction, one exhibit at a time.

As they paused to admire an intricately carved shield of pewter, he leaned closer to her. "I'm going to see what is down there," he said, gesturing to the doorway that led into a long corridor. "I'll be back."

She protested at once. "But there isn't anything down there. That part of the museum isn't even open yet."

"That doesn't mean there isn't anything to see, does it?" With a wink at her, he slipped into the corridor, then hurried down its considerable length to the other end, passing several rooms filled with baskets of broken pottery shards and half-completed mosaics. Clearly, these were working rooms for people at the museum. He halted at the end of the corridor and looked left and right. A long gallery stretched in both directions, lit by square windows set high up in the twenty-foot ceilings. He went left, passing baskets of pottery but not much else. There was no sign of people.

Viola's footsteps echoed on the stone floor, telling him that she was following him, just as he'd hoped.

"John?" she called.

"I'm down here," he called back, and listened as her footsteps brought her closer. He watched as she stepped into the gallery and paused, glancing to her right.

"Viola," he called softly, and saw her turn in his direction. He beckoned to her from where he stood at the end of the gallery. "Come down here and see this."

"See what? There isn't anything down there."

"How do you know? You said yourself you've only been in the new wing once. Have you been this way?"

"No, but I told you this part of the building isn't even open yet. The map says so."

"Forget the map." He took a couple steps backward and made a great show of looking down the two ends of yet another empty gallery. "It seems to me there's plenty to see down here," he said, and returned his gaze to hers, trying to look as innocent as possible.

She frowned, an adorable look of perplexity on her face. She looked down at the map, then back up at him. "What is down there? More pottery, I suppose."

"Heaps of it, and some other things, too."

She took a step closer. "Like what?"

"You want a list? Come and look for yourself."

He vanished around the corner and stepped into a niche that was clearly meant to hold a statue but was empty at present. He leaned one shoulder against the stone wall, waiting, listening to her approach. She was falling for it. She always did, bless her trusting soul. He grinned.

When she came around the corner and saw him standing in the niche, smiling at her, her perplexed frown deepened into a scowl. "You tricked me."

"Of course I did." He straightened away from the wall, laughing as he slid his arms around her waist and pulled her close. "I used to do this all the time, find ways to get you alone. Don't you remember?"

"I remember. Let go of me and stop being ridiculous."

She started to pull away, but he didn't let her go. Instead, he pulled her back into the niche with him.

"Hammond, what are you doing?"

He maneuvered them around in the tight space so her back was to the wall. "You're trapped now. To get out, you have to pay the toll. You remember how these things work, don't you?"

She did. Staring at him from where he had her trapped in the shadowy corner, she licked her lips as if they had suddenly gone dry. "I am not going to kiss you."

His smile deepened as he flattened one palm against the wall and leaned closer to her. With his free hand he toyed with the ribbons of her hat. He pulled, untying them, and her straw bonnet fluttered to the floor behind her. "You fall for this trick every time," he said, fingering the button of her shawl collar. "I think it's because you secretly want me to kiss you, but you just can't be honest and admit it."

"If I fall for your tricks, it's because you are a master of deceit." She moved as if to step out of the niche, as if expecting him to let her pass. He didn't.

Instead, he tightened his fingers around the collar button at her breastbone and cupped the side of her neck in his free hand. "Rules are rules," he said, smiling faintly, caressing her jaw with his thumb. "You have to kiss me first."

"We did silly things like that in our courting days, and we are not courting anymore."

"Aren't we?" he countered with wry amusement, appreciating the arousal he was feeling at this moment. "This seems very much like courtship to me. A great deal of delicious anticipation and heaps of work and ingenuity on my part. I thought after I got married I wouldn't have to do this courtship business anymore, but you are forcing me to take desperate measures."

"Forcing you? Of all the ridiculous—" She

broke off, bit her lip, and once again tried to step around him. He wouldn't let her, and she gave a vexed sigh. "Let me out, Hammond."

"I will, I promise." He slid his arm down from the wall and curved his hand around the side of her waist, still playing with the button of her collar. "But I get a kiss first."

A distinctive male voice echoed to them from the other end of the gallery, interrupting any reply she might have made. "Gentlemen, I know you have been eager for a view of the Romano-British pottery we have collected this year that isn't on display yet. Follow me."

"That's Anthony!" Viola whispered, dropping the map to push frantically at John with both hands. "He will find us."

John didn't move. "So? We're married now, remember?"

"Let me out of here." When he still did not move, desperation entered her voice. "He's bringing those Venetians this way!"

With both hands at her waist to keep her in place, John leaned back to look out of the niche and down the long gallery, where the Duke of Tremore paused, then turned right. A line of elderly gentlemen followed him, and they moved toward the deeper recesses of the new wing. "No, they aren't," John answered her in a whisper. "They are going the other way."

Once they had vanished from view and their

footsteps could no longer be heard, he returned his attention to the vitally important task at hand. "They are gone," he said, moving closer to his wife again. "Now, where were we?"

She glanced around as if trying to find a way to escape, but there was none. She was hemmed in on three sides by stone walls. Cornered, she set her jaw. "I want to leave."

John shook his head. "I want my kiss."

She made a sound of impatience. "Men are such children."

He lifted his hand from her waist to cup her cheek, and the feel of her soft skin against his palm had his desire rising higher. His thumb caressed that tiny mole at the corner of her mouth, and he breathed in deeply of violets. The slow ache of desire inside him began to burn hotter. "My thoughts at this moment are anything but childish, believe me."

A hint of panic came into her face. "I am not going to kiss you!"

Still caressing her cheek, he slid his other arm around her waist. "Fine. I am perfectly content to just stand here and hold you."

"You mean we are going to remain here all day?"

"That depends on you. Come on, Viola. Pucker up." He bent his head, moving his hand back until his fingertips slid into her hair, loosening the complicated knot at the back of her head. A hairpin fell, hitting the stone floor at their feet with a delicate clink.

He brought his mouth closer to hers and watched her lips part. Her thick brown lashes lowered a fraction. Oh, yes, she remembered this game of theirs as well as he did. Just as he had so long ago when they were courting, he held back, controlling the desire in his body, waiting for hers to flare up. He brushed his lips lightly against her cheek, right at the edge of her lips. "One kiss," he coaxed. "Give me just one, and I'll let you go."

"No, you won't." Her eyes squeezed shut. "I know you too well to believe that. You'll just take more liberties."

"Only if you don't say no." He fiddled with the collar button, unfastening it, then pulled the lacy shawl away, exposing the skin of her throat and shoulders above the wide, rounded neckline of her dress.

"What are you doing?" She made a grab for the collar, but he dropped it to the floor.

"Taking those liberties. You dither too long." He bent his head and kissed the bare skin along the side of her throat, inhaling the soft, familiar scent of her. She let out her breath in a little, fluttering sigh. Her neck, her weak spot, his opportunity. He blew warm laughter against her throat, loving it.

Footsteps echoed on stone, and the voices of a

man and woman floated to them from far away. It had obviously occurred to some other man that a museum had plenty of opportunities to get his woman alone.

"You have to let me go," Viola whispered, but not so forcefully this time. "Someone will see us."

Undeterred by something as trivial as faraway voices, he trailed kisses along the curve of her neck and shoulder as he slid his hand down. "They'd have to come all the way down the gallery, and we'll hear them in plenty of time. Besides—" He broke off, forgetting whatever he'd been about to say as his palm curved around the full, round shape of her breast and she gave a little gasp. Layers of fabric impeded him, but his memory of his wife's luscious shape was perfectly clear. The excitement inside him rose like the tide and he forgot whatever he'd been about to say.

She slid her hand between them, curling her fingers around his wrist as if to pull his hand down. He stilled, tense, waiting in agony with her breast against his palm. He remembered the rules they had established long ago. Whether he got his kiss or no, if she stopped him, he stopped. But not before.

Her hand moved, her palm flattened over his, not quite pressing his hand to her breast, but almost. Tacit encouragement. No stopping yet.

John shaped her breast through the fabric with his hand, his fingertips brushing back and forth over the bare skin just above the rounded neckline of her gown. He tasted her throat in countless little nibbles, all the way up to her cheek.

Her breath was coming faster now, and she twisted in his arms. "Someone will see us," she moaned softly, sounding aroused and miserable and angry all at once. "Oh, John, someone will see."

"Better kiss me quick, then."

She made a wordless sound and turned her face toward him, giving him what he wanted. Her mouth touched his and opened, sending shimmers of pleasure through his body. Her hand lifted to spread across his cheek. Her kid glove felt smooth and cool on his skin, her mouth hot and sweet. He closed his eyes, savoring a delight so long forgotten, and yet so familiar. This was Viola; he remembered her taste as he kissed her, he remembered the puffy fullness of her lower lip as he sucked it, he remembered the perfect line of her teeth as he explored them with his tongue.

She broke the kiss suddenly, turning her face away. She stirred in his hold and made a faint sound—a protest, maybe.

Past the blood pounding through him, and her soft little objection, he heard something else, the tap of footsteps turning to come down the gallery toward them, and John knew he was out of time. At least for today.

Wrenching himself away, he pressed one last

quick kiss to the side of her neck, pulled back and let her go. He bent to pick up her shawl collar and hat from the floor and handed them to her. As the footsteps came closer, he straightened his cravat and leaned out of the niche to have a peek, striving to force down his arousal and regain a semblance of sanity. An elderly, stooping gentleman in a dusty black suit and spectacles was coming toward him. Beside him, John could hear the rustle of straw and fabric as Viola shoved on her hat, donned her collar, and straightened her rumpled clothes.

"At last!" John exclaimed, and stepped partway out of the niche. "We have been wandering around forever, trying to find our way, and now here is someone to assist us."

The old man stopped and squinted, peering down the length of the gallery. "Is there someone with you, sir?"

"My wife and I were looking for the new collection of weapons and armaments. We seem to have gotten lost."

"I should say you have. It isn't down this way at all."

John schooled his features into buffle-headed perplexity. "Isn't it?" He turned his head in Viola's direction. "Sorry, dearest. I seem to have led us astray."

He got a none-too-gentle kick in the leg for that remark.

"Did you not get a map when you came in?" the man asked.

"Map?" John pressed his fingers to his forehead as if he were trying to think. "No, I don't believe we did."

"I am Mr. Addison, the assistant director of antiquities." He beckoned with one hand. "I shall direct you and your wife to the armaments."

"I say, that's awfully kind of you." John glanced into the niche and held out his hand to Viola, adding in a whisper, "Collar button."

She fastened it, glaring at him as if this was all his fault. She stuck her chin up to the level of hauteur befitting a duke's sister, brushed back several loose tendrils of hair that had fallen over her face, then put her hand in his and stepped out into the gallery.

"Why, bless me!" the elderly gentleman exclaimed, "Lady Hammond!"

"Good day, Mr. Addison." She was trying to sound dignified, John knew, but there was still a flush in her cheeks, a breathless edge to her voice, and a rumpled quality to her appearance, in which he took a great deal of satisfaction.

"Lost, again, my lady?" Mr. Addison shook his head at her.

She gave the feeble smile of the dim-witted female that only fooled old men and stupid young ones. "It's this new wing, sir. It confuses me."

"I keep telling you to always take one of the maps with you when you go wandering about the museum," he said, answering her smile with an indulgent one of his own. He pushed his spectacles up the bridge of his nose. "Your husband accompanying you today, I see."

John bowed. "Lord Hammond," he introduced himself when Viola failed to do so.

"A pleasure, my lord. Come this way to see the armaments."

They followed a few feet behind Mr. Addison as he led them out of the gallery.

"That was close," John murmured in her ear, laughing softly, exhilarated by the whole experience, especially the gratifying passion he'd aroused in his wife, which had been his goal for the entire afternoon. "I haven't had this much fun in years."

She sniffed. "Don't expect to have any more of it," she whispered back. "Not with me, at least. I have no intention of letting you trick me again."

"No?" He cast a sideways glance at her and grinned. "Now that's a challenge I can't resist."

Chapter 8

$\sim\!\!\infty\!\!\sim$

Viola stared at herself in the mirror of the modiste's dressing room without seeing her reflection or the costume she intended to wear to the charity ball. All she could see was her husband's wicked smile. An outrageous man, he really was, using all manner of tricks and wiles on her just like he used to do, and as he had said, she always fell for it. She would have to watch her step better in the future. He was so good at beguiling her.

He was good at other things, too. She touched her fingers to her mouth, feeling the delicious warmth of his kiss all over again even as she reminded herself he was good at kissing because he'd done so much of it. That true and painful reminder didn't help. It only made her feel more muddled and agonized.

What had happened yesterday? She closed her eyes, thinking of those stolen moments in the museum, and she knew the answer. She'd lost her head, just like the naive girl of nine years ago.

So long since John had touched her like that, but time hadn't made a difference to the way she responded to him. Time hadn't shored up her pride enough to take away the excitement of his hands and his mouth.

She wrapped her arms around herself and opened her eyes. Looking at her reflection, she saw all her confusion and misery looking back at her, and she did not understand her own mind or her own heart. What was wrong with her? Pride had held her together through heartbreak, kept her head high when he turned to other women, helped her pretend to him and to the world that she didn't care what he did, enabled her to find satisfaction in a life of charity work and good friends. Where had all her pride been yesterday?

He would hurt her again if she let him. He would. The deceptions of pulling her into empty corridors and stealing kisses might be harmless ones, but she knew he could lie with his heart in his eyes about the things that mattered most, and she always wanted to believe him. That was what frightened her. How easy it was to believe him.

Do you love me?

Of course I do. I adore you.

A knock on the door interrupted her, and at her call to come in, Daphne entered the modiste's dressing room, wearing her costume of Cleopatra. "Well?" she asked, smoothing the heavy tresses of her black wig. "What do you think?"

I think I am losing my mind.

With an effort, Viola pushed the museum outing of the previous afternoon out of her mind. It was all right to lose her mind as long as she didn't let him steal her heart. She turned to her sister-in-law, relieved by the distraction, and smiled. "Did Cleopatra wear spectacles?"

Daphne made a face. Laughing, she said, "I shall not be wearing them to the ball, dearest! What do you think of the costume?" She toyed with the wide, jeweled collar above her flowing white gown. "Is it too silly of me to choose something like this?"

Viola looked at her best friend in the world, thinking of the woman Daphne had been when they met two years before—shy, so uncertain of herself, so much in love with Anthony and trying so hard to hide it. She was different now. Having her love returned so passionately by her husband and the responsibilities of her role as the Duchess of Tremore had taken away much of Daphne's shyness and replaced it with a measure of self-confidence. But there were moments, like this one, when the shy woman Viola had first met did come peeping through.

"It isn't silly in the least," Viola assured her. "Why should you think it so?"

"I have always wanted to be Cleopatra," Daphne confessed. "I am just uncertain I can be convincing in the role. Even if it is only for a Fancy Dress ball, we are supposed to act out our parts all evening."

"You look very queenly to me," Viola said, laughing. "And Anthony seems willing to be your Marc Antony. He'd take on the entire Roman Empire if you asked him to."

Daphne's mouth curved in a smile that was a bit reminiscent of a cat with the cream jug. "True. I rather like it that way, too. He told me once I have all the power over him because women have all the power in the world over men if only we exercise it properly. It took me a long time to understand what he meant."

Viola sighed. "If you understand it, explain it to me," she said wryly. "I could do with some of that power just now."

Her sister-in-law's smile faded, and Daphne looked at her with a hint of compassion.

Viola couldn't bear that. She turned in a pirouette. "What do you think of me as a French marquise?"

"I think you look lovely. As always."

"Thank you, but what of the costume? Is it authentic?"

Daphne tilted her head. "If you wish to be truly authentic, you will have to powder your hair."

Viola smoothed the dark blue velvet of her over-skirt. "Won't that make rather a mess?"

"At least they don't make it with sugar any longer."

"Hair powder was made with sugar? But wouldn't that attract all manner of insects?"

"That was a drawback, certainly."

"How awful." Though if that would keep Hammond at bay, it might be worth a try. She reminded herself that she wasn't going to think about him anymore. "Does the overskirt hang correctly at the hem?" she asked, turning in a circle again. "It seems a bit crooked."

"It's the hoops, I think, not the sack." Daphne adjusted one of the wide side hoops. "If you don't want to worry about powdering your hair, you could go as a Greek princess of two thousand years ago. Then you could wear a cone of fat on your head instead of hair powder."

"Fat?" Viola faced the mirror again and looked at her sister-in-law's reflection. "Why on earth would I wear fat on my head?"

Her horrified expression made the other woman laugh again. "The fat was perfumed, and in the heat, it would melt, releasing the fragrance."

"You know the most extraordinary things, Daphne. Thank you for the suggestion, but I shall stay with what I have. I cannot imagine what Lady Deane would have to say if I showed up at the ball with perfumed fat on my head." Viola smoothed the overskirt over the hoops at her hips. "Since you know so much, dear sister, how do I avoid getting powder on this dark blue velvet?"

"Wear a wig. Most people did eighty years ago."

"No, it will just get hot and make my head itch. I hate that."

"So that is why you are forever taking off your hats! Now I understand."

A scratch sounded on the door, and Mirelle, London's most fashionable modiste, entered the dressing room. "Your grace. Lady Hammond." She curtsied to Daphne and then to Viola. "I hope you like your costumes? Is there anything you would wish to alter? I am at your disposal."

"I like mine exceedingly well," Daphne said.

The modiste clasped her hands together, gratified. "Your grace is most kind." She turned to Viola. "And you, my lady?"

"Mirelle, what does one use for hair powder? Talc?"

"They make a very fine hair powder for wigs nowadays, my lady. Barristers and judges use it, you see. You could powder your hair with that. But if I may be allowed to give my opinion on the matter, it would be a shame to cover your hair with powder. It is a lovely color, and with the pale blue silk and dark blue velvet, most beautiful, most alluring."

Those passionate moments in the museum

flashed through her mind again, and Viola felt her cheeks heating at the mortifying memory. She wasn't certain she wanted to be alluring. It was too dangerous. "Thank you, Mirelle."

"I agree with her," Daphne put in. "No woman of any era would cover hair the color of yours with powder."

"Then I won't wear it." She told herself it was because powder was messy. The fact that Hammond had always liked the color of her hair had nothing to do with it. She pressed a hand to the low-cut, heavily boned bodice of embroidered, pale blue silk. "But we have another problem. It is a ball, and I shall never be able to waltz or country dance in this. No wonder they only danced the minuet in my great-grandmother's day." She glanced at Mirelle. "Can you have the waistline let out a bit?"

"Only a little bit, or it would spoil the line of the bodice, you see."

"Let out as much as you can, Mirelle. I shall be unable to breathe otherwise." She considered her choice one last time, then nodded. "I do like the gown very much. The embroidery is lovely."

"I am always pleased to be of service, my lady."

Mirelle departed and an assistant helped Viola dress once again in her own clothes. After that, she and Daphne left the modiste. "Mirelle was right, you know," Daphne said as they stepped into Anthony's barouche. "You do look stunningly beautiful in that gown."

Viola leaned back against the carriage seat beside her sister-in-law and gave her a look of chagrin. "There are many beautiful women in the world, Daphne, but beauty is not enough to make a husband faithful. What is?"

Daphne wrapped an arm around her shoulders in an affectionate hug. "I don't know, darling. I just don't know."

"Neither do I," she whispered. "I wish I did."

John knew that in the seduction of one's wife, desperate measures were required. And he also knew he would be forced to endure a certain amount of suffering.

He stayed away from Grosvenor Square for a few days, telling himself that his absence might make her miss him, but the truth was, he needed time to get his own desire back in check. Memories of the museum, of the taste of Viola's mouth and the soft, delicious feel of her in his arms invaded his dreams all three nights he stayed away, and dominated his thoughts for all three days. But it was a sweet sort of suffering.

Monday afternoon he decided he was in control enough to see her again, but this time he doubted he would be able to steal a few kisses in a shadowy corner. Today, his fate was to endure a different sort of torture. He intended to take Viola shopping.

His suggestion that she redecorate the house in Bloomsbury Square had not been met with the enthusiasm he had hoped for, but if she began selecting things for the house, she might begin to feel a part of it, and that could only help his cause. He also knew how much his wife loved to shop.

When John called for Viola at Grosvenor Square that afternoon, he once again suggested the idea of shopping for their house in town, but he found that his idea was still not meeting with any enthusiasm on her part.

"I don't want to go," she said, and sat down on the settee in Tremore's drawing room. "I don't feel well."

"Did anyone ever tell you what a bad liar you are? Put on a bonnet, fetch your reticule, and let's be on our way."

"I told you I do not want to redecorate your house."

"It's yours, too. I pledged my troth when we got married, remember? With all my worldly goods, I thee endowed, and all that."

She folded her arms. "You didn't have any worldly goods."

"I had estates. A title. A few horrid paintings of previous viscounts. What, those didn't count?"

"Why don't you take Lady Pomeroy shopping? She loves Bond Street, and she loves spending Pomeroy's money."

John studied her, and he knew she was flinging Anne in his face to drive him away.

He could tell her about Anne, he supposed.

Opening up the topic was akin to stepping into a pit of snakes, for he'd surely get bitten. He could tell her what an empty amour it had been, an easing of physical needs and nothing more, but he doubted that would make any difference. Talking about it might only make things worse. They would end up in a fight for certain, and what good would it do to rehash the whole thing anyway? His affair with Anne had been over five years ago. The future was what mattered. Besides, no sane man ever jumped into a snake pit.

"Would you prefer to walk to Bond Street or take my carriage?" he asked mildly.

She made a sound of impatience, stood up, and walked to the fireplace. "I told you I don't want to go shopping," she said over her shoulder.

"Viola, you love visiting the shops, and you know how much I hate it. I thought you would jump at the chance to torture me with testing the comfort of chair cushions and picking out Turkish carpets. Not to mention the jewelers, where you can sweet-talk me into spending an outrageous sum for a perfectly useless bauble of rubies and diamonds you can show off to your friends."

She turned around. "I do not need any jewels from you," she said coolly. "And as for the rest, I told you before I have no desire to spend my income from Anthony on your house, even if you are the one who has control of that income."

She was determined to fight with him today, but he was just as determined not to let that happen.

"If you don't wish to shop, then we'll do something else." He thought for a moment. "What if we go calling on all our friends? That would be amusing. We could sit on their settees and hold hands like sweethearts. Married couples never hold hands, especially us. What a shock they will get."

"I am not going to call on my friends and hold hands with you!"

"Oh, very well, if you are going to be so unromantic." He gave her a wicked grin. "We could go back to your brother's museum. I heard there are some very delicious Roman frescoes tucked away somewhere that nobody but the antiquarians are allowed to see. You're Tremore's sister, so we could get in to have a look at them. Let's do that."

She turned her face away. "I don't think so."

"I understand they're quite erotic," he went on, and realized she was blushing. He began to laugh and stepped in front of her, ducking his head to look her full in the face. "Dash it, Viola, you've already seen them, haven't you? Snuck in and had a peek when big brother wasn't looking?"

"Don't be absurd." Her cheeks got pinker, and he knew he was right. The thought of Viola sneaking into Tremore's museum to look at erotic pictures sent his hopes soaring higher.

"Curiosity got the better of you, did it?" he

teased. "I wish I'd thought to look at them the other day when we were there. What were they like? Were they so very wicked? Come on, Viola," he coaxed in the wake of her silence. "You can describe them to me. I am your husband, after all."

She remained silent, blushing furiously, and he knew those frescoes must be very erotic indeed. No wonder Tremore and his wife liked mucking around their estate in Hampshire, digging up those antiquities. John glanced down the length of his wife's body, started imagining some erotic images himself, and lost what little interest he had in taking her shopping.

"You know, the more I think on it," he said, "the more I like the idea of going back to Tremore's museum. There's probably nothing shown in those frescoes we haven't done anyway. In fact, if the room they're in has a lock on the door, we could try some of—"

"All right, all right!" she cried, lifting her palms toward him as if to stop any more of his words. "We shall go to Bond Street, for heaven's sake!"

She turned away and strode out of the drawing room, her pale yellow silk skirt and lacy petticoats churning up behind her heels with the force of her strides.

"But I've changed my mind," he called after her, laughing. "I want to go to back to the museum with you and look at the naughty frescoes."

"Not a chance!" she shot back over her shoulder

as she left the room. She returned a few minutes later, a straw bonnet trimmed in purple and yellow pansies on her head and an embroidered reticule in her gloved hand. Pausing in the doorway, she said, "Well, come along then," and vanished, starting toward the stairs without waiting for him.

It was only a distance of two blocks from Grosvenor Square to Bond Street. Since she had expressed no preference and it was such a fine day, he suggested they walk. She agreed, but when he offered her his arm, she did not take it, and they walked toward Bond Street side by side without touching. Two footmen followed a discreet distance behind, ready to carry packages for them if necessary.

When they turned onto Bond Street, she paused, and he halted beside her. "What do you wish to buy?" she asked.

"I have no idea. This is your territory, not mine. The only shops I frequent are boot makers and booksellers. And occasional visits to my tailor." He made a open-handed gesture to the street before them. "Lead the way."

She glanced around, thinking for a moment. "Perhaps Bell's would be a good place to start."

"Bell's?"

"Drapers. I heard they have some very beautiful new velvets, and you need new draperies in several of the rooms. The ones you have are a bit down-at-heel." She tapped one gloved finger against her lips, considering. "Although, you might want to have some of the rooms repainted first. We'll have to see."

A memory struck him and he began to laugh. "Remember when you started redecorating Hammond Park?" he asked as they resumed walking. "You painted the master chamber that deep red color, and you hated it once it was done. I loved it and wanted to keep it like that. We had a huge row over it."

"And you won," she answered, pausing before the drapers shop, waiting as he opened the door. "You usually did in those days," she added over her shoulder as she walked through the door. "It's galling to think how many times I gave in to you."

He followed her inside the crowded shop. "I don't know," he murmured beside her. "I rather liked having to sweet-talk you into seeing things my way. If I recall, it always took quite a few kisses to persuade you to my side. That was the fun part."

"I wish you would stop bringing up things like that!"

She blushed again, making him laugh as he followed her to a long counter where sample swaths of velvet were laid out in piles. This season's most fashionable colors, no doubt. He halted slightly behind her, looking over her shoulder at the fabrics.

"Does it bother you when I mention how we

used to kiss and make up?" he asked softly, so the ladies milling about would not hear.

She looked up at him in exasperation. "Must you hover beside me like a shadow?" she asked, and took a sideways step away from him.

"Not going to answer that, I see." He circled the counter, moving to stand opposite her. "You know, you are as prickly as a chestnut today."

"I have five good reasons," she shot back in a whisper. "No, six, if you count Elsie."

He did not respond to that. Instead, he held up a swath of moss green velvet, knowing she was fond of that color. "What about this?"

Viola looked at it, head tilted to one side. "It would be nice in your library," she said after a moment. "With those butter-colored walls and all the leather books, it would look quite attractive. What do you think?"

"Do you like it?"

She looked down at the fabrics spread over the table. "It does not matter if I like it."

"It matters to me, Viola."

She did not reply. She stood with her head bent, rubbing velvet between her gloved fingers.

"Do you like it?" he repeated.

She shifted her weight from one foot to the other, sighed, looked at him. "Yes, yes, I like it. All right?"

A small concession, but he'd take it. He grinned. "I knew you would. That's why I picked it."

"How would you know I liked it?"

"You like green. I remembered. Rather good of me, don't you think?"

"You needn't look so pleased with yourself." With that, she lapsed into silence, broken only by an occasional inquiry as to his opinion about various fabrics.

They made their way along the counter, and she continued to speak in such impersonal terms it was as if he had hired her to decorate his house. He wanted a smile, a laugh, a kiss. Damn it all, he wanted to please her.

When he spied a swath of fabric in a color she loathed, that gave him an idea, and he grabbed the piece of velvet. "I've changed my mind about having that green in the library," he said. "I want this instead."

She looked up, stared at the fabric in his hands, then looked at him as if he'd lost his mind. "What?"

John strove to seem serious. "Yes, I like this one much better than the green."

"It's orange," she said in horror.

He looked at it, pretended to think the matter over, then looked at her again, all wide-eyed innocence. "I like orange. What's wrong with orange?"

"I hate it! It's an awful, lurid color."

"But, Viola, I like it."

Her expression became downright mulish. "Our library is not going to have any orange!"

"At last!" he cried, and tossed the swath in the air, earning himself stares from the matrons around them and a baffled look from her. "A victory at last."

She cast an uneasy glance around. "What are you talking about?"

He grinned at her, and he didn't give a damn if every lady in Mayfair was in the shop. "You called it our library."

She jerked her chin, looked sideways. "I did not," she muttered.

"You did," he said, "and you can't take it back."

She returned her gaze to his. "That was a trick, Hammond," she accused. "You don't really want orange, do you?"

"Of course not. But it doesn't change the fact that you called it *our* library. You know what that means?" He gave her a triumphant look. "I get a point."

"A point? What are you talking about?"

"If I get enough points, I win."

"Points, indeed. Are we playing another game, then?"

"The same game. It's called 'Winning Viola.'"

Despite her best efforts, a tiny hint of a smile touched her mouth. "So I am to be the prize in this game as well as your competitor?"

"Well, yes. How many points do I need to win?"

She made a sound that might have been a laugh, but she pressed her fingers to her lips, smothering it at once. After a second or two she lowered her hand and once again began sorting through the samples on the counter.

"How many, Viola?

"Thousands and thousands."

"Not fair. Give me a number."

"All right." She paused, then said, "Eighteen thousand, seven hundred forty-two."

"It that all? You are being far too easy on me. That means, of course, I get another point."

That made her look up again. "Whatever for?"

"If you really hated me as much as you keep saying you do, you'd have told me I needed a million points at least. See how this game works?"

"You are so outrageous!" She held up piece of fabric in a sort of beige color with gold leaves embroidered into it. "What do you think of this for your music room?"

"What about this instead?" He held up a swath of lavender velvet, and though he once again tried to look serious, this time he couldn't quite manage it.

She smiled, wider this time. "Lavender, John? Surely not for the music room. But it would be the perfect color for your bedchamber."

He set down the sample and leaned over the counter, closer to her. "Would it get you there?" he asked in a low voice.

She didn't even hesitate. "No."

"Never mind, then," he said, and straightened. "I was willing to make the sacrifice, but it would be in vain, I see. Given that, there is only one useful purpose for velvet this color."

"What purpose?"

"A coat for Sir George."

This time she did laugh, and his spirits lifted another notch. "That poor man," she said. "You and Dylan truly have it in for him. Have the two of you been composing limericks about him again?"

"No, but we did come up with one for Lady Sarah Monforth. She is one of your dearest friends," he added slyly, "So I'm sure you want to hear it."

"I don't."

With a glance around to make certain no one was within earshot, he once again leaned over the counter. In a low murmur he said, "There once was a lady named Sarah, with a heart as dry as the Sahara. Bedding her would be as cold as the sea, and talking to her like having malaria."

She burst into laughter, forgetting for the moment that she was supposed to hate him. "That is one of the most dreadful limericks I have ever heard," she told him, still laughing.

He laughed with her. "I know, but I think I get at least ten points for it."

"Ten? I shall give you two. It's so awful it doesn't deserve more."

"Of course it's awful. Think of the subject. Besides, have you ever tried to rhyme anything with the name? It's rough going. And having been forced to endure that lady's conversation at dinner more often than any man should have to do, I feel malaria was a kind way of describing it. Accurate, too."

"Accurate? How so?"

"Around her, I always get this dazed, rather ill feeling. It comes of having to listen to someone whose mind is truly empty of any brains at all."

She laughed again, and as he looked at her, at the gold highlights of her hair and the radiance of her smile, he caught his breath. Eight years may have changed both of them, but one thing was still just the same. When Viola smiled and laughed, it was like the sun coming out. He knew he was going to need more limericks.

Suddenly, all her laughter stopped and all that radiance went out of her face. The sun went behind a cloud, and it was as if a chill wind had just whispered through the shop. He turned to see what had brought that terrible look to her face.

A pretty, brown-haired woman in a cherry-red hat was leaning over the counter in the center of the room, looking at bolts of fabric and smiling as she talked with the other women surrounding her. She looked up and caught his eye. When she gave him a nod of recognition, a fleeting tenderness came into her face. He bowed in response, and she looked away.

Lady Darwin.

A long time since he had last seen the baroness, he thought. Two years, at least, perhaps longer. She looked well, and he was glad of it. Peggy had always been a warm, kind woman.

He watched her glance past him, and he turned back around just in time to see Viola vanish out the door of the shop. He felt a sinking feeling in his guts, fearing that any progress he had made toward wooing back his wife had just disintegrated into ashes.

Chapter 9

*H*ell.

John started across the draper's shop in pursuit of his wife, but by the time he made it around the long counter, two stout ladies carrying parcels had stepped into the doorway ahead of him, each of them insisting that the other lady go first. He had to wait until they finally settled upon precedent as the proper order of departure, and it seemed an eternity before he was able to exit the draper's shop. He stepped onto the sidewalk just in time to see his wife turning the corner onto Brook Street, walking as fast as she could. "Viola, wait!"

He raced after her, calling her name, oblivious to the stares of the people he passed, not caring that this was Mayfair—proper, well-mannered Mayfair, where no one shouted and no one ever ran anywhere.

He caught up to her at the corner of Davies Street. "Where are you going?"

164

"Home."

He put a hand on her arm. "Grosvenor Square is not your home."

"It is now." She jerked free of his hold and kept walking. "And it will be forever, if I have my way."

"Can we talk about this?"

"You want to talk instead of leaving?" she shot back without looking at him. "That's a refreshing change for you, but no. I don't want to talk because there is nothing to say. I don't want to see you. I don't want to spend time with you. I don't want to pick fabrics for *your* library. I want you to go away and leave me be. Don't like having Bertram as your heir? That is your misfortune and no concern of mine!"

They reached the end of the block and started to cross Duke Street, but a lorry was passing and he grabbed her to keep her from stepping in front of it. "Careful, Viola, for God's sake!"

She waited until the lorry had passed, then pulled out of his hold again and started across, though this time she did look where she was going. He stayed beside her until they reached the other side of the street, but when she turned into the square, he stopped and watched her walk away, waiting to see if she would even look over her shoulder to see if he was following. She did not.

He wondered if he should even bother to follow. He'd asked if they could talk, but as she had so accurately pointed out, there was nothing to say.

He watched her cross the square toward Tremore's house, and he slammed his fist into his palm with an oath of frustration. Deuce take it, they had just started to get along.

Seeing Peggy Darwin was the worst thing that could have happened. He couldn't help wondering if this was going to occur every time they were out together. If so, he hadn't a prayer.

She still didn't look back to see if he was following. Perhaps he should just let her go.

Of course you'll walk away. You always do.

Not this time. John strode across Grosvenor Square and entered the house just as she was reaching the top step of the curving staircase. "Viola, wait."

She did not stop.

"Now who is the one walking away?" he shouted after her.

His words echoed back to him down the stairs, but there was no reply. Ignoring the curious stares of Tremore's servants, he took the stairs two at a time, racing to catch up to her, though it wasn't until she turned down a corridor on the second floor that he managed it. He got there just in time for her to slam the door in his face, but he grabbed the handle and shoved it open before she could even think about locking it.

This was Viola's bedchamber. Her maid, Celeste Harper, was in the room, laying out gowns on the bed. "Harper," he said quietly, "leave us."

"No, Celeste," Viola countermanded him, "stay right where you are."

John said nothing more, but the maid knew he didn't have to. The lord and master was the one who paid her wages. She gave a quick bob of a curtsy to both of them and went scurrying out.

"How dare you follow me into my room this way and order my maid around!" Viola cried the moment the door was closed. "This is not your house. Get out of here at once or I'll have Anthony throw you out."

"Hiding behind your brother's coattails won't solve anything."

"Get out. Go find yourself some welcoming feminine company."

"I am not going to do this anymore. By God, I'm not! I am not going to be in a continual war with you and have you throwing things in my teeth that I cannot change. There is nothing I can do about the past. There is nothing I can say."

"What do you mean there is nothing you can say? Why not try something witty, something clever, something to make me laugh and deflect from the unpleasant situation at hand. Isn't that what you always do?"

That cut him, deep, but he refused to let her see how much it hurt. "Oddly enough, my dear, I cannot think of a single witty comment. It's beyond me just now to even try to make you laugh. I wish to hell I could. There is nothing I can say about Peggy or Anne or Elsie or any other woman I've been with. You are going to have to get over it."

"Just forgive and forget? Is that it? How convenient for you."

"Do you want me to tell you about Peggy so you have even more reason to despise me?" he asked, frustrated by the futility of it all. "Do you?"

She did not answer.

"Some of the women I've bedded I haven't given a damn about," he went on, goaded by her silence. "Like Anne Pomeroy. She used me, I used her. Sordid, but there it is. Peggy was different. Peggy and I came together with one thing in common. The loneliness of our empty, meaningless, sensible marriages."

Pain shimmered across her face, pain that hurt him, too, but he did not stop. "Peggy and I consoled each other. Believe me, we both needed consolation."

"Don't!" She clamped her hands over her ears. "I do not want to hear this."

"You must want to hear about it, since you keep bringing it up and hammering me with it. Peggy and I were lovers for over a year. She was a merry companion and a warm, loving woman. And both of us enjoyed it for exactly what it was for as long as it lasted."

"It's bad enough I have to see your lovers everywhere. I don't have to stand here and listen to you talk about them."

She tried to walk around him, but he stepped in front of her. "Why not? Would it really bother you?" He saw the pain in her face and knew he was causing it, but he didn't stop. He pushed harder, feeling defensive, feeling cruel, feeling—damn it all—guilty. "Do ice queens ever need anyone?"

She turned her face away. In profile he could see her lips quiver, press together in a hard, tight line.

"I could say that my affair with Peggy meant nothing, because that's what men always say to their wives, but in this case, it would be a lie."

"As if lying is so hard for you."

"It wasn't nothing. But it wasn't love, or anything close to it. It was two lonely people who had a fondness for each other and needed the warmth of human contact."

"Peggy Darwin was in love with you!"

"Nonsense."

"It's not nonsense. She was mad for you, and everybody knows it. Everybody but you."

She started to turn away, but he grabbed her by the shoulders. "It wasn't love, Viola. It was lust and someone to talk to afterward, a way to ease loneliness, and that's all it was."

She shook her head in disbelief but wouldn't

look at him. He grabbed her chin and lifted her face, and he saw the streak of a tear. It fell onto his hand and burned his skin like acid.

"Christ almighty!" He let go of her and backed up against the window, hating her for eight years of walls between them, hating himself more for giving her so many reasons to build them. "What do you want from me? Devil take it, woman, what do you want?"

"I don't want anything from you. It's you who wants something. Something I can't give you. It's gone, John, and you cannot get it back. Some things just aren't reparable." With that, she turned and ran for the door.

"How many times do I have to say it? I cannot do anything about the past."

"Yes, you can." She halted in the doorway and whirled around. "You can learn from it. I did. I learned never to trust you again."

With that, she was gone.

He leaned back against the window and stared at her bed in her brother's house, at the pale, magnolia-pink gown that lay across it, and her laughter from earlier echoed through his mind. He'd decorate every house he owned with pink wallpaper if it would make her laugh and smile. If it would do any good. But it wouldn't.

He turned his back on the bed and stared out the window, fighting the urge to smash his head through the glass. "Damn," he mumbled, regretting the harsh words he had spoken moments ago, cruel words, meant to hurt. "Damn, damn, damn."

They had been down this road so many times before, where Viola was cold and he was angry, where she was hurt and so was he, where she could not forgive and he said to hell with it. When he walked away and found a woman who didn't judge him, didn't cut him into pieces, and didn't despise him. Perhaps she was right that some things weren't reparable. No matter what he said or did or tried to do, it wouldn't be enough. He could take a vow of celibacy and move to a monastery in Italy and it wouldn't be enough. As long as he was breathing, it would never be enough. Not for Viola.

A couple walking down below caught his attention, and he realized it was the Duke and Duchess of Tremore. They were strolling side by side along the path at the edge of the oval park below, and Tremore himself was pushing a pram in front of them. They were taking baby Nicholas for a walk. Beckham, the nanny, trotted along a few paces behind.

John watched as they stopped beside a wrought-iron bench. The duchess lifted Nicholas from the pram, then she sat down, standing the baby on her knees, her hands holding him around the waist. Her husband sat down beside her, draping an arm across the back of the bench, behind his wife.

They were like any couple fortunate enough to be happily married, laughing and talking and taking their baby son for an outing in the park.

They were a family.

Just then Viola emerged into view, crossing the thoroughfare in front of the house to join them. Her hat was in her hand, and her tawny hair shone like gold in the sun.

She halted in front of the bench, tossed the hat onto the grass beside the bench, then reached out her hands to take Nicholas from his mother. She lifted him high into the air above her head and spun in a slow circle, head thrown back as she laughed up at the baby. Something as hard and painful as a physical blow hit John in the chest.

He tried to turn away but felt paralyzed. He flattened his palms against the glass panes on either side of his face and stared at his wife holding a baby that was not his son, and he had never felt more helpless, more angry, or more bereft in his life. Maybe he should tell Viola, he thought. No doubt his pain would be a great comfort to her.

"My goodness, he's getting big!" Viola lowered the baby from over her head and cradled him against her as she sat down beside her sister-in-law on the bench. "I cannot hold him up that high for very long."

"He does love it when you do that, though."

Daphne reached for the child, but Viola turned away, keeping the baby out of his mother's reach.

"Let me hold him," she pleaded. "I haven't had a chance to hold him all day."

"But it's time for his nap."

"Just a few minutes." She hugged the baby tight against her shoulder, but he began to wriggle in her hold, so she stood him on her lap, gripping his hands in hers. The baby's fingers curled tightly around her own, and a frown of concentration puckered his forehead as he stood on her knees. "Steady as can be," she said, watching him. "He's going to be walking any day."

"He is very close," Daphne agreed. "He pulls himself up, but every time he takes a step, he immediately falls back down."

"He was doing that all morning." Anthony leaned around his wife on the bench to look at Viola and the baby. "When he was in my study with me after breakfast, he kept grabbing onto the edge of an ottoman and hauling himself up. Every time he fell down, he tried again. Stubborn fellow, my son."

"That is no surprise," Viola said. "He—"

The clatter of wheels on the cobblestones interrupted her, and all three of them looked up from the bench as John's carriage came to a halt in front of Anthony's house about twenty yards from where they sat.

Viola watched as John came out the front door

and climbed into the open landau, a frown like thunder on his face, and she was glad he did not glance in their direction.

"How fiercely Hammond is scowling," Daphne murmured as the carriage jerked into motion. "Whatever can be wrong with him?"

"Indigestion?" Anthony suggested, sounding hopeful.

"Anthony, really!" Daphne rebuked him. "That was a most unkind thing to say."

"I am the cause, I suspect," Viola murmured, lifting Nicholas to rest his head on her shoulder as she watched the landau roll away. It turned out of the square and vanished from view, and she wondered if John intended to spend his evening seeking out another woman for *consolation*. If he found one appealing enough, he might stay away. That thought should have brought hope, but somehow it did not. It only made a sick little knot form in the pit of her stomach. She held the baby tighter.

"Did the two of you have a quarrel?" Daphne asked.

Viola turned her head to look at her sister-in-law. "Don't we always?"

Anthony gave a sharp sigh and rose to his feet. "If the pair of you are going to talk about Hammond, I shall leave."

"We are not going to do anything of the sort," Viola assured him. "My husband is the last thing I want to discuss. Stay."

Anthony shook his head. "No, really, I should be going. I am meeting Dewhurst at White's to discuss our proposed revisions to the Reform Bill. I shall be back well in time to escort the pair of you to Monforth's rout this evening."

Viola shook her head. "I am not going. I cannot abide Sarah Monforth. I shall claim the vapors and stay home."

"I have more reason to dislike Lady Sarah than you do," Daphne said, laughing. "Anthony almost married her instead of me."

"A thought which still makes me shiver when I think on it," Viola said.

"Neither of you have cause to dislike Lady Sarah," Anthony protested. "I didn't marry the woman after all."

"Dear brother, even that blessed fact is not enough to make me like her. Daphne, I say we should both stay home. We could play piquet and get tipsy on madeira."

"And leave Lady Sarah an open field to flirt with my handsome husband?" Daphne asked with mock severity. "Never!"

"As if it would matter." Anthony pressed a kiss to the top of his wife's head. "I shall return by seven o'clock to fetch you." He walked away, leaving the two women alone.

"Are you really going to abandon me to Lady Sarah and stay home?" Daphne asked.

"Yes. I intend to spend a quiet evening." She

kissed the top of her nephew's head. "Nicholas shall keep me company. He is a better conversationalist than Lady Sarah."

Daphne laughed. "When you say things like that, I almost feel sorry for the woman. I am so glad you never took a dislike to me!" Something past Viola's shoulder caught her attention, and she made a sound of dismay. "Oh, Viola, there goes your bonnet!"

Viola turned and saw that the spring breeze was sending her hat tumbling across the grass. She handed Nicholas back to his mother and ran after it. She had to chase it for quite a few yards but was finally able to catch it by the brim just before the wind whipped it out of her reach again.

Breathless, she returned to her seat beside Daphne.

"You'd best put it on," her sister-in-law advised, patting baby Nicholas on the back as Viola sat down beside her.

"I shan't!" Instead, she put the bonnet in her lap, wrapping the ties securely around her fist. "With this wind, I should have to use my hat pin, and that would surely give me a headache."

"You do loathe hats. You are forever taking them off."

I remember how you'd always tear off your hat and toss it up in the air, laughing.

She had forgotten about that, about riding horses on the downs with John. She had forgotten so many things. The blackberry jam. The way he kissed her neck. The way he used to trap her in corners and steal kisses from her. The way he made her laugh. The hot desire in his eyes. How much he could hurt her.

"One of your blossoms is torn." Daphne shifted Nicholas to her other shoulder and reached over to touch the shredded edge of one of the purple and yellow pansies that trimmed her bonnet. "I don't believe it can be mended."

Viola stared down at the bouquet of silken blossoms. Violas. Her namesake flower. She'd had them in her wedding bouquet. "Some things can never be mended," she whispered.

"Perhaps we should go shopping tomorrow so you can get a new one. You can accompany me to Bell's while we are out."

Viola's fingers clenched around the brim of her hat. "The drapers?"

"I heard they had some fine velvets just now. I wanted to have a look at them."

The image of a pretty woman in a red hat laughing over bolts of velvet flashed through her mind. "They are not so very fine."

"Have you seen them, then?"

"Hammond and I were in Bell's this afternoon." She paused. "Lady Darwin was there. That was why John and I quarreled. She was his mistress four years ago.

"He has no mistress now. He broke from Emma

Rawlins, and I heard she has gone to France."

"It doesn't matter, Daphne. He'll just find someone else. He always does. And then I will have to see her, and hear people talk about her, as I have all the others." Viola could feel Daphne's steady gaze on her, and she sighed. "It should not have hurt to see Lady Darwin in Bell's today, but it did. The look on her face. She was in love with him once. I know it. And I know she is in the past, but it still hurts, Daphne. It hurts every time. With every woman. Yet he expects me to begin living with him again as if none of that ever happened."

Daphne was silent for a long moment, patting Nicholas's back and staring dreamily into space through her gold-rimmed spectacles. After a moment she returned her gaze to Viola and asked a wholly unexpected question. "Would it be so very terrible living with Hammond again?"

Viola stared at her sister-in-law, astonished. "After what he has done, how can you ask me that?"

"I know all about Lady Darwin, and Emma Rawlins, and all the other women, but would it be possible for you to put that behind you? Can the two of you not make a fresh start? Begin anew?"

She didn't want a fresh start. Or a new beginning. She did not want John. He wasn't worth the pain. "One cannot have a fresh start with a man who is a liar and a philanderer," she said, trying to harden her heart again. "He has proven himself unworthy of trust time and again."

"Trust takes time, something you two have had little of, apparently, despite being married nearly nine years. Perhaps time is what you need to find common ground and learn to live amicably."

Viola stirred on the bench, feeling prickly and defensive. She tugged at the torn pansy, ripping it out of the bouquet. "Hammond and I have no common ground and we never lived amicably, even when I still had romantic stars in my eyes about him. We fought all the time."

When we weren't making love.

She made a fist around the silk flower in her gloved hand, thinking of the topsy-turvy days when she and her husband had lived together—the passionate quarrels and the equally passionate reconciliations. She did not want to fight with Hammond, but she did not want to make up with him, either. And she most certainly did not want to talk about him.

Daphne, however, seemed determined to have a conversation on the topic. "Both of you are older, wiser now than you were then. Is there no way the two of you could just learn to get along?"

"Is that what a marriage is?" she asked, looking at her sister-in-law. "Merely getting along?"

Daphne's violet eyes were grave behind her spectacles. "Believe it or not, yes, most of the time. Not very romantic, I suppose, but true."

Getting along with Hammond not only sounded unromantic. It sounded impossible. "You are happily married. You don't understand."

"I understand your pride, and you have good reason to mistrust him after what he did. But men have pride, too, a great deal of it. Hammond more than most, I suspect. And he is certainly not one to wear his heart on his sleeve."

"He does not have a heart."

"I think he does. He hides it well. He is, in fact, a great deal like me."

"What? That is nonsense!"

"It is true. You are very different from me, Viola, for you are openly affectionate and trusting toward every person you meet. Until they give you a reason not to be. Then you can be—pardon me for saying this—you can be as cold as winter in Scotland."

That stung. It echoed John's description of her. She swallowed hard. "You are saying I am unforgiving? That I am . . . that I am some sort of ice queen?"

"I am saying your passions are very strong and long lasting. You see things in very stark terms. Black or white. Good or bad. Right or wrong. Friend or foe. Not everyone is like you, dearest. I am not. I have the impression the viscount is not. We are both more moderate, I think, than you. More temperate. We have just as much pride. We simply express it differently. Usually by hiding how we feel."

"I cannot believe you compare yourself with him. You are nothing like him! You would never lie. You would never toy with someone's affections. You would never be unfaithful to those who love you. You would not walk away from difficult situations. If you wronged and wounded another person, you would acknowledge it and regret it and try to make up for it. I know Hammond better than you, and you don't know what you're saying."

Daphne put a hand on her shoulder. "You loved him once. I know that much."

Tightness squeezed her chest, and she grimaced. "That, I believe, is common knowledge. That makes it all the more mortifying to be played the fool, does it not?"

The baby stirred in his mother's arms, and Daphne resumed stroking his back. "It must be hard on a man," she said thoughtfully, "to be despised by a woman who once loved and adored him so much, to watch her turn her back on him. Turn him out of bed." She met Viola's gaze over the sleeping baby's head, her cheeks pink. "The physical side of . . . of . . . things is very important to a man, Viola. Even more important than it is to us. I think you already know that."

She could not believe what she was hearing. "Are you taking Hammond's side?"

"I am not taking his side. I am *seeing* his side."

That her dearest friend in the world would take Hammond's part was too much to endure. "He has no side," she flared, "at least not a justifiable one. He was a fortune-hunting scoundrel. He lied to me, he walked out on me, and he has been with woman after woman after woman. And society blames me for all of it."

"Not all of it. Society has its share of condemnation for him, too. I have heard the talk. There are many who deem Hammond less than a man for not dragging you to bed and forcing an heir on you long ago. Having his masculinity called into question would be a very hard thing for a man to endure, I should think. Hammond acts as if he doesn't care what others say of him, but I imagine he covers a lot of his feelings that way."

Viola rubbed the side of her neck with irritation, thinking of those passionate moments in the museum. "I don't see why anyone would question his masculinity. With all the women he's had, he hardly needs to prove it."

"Is it so difficult to imagine why he turned to those other women?"

Peggy and I consoled each other, and believe me, we both needed consolation.

"You are being cruel, Daphne. Cruel to say this is my fault!"

"I did not say any such thing," Daphne answered with her usual calm equanimity. "I am merely speculating on what a man like Hammond might have thought and felt during the past eight years. I do not know him well, and I could be completely wrong about his character. Anthony would say I was, for to his mind, Hammond should be hanged, drawn, and quartered for doing anything to hurt his baby sister. Your brother worships the ground you walk on, you know that."

"Anthony hates Hammond because Anthony is a very good judge of character. Better than I am, obviously."

"Really?" Daphne smiled. "You are the one who looked at a plain, shy young woman with low connections and thought she would be a much better wife for your brother than Lady Sarah Monforth. Anthony didn't see me in a favorable light at all, if you remember."

"It did take him a bit of time to come around to my way of thinking. But I was right about you."

"If you were right about me, then perhaps you are a better judge of character than you think. You fell in love with Hammond, and even though you were young, I cannot believe you were ever a fool. He must have had some good qualities, and you must have sensed them in his character, or you would never have fallen in love with him in the first place."

"I fell in love with him when I knew nothing of his character." She shook her head impatiently. "It hardly matters anyway. I am not in love with him now. That love is gone, and once love is gone, you cannot get it back."

"I did. I fell in love with Anthony twice."

"Daphne, stop this. I do not want to be in love.

Not with Hammond. Not ever again. I don't want it, I tell you!"

Her raised voice woke the baby, who stirred and began to cry.

Viola had a most stupid desire to do the same. "All this talk of love is pointless," she said in a more moderate tone.

"And what of the other purpose of marriage?" Daphne asked as she rocked the baby and tried to soothe him back to sleep. "What about children, Viola? Do you not want children?"

That question felt like a knife going in. She had long ago resigned herself to never having children of her own, had come to accept it. "Society blames me for Hammond's lack of an heir. Do you blame me, too?"

"It is not a question of blame, dearest. I simply asked if you want children."

"Of course I did!" she cried, stung. "I always wanted them. All my life, I had known what I wanted. I used to dream of it—a wonderful husband to love who loved me, and we'd have a whole brood of children. When I married John, I thought I was getting my dream come true." She choked and her eyes began to blur. "That was when I a stupid, romantic girl."

"There is nothing stupid about wanting a husband and children to love. You have the husband already. He wants children, too. Viola, have you stopped to think that this might be your second chance to have your dream come true?"

"With Hammond?" She shook her head. "No, Daphne, no. Even if I did ever develop some . . . some renewal of affection for that man—which is highly doubtful—what difference would it make? He doesn't love me. He never has and he never will, and I don't love him anymore, and I never will. And that's all there is to that."

"If you say so."

"I do say so. Besides, even if love has nothing to do with it, even if marriage is all about getting along, Hammond and I are doomed by that alone. Let's not talk of it anymore."

Thankfully, Daphne let the matter drop, but in her own mind, Viola could not stop thinking about it.

She and Hammond would never be able to just get along. Because he still made her weak in the knees when he kissed her neck or touched her cheek. Because if she gave him an inch, he'd always take a mile. Because if she let herself believe in his smile and his laugh and that heated look in his eyes, she would be deceived again. If she let him take her to bed, she would run the risk of falling in love with him again. All of that could only lead to one conclusion. Her broken heart. Again.

Viola stared at the pansies in her hat. Wedding vows meant nothing to him. If she gave him what he wanted, he would still leave her in the end. He desired her right now, she knew that, but she also knew that love and desire were not the same thing. Hammond had desired many women. She was just one of many.

She lifted her fist and opened her hand. The bit of purple and yellow silk floated away on the spring breeze. When unaccompanied by his love, a man's desire was like the wind. It had no substance, and it was impossible to hold onto. She would do well to remember that.

Chapter 10

The clash of swords and the curses of men were the prevailing sounds as John walked through the doors of Angleo's. When it came to fencing, any man worthy of being called a Corinthian honed his skill with a blade at Angleo's.

Dylan Moore was already there when he arrived. The two men practiced together almost daily, but they had not done so very much of late. John had been too preoccupied with trying to win over his wife to think about much else.

An entire week had gone by since they had seen Lady Darwin at Bell's. Since then, he had tried several times to talk to Viola, but she refused to see him. Today, her three-week reprieve was over, but when he went to fetch her, he found her trunks were not packed, she had once again refused to see him, and her damnable brother told him to leave. Unless he wanted to force the issue by legal means, he and Viola were at stalemate. He did not know what to do.

He was feeling like a boiling kettle with the lid on. After leaving Grosvenor Square this afternoon, he had sent Dylan a note asking to meet at Angleo's for sparring practice this evening, because he had finally reached his limit and knew if he didn't let off some steam, he was going to explode.

His friend looked up as he entered the practice room. Already down to his shirtsleeves and ready to start, Dylan slashed through the air with the foil in his hand. "You ask me to meet you and then you arrive late."

John didn't say it was because he was going out of his mind. He didn't say it was because he was preoccupied, frustrated, baffled, and—worst of all—helpless.

He glared at Dylan as he tore off his coat, waistcoat, and cravat and tossed them to the boy standing by the door. The servant then left the room, and John took his favorite foil down from the hook on the wall. "You'd best watch your step this evening," he warned. "I'm in a foul mood and I intend to take it out on you." He slashed the blade through the air. "Women are the very devil."

"Matrimonial troubles?" Moore asked, looking at him with sympathy.

"You don't know the half of it."

The two men faced each other, stepped into positions en garde, crossed blades, and began. John lunged first, and the blades of the two men clanged, echoing through the room.

"Gossip is flying all over town," Moore said, parrying the thrust. "I have heard that Lord and Lady Hammond may be reconciling. Or it may be that they are not."

"Reconciling?" John pulled back, and immediately lunged twice more, forcing his opponent to retreat several steps with the use of his blade. "I am inclined to doubt it myself. It takes two to reconcile."

Once again Moore managed to parry, for the two men were equally matched, and John was soon the one retreating. Within moments they were back to the center of the room.

"Sitting together at Covent Garden," Moore said as they circled each other, foils pointed. "Picnics and carriage rides." He began to laugh. "Kissing your own wife in Hyde Park, Hammond? Taking her to museums? Going shopping for draperies together? That sounds like reconciliation to me."

"It was more like a temporary lull between battles. Excellent show at Covent Garden," he said, trying to divert the conversation. "Brilliant symphony. Best thing you've written in years, I thought."

"Thank you." Moore lunged, John parried, and the swords of the two men clanged together. "I did hear that Lady Darwin went shopping last week, too. I take it the lull is over and the battle is raging?"

He might have known Moore wouldn't let it drop. The man delighted in needling his friends. "Is my marriage any of your affair?" he asked as the two men began circling, gazes locked, each waiting for the other to make the next move.

"No." Moore gave him a mocking grin. "Couldn't pet her and soothe her and get her back with a kiss or two, eh?"

John refused to be provoked. "Apparently not," he answered lightly.

"Told you to go to the devil, did she?" Moore knew enough about women that an answer wasn't necessary, and he didn't wait for one. "When you decided you needed a son and approached her with the notion, what did you think would happen? Thought she'd see the necessity of it, did you? That she'd understand and do her duty?"

"Sod off."

Moore began to laugh, and there was a great deal of sardonic amusement in it. "Or perhaps you thought your wife would just fall back into your bed after a few weeks of wooing because you are such a legendary lover?"

Moore's mockery on top of Viola's condemnations pushed John even closer to the edge of reason. "I don't have a wife!" he said, and struck first. His opponent parried, and the two men paused again, blades pointed down, wrists crossed. "I haven't had a wife for eight and a half bloody years."

"No? If you don't have a wife, who is that lovely blond woman who goes about calling herself Lady Hammond?" Moore pushed with his wrist, forcing their blades in an arc toward the ceiling, then he ducked past John, turned so their positions were reversed, and lunged with his blade.

Anticipating the move, John ducked sideways and evaded it. He stepped around his opponent and, by the time Moore turned around, had him dead to rights. He planted the tip of his foil right against his friend's chest. "A hit," he declared, then turned and stalked away.

"You know who I mean," Moore went on as he followed John to the center of the room. "Petite," he prompted as the two men faced off. "Hazel eyes. Pretty mouth. I seem to remember seeing you marry a woman of that description almost nine years ago."

"Two people living in separate houses and sleeping in separate beds is not a marriage." He lunged, striking Moore's foil with his own. "It's a joke," he said, and lunged again. "It's been a joke almost since the beginning, and everybody knows it."

Steel slid against steel as Moore parried and spun away. When he turned, both men paused a few feet apart, breathing hard, blades poised.

Moore looked him in the eye. "A joke, Hammond? I don't see you laughing. Seems the joke might be on you."

John did not reply. He feigned left and thrust right, thinking to catch the other man in the chest again, but his opponent wasn't fooled. Moore sidestepped the move, and John's blade hit the wall. Before he could recover, the other man came up underneath, and John was the one caught in the ribs.

"Hit," Moore said. "You are not concentrating."

"Indeed? Yet I managed to get a hit on you moments ago."

The two men moved to en garde, crossed foils, and began again. For several minutes they were silent, the only sound the clash and rasp of striking blades, but it didn't take long for Moore to start in on him again. "I have a suggestion for you." He lunged and missed, then pulled back. "It might help you make peace with your wife."

"You've been married for, what, seven entire months?" John countered as he wiped sweat from his brow with his free hand. Now it was his turn to be mocking, and he laughed. "Wait at least that many years, then give me advice on the subject of matrimony."

"I am serious, Hammond." He stepped back and pointed his foil toward the ceiling to stop their match. "Listen to me, will you? You know I do not usually interfere in the affairs of my friends, but I have a suggestion for you. You won't like it, but it might help things along."

John heard the sincerity in Moore's voice, and it made him curious. "What suggestion?"

"Tell Viola you want to be friends."

That was absurd, and he showed what he thought of it by his sound of contempt. "I thought you said you were being serious. Viola and I friends? What an idea!"

"I am in earnest. Become her friend."

"Good God, man," he said with a humorless laugh, "where have you been for the past eight and a half years? Viola loathes me. You are out of your head if you think she and I could ever be friends. In the nine years we've known each other, she and I have been many things, but we have never been friends."

"All the more reason to give it a try, then. Besides, it worked for me. Grace and I were friends before we ever became lovers."

"She was your mistress."

"After she became my friend."

"If that is so, it was not at your instigation. I know you, Moore. It had to be Grace's idea."

"It was. I loathed it, I admit, but in the end it was the best thing that could have happened to me."

"You were a courting couple. Viola and I are already married. The two are entirely different." He made an impatient gesture with his foil. "Come on. Let us get back to the match."

"Why are they different? I am a married man

now, and I do not see a difference. Grace and I are still friends."

"You and Grace don't fight like cats and dogs. She doesn't despise you." John moved to en garde position and beckoned with his blade. "Are we going to fence or talk?"

"Viola might fall in love with you again. Is that what you're afraid of?" Moore mirrored John's stance and lifted his blade to cross John's. "Or perhaps you're afraid you'll fall in love with her."

Those words caused something inside John to snap. "Love, love, love!" he shouted, his simmering emotions finally erupting. "I am sick to death of that particular word!"

He struck hard and fast with his blade, using every bit of his skill to drive Moore back toward the wall. Thinking of how many times Viola had thrown her love for him in his face, remembering how she had talked of his liaison with Peggy Darwin as love, he felt savage and resentful, and he took out his frustration on his opponent, attacking until he finally caught a vulnerability and jabbed his foil against Moore's belly. "Hit."

The other man looked at him, clearly astonished by his vehemence. "I believe I struck a nerve."

Breathing hard, John stepped back and lowered his blade. He turned away. "Love. People fling that word around all the time, especially women, and what does it mean? When most people use the term, they mean simple, ordinary lust. Or idealistic infatuation. Sometimes both together. Is that love?"

"If you do not know the answer to that question already, I cannot answer it for you." Moore followed him to center. "I know I found it."

"How?" John demanded, facing him. "How did you find it? And when you found it, how did you know it was genuine? Cupid fired his arrow and angels sang and you knew? Is that it?"

"How disdainfully you speak of love. I never realized just how deep your cynicism runs, Hammond. You are more contemptuous of love than I ever was, if that is possible."

"I am not a cynic about love, nor am I contemptuous of it. I just—"

I just don't know what it is.

That realization froze him in place. He stared at his friend, looking through him as if he were not there. In his mind, he saw his wife holding a baby in the air and laughing. That queer, empty feeling returned, the emptiness that had been haunting him like a ghost for the past week. Emptiness inside himself that he had always pushed aside and covered up, but had been there ever since he could remember.

"Hammond?" Moore's voice interrupted his thoughts. "Whatever is the matter?"

"What?" John blinked, staring at his friend, trying to think.

"You're standing there, staring at me, looking dumbstruck. Are you unwell?"

"No," he answered, forcing himself to say something. "Perhaps. I don't know." He shook his head, trying to clear his mind. "Let's end for today."

What was love, really?

He asked himself that question as the two men put away their blades, retrieved their coats, and left the fencing gymnasium.

The beautiful May afternoon had turned into a cool, cloudy spring night. As he and Moore stood on the sidewalk outside Angleo's waiting for their carriages, his friend spoke again, all mockery gone from his voice. "Hammond, think about what I said. Suggest to Viola that the two of you become friends."

"And as I told you, she will never agree. She will probably laugh in my face."

"At least make the suggestion. It might help the two of you get along better if you could convince her to be friends."

John gave his friend a wry, sidelong glance. "A man and a woman getting along out of bed leads to them getting along in bed, is that it?"

Moore grinned at him. "That depends on how good a friend you can be, now, doesn't it?"

Despite his black mood, Moore's sardonic wit was infectious, and John couldn't help a laugh at that as the other man's landau pulled up in front of Angleo's, its top up against the chance of rain. "You really are a devil, you know."

"Of course I am," Moore answered as he stepped into his carriage. "I may be married, but I still have a reputation to maintain." His landau pulled away, and he left John standing on the sidewalk.

Dylan leaned back on the seat of his carriage, smiling to himself. A devil he was, indeed. He knew full well what Hammond was feeling at this moment, and it was about to get worse. The viscount was just desperate enough to give friendship with Viola a try. Poor fellow. Friendship with a woman you wanted to bed so desperately was hell on earth.

Still, one usually had to go through hell to get to heaven. In the end, Hammond might get the son he wanted, but more important, he might gain back a loving wife. Dylan knew the worth of that was beyond measure.

He liked Hammond, had a great deal of affection for Viola, and hoped they took his suggestion to heart. They might find themselves happily married for a change.

That thought made him want to laugh. Dylan Moore in the idealistic role of matchmaker. Who would have thought it? He couldn't wait to get home and tell Grace.

* * *

The notion of friendship was not what was running through John's mind as he waited for his carriage. It was instead the notion of love.

What was love? Poets wrote about it, people like Moore made music out of it, everyone was constantly falling in love or talking about it or suffering for it, but what was it?

He thought of Moore. Of all the men in the world, he would have picked Dylan as the one man who would never marry. Yet, he had. He had married his mistress. John could not fathom what it was about Grace that had caused England's most notorious rake to fall in love with her. She was a beautiful woman, certainly, and a kind, loving sort of person. But Moore was mad about her, crazy in love with her in a way that was almost frightening in its intensity.

John's carriage pulled up to the curb. He started toward it, then stopped, and on impulse waved the vehicle away and decided to walk home. It was a long way, but he felt like walking. The evening was cool and the bracing air felt good against his skin. He could always pick up a hansom cab if it started to rain.

There were different kinds of love, he supposed.

He thought of his sister, Kate, dredging up memories of when he was a small boy, vague memories of her hugs and her laughter and the terrible hole inside him when she died. He had loved his sister. He knew that much.

He thought of Percy and Constance, friends he had always cared about, who always cared about him, friends whose affection and trust were beyond question. He had spent a lot of time not thinking about Percy, because when he did, it hurt like an open wound. It hurt because he had loved his cousin like a brother. He loved Connie, too, with an affection and respect he gave to very few, but had he ever been in love with her? He thought of her words to him at Percy's funeral, and knew the answer had to be no. When she married his cousin instead of him, he had gone on a seven day drinking binge, whored around for several months, and gotten over it. If that was real love, true love, did a person recover so easily with such shallow methods? Surely not.

Ahead of him the sidewalk broadened into a wider thoroughfare, and that sight brought him out of his reverie. He came to a halt, and realized he was going the wrong way. He should have turned east at Brook Street, but instead he'd turned west and now was staring straight at the imposing wrought-iron gates that surrounded the park at Grosvenor Square.

Damn. Hadn't he had enough of this place? If he had any brains, he'd leave now, walk away, go find himself a woman who would welcome him into her bed.

But instead of turning around, John ventured forward into the square until he was at the park gates. He wrapped his hands around the bars, staring between them at the place beside a wrought-iron bench where his wife had been holding Nicholas a week ago today.

He thought of his parents, who had never had any love, nor even affection, between them, and the irony of how his marriage had turned out was not lost on him. The coldness of his mother and father toward one another was something he remembered from his boyhood with vivid clarity, and despite all his efforts these last nine years to be as unlike his father as possible, he had managed to make his marriage exactly the same loveless sham his father's had been.

It began to rain, a light drizzle that dusted his coat and dampened his linen. The air was decidedly chilly now, and he knew it was stupid to stand here. He should go back before the rain changed from a light drizzle into a downpour and he got soaked.

He turned around, but instead of leaving, he leaned back against the iron bars and stared up at the lamplit drawing room of Tremore House. A glint of gold hair passed the window. Viola's hair.

He thought of the girl she had been nine years ago, the open, vulnerable, passionate girl who had adored him in a way she had defined as love. He had wondered then, and he wondered now, how anyone could fall in love in one night, after two dances and a bit of conversation, without any knowledge of the other person. That couldn't be love because it wasn't real. He hadn't trusted it then. He didn't trust it now.

He knew from the start he'd had a power over her, but to this day he did not understand it. He did not understand her. Against the wishes of her brother, knowing he was stone broke, knowing he was irresponsible, knowing his wild, ne'er-do-well reputation, she had married him three months after meeting him, when no woman with sense would have married him at all. Because she had loved him. He thought of Percy down on his knees in the mud threatening suicide if Connie didn't marry him. All because he'd loved her.

John raked a hand through his wet hair and rubbed rain off his face. What was it about love that made people lose all their common sense?

He remained standing by the park for a long time, lost in drizzle and mist, looking up at the windows of Tremore House, and for the life of him, he could not find an answer.

Chapter 11

Viola went to bed early. Anthony and Daphne had gone to a ball, but she had a headache and decided to stay home. She took a warm bath, drank a cup of the cook's willow bark and peppermint tea, dressed in her nightclothes, and crawled into bed at nine o'clock. But though the tea soothed her head, falling asleep proved more difficult. Accustomed to the late hours of the season, she could not fall asleep. After an hour of tossing and turning, she gave up and went downstairs in search of Quimby. She told the butler she would be in the library and asked him to have a dish of ordinary tea prepared for her and sent up.

She then went to the library, accompanied by a footman who made up a fire for her against the damp chill in the air. His task done, the footman departed, and Viola took a book from one of the shelves. She curled up in a corner of the settee, thinking to read until she got sleepy.

But she had no chance to get sleepy. The steam had not even cooled on her tea, and she was only on page two of a Dumas novel, before a voice interrupted her. "Hullo, Viola."

Startled, she looked up to find John in the doorway. She snapped her book shut and jumped to her feet. "What are you doing here?"

"Getting warm and dry." He leaned one shoulder against the doorjamb, and as she watched him, she realized how disheveled he looked. He was not in evening clothes. He was still dressed in a morning suit. It was rumpled and damp from the light rain outside. His hair curled at his collar the way it always did in damp weather, and his linen was limp. He had not even shaved. The shadow of beard on his face was something she hadn't seen for years. Not since the days when they had slept together and she woke every morning to the raspy feel of his cheek against her shoulder.

She had spent all week avoiding him, and now, just at the moment she let her guard down, here he was. She knew she ought to tell him to leave, but instead she just looked at him, remembering the burn of beard stubble on her shoulder when he used to kiss her awake.

He might have come to get warm, but she was beginning to feel the heat, and it had nothing to do with the fire in the grate. She brushed back a tendril of hair that had come loose from her braid and curled her toes into the lush softness of the carpet beneath her bare feet, keenly aware of her own state of dishabille. "Quimby should have announced you."

"Don't be cross with Quimby. He is a most excellent butler. He tried to tell me you were not at home, but I knew that wasn't true. Since your brother isn't here to prevent it, I pulled rank on the butler and came upstairs anyway. Terribly rude of me, but there it is."

"How did you know I was home?"

"Because I've been down by the park for the past two hours. I saw you in the drawing room earlier, just as it was getting dark, before the maids drew the curtains."

"Two hours!" Viola stared at him in astonishment. "By the park, in this weather? Whatever for?"

"Can't you guess?" He straightened away from the door and came into the library, but stopped some distance from where she stood. "I was working up the nerve to come and say let's make up."

He wanted to make up. She knew what that meant. He looked sorry. She knew that meant nothing. Before she could speak, he did.

"When we quarreled, you said you don't trust me, and you have every right. I just—" He drew a deep breath and let it out slowly, as if trying to think of what to say next. "I just wanted to see you."

"That's what you came up here to say?"

"Yes." He smiled a little. "Very tame, I know, especially after spending two hours in the rain working on it, but I was getting cold."

That warmth began spreading through her like warm honey, and she tried to remind herself it was all just words. He could say anything and make it sound like God's truth. How could she ever believe anything he said? She wanted to believe it, though. She did.

The seconds ticked by. The clock struck half past ten.

He stirred. "I'll go," he said, and backed up a step. "I can see you wanted to go to bed early."

"You don't have to leave."

What was she saying? But the words were out of her mouth now. She could not take them back, and she tried at once to qualify them. "I mean . . . you are cold and ought to get warm first. If you don't, you could catch a chill, and . . . and . . . that would be bad." Her voice trailed off.

John turned back around. "Do you want me to stay?"

She looked down, acutely self-conscious. She did, God help her. "Yes." She looked up and saw him smile. "For a while," she amended at once.

His smile got wider, the wretched man.

She sat down on the settee. "I thought we might talk about things."

The smile vanished, and he groaned, lifting his

gaze heavenward. "Lord help me. First standing out in the rain, and then talking about things." He gave a sigh and pulled off his wet coat. "I don't suppose those things will be easy things? Irish politics, for instance? Or how to lessen poverty within the British Empire? Or what the ramifications would be of repealing the Corn Laws?"

How did he manage it? He could always find a way to make her smile. She sat down on the settee, and after draping his coat onto the back of a chair by the fire, he sat down beside her. "What do you want to talk about?" he asked.

She thought a moment. "I don't quite know," she said with a little laugh that sounded just as nervous as she suddenly felt. "I always thought if we ever sat down and talked, I'd have plenty to say, but now I am at rather a loss."

"We used to find many things to talk about."

"And argue about."

"True enough." He shot her a wry look. "That hasn't changed, in case you hadn't noticed."

"I noticed." She paused, then said, "We have been married almost nine years, and yet, I do not know you, John, not really. In many ways I do not understand you. I don't believe I ever did. During our courtship and the early days of our marriage, I was always open with you. I told you so many things about myself, my family, and the things I want and like and what I think. But whenever I asked you things about yourself—what your childhood was like, or how you felt about—oh, I don't know—anything *personal*, you would always make some offhand joke and change the subject."

"And?"

"You may be my husband, but you are a stranger to me. I feel as if we should remedy that but I do not know how. If I ask you things, will you tell me?"

"About my childhood? It was a nightmare. Enough said. Believe me, you don't want to hear it, and I certainly cannot bear to talk of it. And anyway, isn't it more to the point to be talking about us?"

"If I ask you anything about us and you don't wish to discuss it, you will divert the conversation."

He didn't speak for a moment, then said, "No, I won't. Ask your questions. Fire away." He leaned back against the sofa and turned his head to look at her. "Be warned. I cannot guarantee you will like my answers, but they will be honest ones. Fair enough?"

Faced with exactly what she had asked for, Viola thought a moment, wondering just how blunt her questions should be. But he'd said she could ask him anything, so she was going to take advantage of the opportunity. "Did you love any of your mistresses? Any of them?"

"No."

"Did you love me, John?" She already knew the answer, but she had never heard him admit it. She wanted to hear it from him. "When you asked me to marry you, and you told me you loved me, did you mean it?"

"I . . . " He rubbed a hand over his eyes and let out his breath on a sigh. Then he lowered his hand and met her eyes. "No."

There it was. The stark and brutal truth. He did not try to explain his actions or justify them. This was the answer she had expected, a confirmation of what she had known for over eight years, but even now it had the power to hurt her. Still, better an honest, hurtful answer than a lie. She'd had enough of those.

"Do you—" She hesitated. Asking him questions was so much harder than she had thought it would be. She sucked in a deep breath and tried again. "Do you have any children by any of the women you've had?"

"No."

"Are you sure?"

"Yes. There are ways to prevent . . . there are sheaths a man can use. They don't always work, but—" He broke off and stirred beside her, uncomfortable. "God, Viola, do not ask me to discuss things like that with you. I cannot do it."

"Many people say Peggy Darwin's youngest son is yours, even though Darwin claimed him."

John moved closer to her. "No, Viola, no. I told you, he is not mine. I know that rumor has been flying around for years, but it is not true."

"Because of these . . . sheaths that don't always work?"

"And because I can do arithmetic. Peggy and I broke off our liaison a year before William was born, and no child takes twelve months to come out of the womb. No woman has ever come to me with word of a child by me."

Even though she knew he could be lying, she believed him. She chose to believe him, and with that choice came a profound sense of relief.

"May I ask a question?" He paused, then said, "You loved me. Why?"

Taken aback, not only by the question but also by the sudden intensity in his voice as he asked it, she stared at him. "Why did I love you?"

"Yes, why? I mean, you didn't even know me. Even nowadays, as you said, we don't know each other. Yet, you tell me that you loved me. That is something I find baffling, Viola. Why on earth did you ever fall in love with a bloke like me?"

He was frowning, and there was something in his face, something that reminded her of a school-boy who was waiting for an explanation of a complicated mathematical problem. He was expecting an answer that made sense. She lifted her hand helplessly. "Heavens, I don't know. I suppose because you made it so easy. Whenever I was with you, everything in the world was good and right, and I was happy. The sky was bluer and the grass was greener—" She broke off, looked away. "That sounds silly, I know, but it's how I felt. I can't tell you why, but I did love you." She swallowed painfully and looked at him. "I loved you more than my life."

He reached up one hand to touch her face, spreading his palm across her cheek, his fingertips stirring the hair at her temple. "I never meant to hurt you, Viola. God, if you believe nothing else I ever say, believe that. When we married, I hoped to be content. That's all one can really expect from life anyway. But that wasn't enough for you, was it? Being content?"

She moved away from him. "If you've ever been in love, you shouldn't have to ask that question." Struck by her own words, she studied him at the other end of the settee, and the few feet she had just put between them seemed like miles. "Have you ever been in love?"

He looked away. "No."

Perhaps he was incapable of loving anyone. She did not say it, but that unspoken conclusion hung in the air. She turned, leaning back against the settee, and stared straight ahead. "You've never been in love with me or any other woman. You certainly are not in love with me now. So give me one good reason why I should consider coming back to you. Other than I am your wife and I have no choice and our society lives by certain rules."

"All right." He began moving toward her, easing his way across the settee to her side. "Because I make you laugh. Because when I kiss you, you get all soft and shivery, and I like that. I have always liked that." He put his arm around her, ignoring the way she stiffened. "Because whenever I touch you, everything in the world goes away, and it is only the two of us. Because even when we are fighting, half of my mind is trying to figure out how to get you out of your clothes. That is as honest an answer as I can give you."

She would not be beguiled by it. "You never feel these things, of course, with any of the other women you've had."

"It is not the same."

"How is it different?"

He made a sound that might have been a laugh. "Because no other woman in the world ever makes me so insane that I want to smash my head through a window."

"Not good enough."

"Because you are my wife, I am your husband. Because I want children, Viola. I think you want them, too."

"What you mean is that you want an heir."

"No, that is not what I mean." He must have realized how unbelievable that sounded, given that was his whole reason for trying to come back to her, and he amended his answer at once. "I mean, I need an heir, yes, but I want children. Isn't that what marriage is for?"

"Because marriage is a sensible decision," she said, a dreariness coming over her as she spoke.

"For me and for most of the people we know. Not everyone looks at marriage the way you do, Viola. It isn't always about love. That is one of those rules that govern our lives."

He was right about that. She thought of the titled families they knew. Anthony and Daphne were an exception—for most couples of their acquaintance, marriage was not about love. It was about alliance and securing heirs, then going on to lead separate lives and have lovers of one's own choosing. She saw the future stretched out before her—a future that she had thought to avoid when she married John—a loveless marriage.

She could take lovers, she supposed, to ease the wretched loneliness, if she wanted them, but she could not imagine being touched by any other man but John. Still, something prompted her to ask the question. "The rules apply to us, too, I suppose? I mean, I could be like Peggy Darwin and take a lover of my own, if I wanted one."

"No, you could not!" The words came out of him with unexpected force, as explosive as gunshots in the room.

"But you could. In fact, you already have. That's hardly fair."

"Too bad." Turning, he looked at her, defying fairness. "My heir, Viola, no other man's. That's part of the rules, too."

"But what about after that? You go your way and I go mine? Then you can have as many lovers as you please, just like before? The only difference being that I shall be free to do the same? Is that how it works, John? If I come back to you, is that how it will be for us, too?"

"I hope not."

"Without love, how else could it be?"

"To my way of thinking, that depends on you. Are you going to turn me out of bed? Because if you are, I will eventually go get a mistress. It is that simple."

"How convenient for you that the entire future of our marriage rests with me."

"So it does."

She might have laughed at that, except there was nothing amusing about the situation. "And if I am a faithful wife, will you be faithful to me in return?"

The defiance melted away, and sulkiness stole into his face like shadows. He folded his arms. "No man ever answers a question like that."

"No? Why not?"

"If I say yes, you will not believe me. If I say no,

I ruin any chance of ever getting you into bed again. If I say I don't know, I am condemned for not giving a definite answer. No matter what I say, it's the wrong thing, and I lose."

"This is not a game! It is not about winning and losing. I want—" She broke off, and amended her words. "No, I *deserve* an honest answer to my question. If I came back to you, and I were a faithful wife who gave you children, would you be a faithful husband to me?"

"I don't know."

She shook her head, staring at him in disbelief. "You don't know? What sort of answer is that?"

"An honest one! I told you, that is a no-win question for a man. No matter what I answered, it wouldn't satisfy you. Would I do my best to be a faithful husband? Yes. Would I succeed? Again, that depends on you. Can you be a good wife to me? Can you be a loving, affectionate companion? Can I rely on you not to dissolve into tears and shut your bedroom door to me? Can I rely on you not to turn into the unforgiving ice queen when things don't go your way?"

That hurt. She bit her lip, looking at the resentment in his face, resentment directed at her when she did not deserve it. "That is a cruel thing to say."

"You wanted the truth."

"For heaven's sake!" She jumped to her feet, truly angry now. "You talk as if I am being unreasonable. It is not unreasonable for a woman to expect her husband to be faithful!"

He also stood up. "Nor is it unreasonable for a man to expect his wife to make fidelity worth his while!"

The sound of sobbing from the other side of the closed door interrupted any reply she might have made. Both of them turned as the door opened and Beckham came in, a wailing Nicholas in her arms and a distraught look on her face.

"Forgive me, my lord," the nanny said to John with a quick curtsy.

Viola was rather relieved by the interruption. She was beginning to understand what he meant about how she might not like his honest answers to her questions. "What is it, Beckham?"

"So sorry, my lady, but I am looking for Mr. Poppin."

"Oh, dear." She looked at Nicholas. "Poppin's gone missing, has he?"

"I am afraid so," Beckham answered. "I know the baby was in here with her grace earlier this evening, so I was hoping they had left Poppin in here."

Viola took a glance around the library. "I don't see him."

"Who is Mr. Poppin?" John asked over the child's sobs.

"His favorite toy, my lord," the nanny explained, and returned her attention to Viola. "I

can't think how I tucked him in without noticing
it was missing, but I must have done. He fell
asleep without it, he was so tired. But then something woke him, and he must have discovered the
toy wasn't there, because he just started crying his
little heart out. I don't believe he's going back to
sleep without Mr. Poppin."

Viola looked at the baby, who was sobbing as if
the end of the world were at hand. "What's wrong,
Nicky?" she crooned, and reached for him. She
pressed kisses to his wet face. "Poppin playing
hide-and-seek with you again?"

Nicholas would not be soothed by a few little
kisses. He wailed louder, and Viola looked at
Beckham with a sigh. "We are going to have to
find that toy."

"It seems so, my lady."

She started to hand the baby back to the nanny,
but John's voice stopped her. "May I—" He broke
off, clasped his hands behind his back, and looked
away. "Never mind."

Viola looked up at him, studying his profile.
There was no anger in his face now. He looked
grave and uncomfortable. Almost embarrassed.
She could not remember John ever looking embar-
rassed, and she could not help being curious.
"What were you going to ask?"

She watched as he shifted his weight from one
foot to the other. He did not look at her, though he
did cast an uneasy glance at the nanny before re-

turning his attention to the baby. "I only wondered if I might hold him," he muttered, "but then I realized it sounded too silly for words."

"You want to hold Nicholas?" she asked in astonishment, uncertain she had heard him right. Men never wanted to hold babies, especially not those who were wailing at the top of their lungs. But he gave a quick, jerky nod, and she realized he meant it.

"It isn't silly at all," she said, and stepped closer to her husband. "Here."

She started to hand Nicholas over to him, but he did not reach out take the baby from her. "I don't know how to do this," he said, looking suddenly panicky.

She settled Nicholas against her shoulder again to demonstrate. "Just like this. You see?" After a moment he nodded and she turned the baby around. Leaning closer to her husband, she handed the sobbing child over to him.

He took the baby in a way that was tentative, uncertain. She could scarcely believe it. First embarrassment, then uncertainty, from John, of all men. What an odd evening this was turning out to be. He pulled Nicholas against his chest, the baby's bottom resting on his forearm, his hand against the baby's head, holding him in the exact position she had.

At that moment, for the inexplicable reason known only to angels, Nicholas stopped crying.

In the sudden silence, Viola stared at her husband. He looked as if he were holding a miracle in his hands, and she felt the world caving beneath her feet. Arguments and unfair words and expectations dissolved away, and a queer, piercing, painful joy hit her in the chest. She could not move, and she hoped it wasn't Cupid who had just fired that arrow into her heart.

"Bless us all," murmured Beckham. "You've a way with babies, my lord."

John pulled back a bit to look into the face of the child in his arms. "Deuce take you," he said, laughing as if amazed.

The baby stared at him, a frown of puzzlement puckering his brow, as if uncertain what to do in the arms of this stranger. Then, his face still streaked with tears, he smiled and said something unintelligible that sounded suspiciously like a coo of affection.

John pressed his forehead to that of the baby. "If people find out about this, I shall take no end of ribbing at the club. We'd best keep this between ourselves, old chap."

The baby gurgled in reply, and Viola watched as he lifted one hand to bat at her husband's cheek. John turned his head, blowing air into the baby's palm, making him laugh, seeming to charm Nicholas without any effort at all. Even babies were not immune.

He bounced the child, settling him more firmly

in the crook of his arm, appearing much more comfortable with holding him now than he had a few moments before. "What a handsome fellow you are when you're not crying. You have your mother's eyes, I see. No lady's heart shall be safe twenty years from now."

The baby stirred and pressed a hand against John's chest, burying his fingers in limp linen ruffles and cravat silk. He made a distressed sound and looked about him, wriggling.

"Not interested in being the heartbreaker of the ton, eh?" John said. "I cannot say I blame you. Women were designed to turn men's entire lives into chaos at every possible opportunity. Best to steer clear as long as you can."

"That is a terrible thing to say!" Viola protested. "Nicholas, don't listen to him."

"He won't," John told her. "We men never steer clear. That would be like compass needles not pointing true north. It's just not possible."

The baby pushed against John's chest with both hands. "Pop," he said. "Pop-pop."

"Yes, I know," he said with a nod of complete understanding. "Thank you for reminding me of the important business at hand." He began walking around the drawing room, the baby in his arms, making a great show of looking for Mr. Poppin. As he peered behind the pianoforte, under tables, and between chairs, he continued talking to his nephew in worldly-wise accents. "The devil of it, my boy, is that women are more important to us than anything else, and they know it. Not that any of the fair sex would ever use this fact against us, mind you."

He bent at the knees with the baby in his arms, looking under a round rosewood table. "But it's important for a fellow to keep his wits about him."

He straightened and paused to look at his nephew. "Be especially careful of the no-win question," he advised the baby, who was staring back at him in grave fascination. "They will get under your skin with that one every time. Mark my words."

Viola let out her breath in a huff, but John paid no heed. "Of course, in such circumstances," he went on as he started in her direction, "we often do the worst possible thing—retaliate and say something hurtful." He paused close to where she stood, and met her gaze. "We always regret it afterward and feel like dogs."

He resumed his search, walking past her without another word.

She had just gotten an apology. In all the fights they'd had in the nine years they had known each other, John had never given her an apology for anything before. Had never come close. It was still just words, but words that he had never said to her before.

Stunned, she turned around, watching as he circled to the other side of the settee, where he gave a cry of triumph.

"Ah, here we are!" One arm securely around Nicholas, he bent at the knees, going down behind the settee. He came up with a brown, furry toy bear. "Mr. Poppin, I believe."

With a shout of delight, Nicholas wrapped one arm around the toy. He leaned against John's chest with a hiccup and a gratified sigh, and buried his face against John's neck. His free hand flailed in the air, then patted the man's beard-roughened cheek and finally came to rest in a fist on the silk of his aubergine waistcoat.

Her heart constricted, and she turned her back because it hurt her eyes to look at them. She thought of what he wanted from her and what he was not willing to give in return. Blinking, she stared down at the books scattered on top of the writing desk. A baby was impossible. It had to be impossible. That dream was long gone.

"Well, well, this is an amazing thing," John said.

She made a show of straightening the books into a pile and forced herself to speak. "What is amazing?"

"There is at least one member of the Tremore family who is on my side."

She stiffened, trying to prop up her protective walls. "Don't get too conceited over it," she said, and steeled herself as she turned around to look at him again. "I hate to tell you this, but Nicholas likes everyone."

"That may be so, but I am special. I rescued Mr. Poppin." He kissed the top of the baby's head. "Your aunt doesn't like me, Nicky," he murmured, "but I know she would listen to you. Put in a word for me, would you? There's a good chap."

She gestured to Beckham to take the baby. The nanny walked over to John's side. He hesitated, reluctant, but Viola could not bear the sight of him holding the baby any longer. "He ought to be put back to bed, Hammond. It's late."

"Of course." He handed the baby over to Beckham, who took the child and departed for the nursery. Nicholas was either too exhausted or too happy at the return of Poppin to feel deprived of his uncle's charm. Not a single sob echoed back to the drawing room from the other side of the closed door.

The silence was awkward and deafening.

He took a step toward her. "Viola—"

"It's very late." She took a step back and ran into the writing desk behind her.

"It's not that late." He continued walking toward her with slow, deliberate steps, giving her plenty of time to evade him. For some stupid reason, she didn't.

He came to a halt in front of her. His lashes, thick and dark, lowered a fraction. He took the braid of her hair in his hand, lifted it to his mouth and kissed it, breathing in deeply. "Violets."

She began to shake inside, and she curled her fingers around the edge of the writing desk behind her. She thought of all the impossible, romantic dreams of her girlhood, and reminded herself they were dead dreams now.

He moved the braid over her shoulder and let it fall down her back. Then he lifted both hands to her face. He ran his fingers along her cheekbones, lightly traced the sides of her nose, shaped the arch of each of her brows. He pushed his fingers into the hair at her temples and cupped her cheeks, caressing her lips with his thumbs. He did it all without looking into her eyes, keeping his gaze focused on his hands and her features as he touched them. There was deliberation and intent in every move.

Caressing the mole at the edge of her lips with the pad of his thumb, he lowered his other hand to her waist and bunched delicate muslin in his fist. "I did come here for a reason," he reminded her, and that was when he looked into her eyes. "I came to kiss and make up."

"You didn't say anything about the kissing part."

"Tricked you again." He tilted her chin up and covered her mouth with his.

John's kiss, as potent now as it had been in the

museum, as potent as it had always been, making it so easy to forget that anything else in the world existed. John's hands, so sure, sliding to her hips, pulling her closer, his fingers spreading across her buttocks. John's mouth, coaxing hers to open.

One of her hands came away from the desk, lifted to his unshaven cheek and touched skin rough like sand. Her lips parted. The strands of his hair were like damp, heavy silk in her fingers as she slid her hand to the back of his head and deepened the kiss.

His tongue met hers and his hands tightened on her hips, holding her imprisoned against the desk as he tasted her. The kiss stung, burning where his beard stubble rubbed the skin around her mouth. Mornings with John, erotic images that had taunted her for years, images she had finally thought forever buried, came raging back to taunt and tease her now. Images of his hands touching her in the morning sunlight in a big mahogany bed at Hammond Park ran through her mind, sending electrifying excitement pulsing through her body now, impelling her to press her body closer to his. Her arm came up around his neck.

He made a rough sound against her mouth and broke the kiss. He leaned sideways and with a sweep of his arm cleared the desk, sending the stack of books toppling off the side and onto the floor. Then his hands cupped her buttocks and he lifted her to set her on the desk.

He reached for the sash wrapped around her waist, untying the bow with a hard, quick tug. He parted the edges and pulled her dressing robe apart. His fingertips touched her breasts through her nightgown, brushing back and forth over the hardened nipples. Pleasure rose within her, pleasure long forgotten, pleasure that made her gasp and shiver with excitement. Her hand tightened in his hair and she pulled him closer, guiding his head down to her breast.

He laved the tip of her breast with his tongue, dampening the muslin. His hand came up to embrace her other breast, his thumb and forefinger closing to tease her nipple through the thin fabric. Sharp sensation rose with each pull of his mouth and each roll of his fingers as he suckled her and touched her and teased her through her nightdress.

She cradled his head in her hands, trying to pull him even closer. She was lost in the hot, demanding urgency of his hands and his mouth. It had been so long since she had felt John's hands on her, so long since she had felt this wild, sensual drive. She could hear the soft, hushed sounds that came from her own throat, sounds of desperate want and aching need. She heard herself moan his name.

He straightened, moving one hand to the top of her nightdress. He began slipping pearl buttons free as he used his other hand to yank the hem of the nightgown upward, above her knees. "God," he groaned against her throat, "how I've missed this."

Missed what? Having a woman?

Those questions sprang into her mind, and with them came reality, as cold as ice water washing over her. Good lord, what was she doing?

She stiffened as his hand moved between her thighs, and she clamped her legs tightly together, putting a stop to this madness before it went any further. "No, John," she gasped, seizing his wrist. "No."

He went rigidly still, his hand wrapped around her inner thigh, his harsh breathing mingling with hers. "Viola." His hand stirred against her hold, slid up her thigh an inch or two.

She pushed at his wrist. "Let me go."

He hesitated, and it was that moment of reluctance that galvanized her. "Let go, let go, let go!"

Panicking, desperate, she slammed her palm into his shoulder, shoving him. She twisted sideways, hurling herself off the desk, stumbling over the hem of her robe in her haste to get away from him. "Out of my mind," she muttered, shaking her head. "I must be out of my mind. What am I, a glutton for punishment?"

"Viola—"

The sound of his voice had her coming to a halt a few steps away from him. She whirled around, wrapping her robe around her body to shield every part of it from his view. "I cannot believe how eas-

ily I make a fool of myself over you and how often."
She pressed her fingers to her forehead, once,
twice, three times, wondering what happened to
the brains inside. "I can be so, so stupid."

He looked at her, still breathing hard, his face
conveying a disbelief quite different from hers. He
took a step toward her, reached for her, tried to
touch her.

She evaded him, moving farther out of reach.
"I can't even blame you for it. That's the worst
part. It's not as if you lied to me this time or anything. You have admitted that you have never
loved me. You could not even promise to be faithful to me. Yet thirty minutes later I was ready to
lay my body down for you to take. Where on
earth are my brains? Where is my self-respect?"

"Self-respect?" He rubbed his hands over his
face, gulping deep breaths of air. "God, woman,
your self-respect isn't the problem. Neither are
your brains. It's your timing."

"Eight years without you, building my own
life," she went on, ignoring him, lecturing herself,
"and after only a few outings with you and a couple of stolen kisses, I am behaving as wantonly as
one of your bawds."

"You are my wife! There is nothing bawdy
about wanting to make love with your husband.
And you wanted to, damn me if you didn't. Why
did you stop?" He raked his hands through his
hair and turned away with another oath. "Hell,

Viola," he said over one shoulder, "sometimes I despair of ever understanding you."

"I would like you to leave."

He walked across the room, putting even more distance between them. His back to her, he straightened his clothing while she straightened hers. Neither of them spoke. After a few moments he walked over to the chair where he had left his coat earlier in the evening. He put it on. "The three weeks are up. I shall come for you tomorrow at noon. You'd better decide tonight which house you want to live in. If you don't, Tremore can expect a demand from the House of Lords the day after."

She started to refuse, but when he turned around to face her, she closed her mouth and gave it up. There was defiance in his face now, defiance of her wishes, challenge in the lift of his brows, pride in the grim, determined set of his jaw. She knew that countenance very well. Arguing was pointless.

"I gave you my word," he reminded her in a hard, tight voice, and added, "I want a willing mate, so you needn't worry about having to lay your body down for me to take. Far be it from me to treat you like a bawd."

Bowing, he left her.

All very well for him to tell her not to worry. Worry wasn't really her problem. It wasn't worry that gnawed at her. It wasn't worry that made her insides twist with dread and made her want to board the next ship headed for France.

It was how the man who had hurt her so much, the man she ought to despise, could hold a crying baby in his arms and make him laugh. It was how he could still make her laugh, too, even after all he had done. It was how he could make her melt into a puddle when he kissed her and how he could light her on fire when he touched her. She wasn't a foolish girl anymore, but she still wanted that man. She could fall in love all over again with that man. It would be so, so easy. Easy to say yes and give him what he wanted, having nothing in return. Not even a promise he would be faithful.

No, she wasn't worried. She was terrified.

Chapter 12

~~~~~ ⌒⌒ ~~~~~

It wasn't until the cold light of day that John's desire and anger simmered down to a point where his brain began to work again and he could think clearly. And he had to think. He had to figure out what his next move should be.

He stared down into his plate and idly pushed kidneys and bacon around with his fork. If he'd been thinking at all last night, which was doubtful, it had been about taking advantage of the blessed opportunity he'd been given as quickly as possible. He probably should have gone more slowly—wooed, coaxed, eased her into her bedroom upstairs. But he hadn't. And then he had compounded the problem by getting autocratic and reminding her that the three weeks were up. If she didn't come with him today, he'd have to go to the House, for he could not back down. Even then, when they were living together, he would still have to do some serious wooing to get her into bed.

He dropped his fork into his plate with an exasperated oath. No man should have to put up with this from his wife. Most other men in his situation would drag her into the marriage bed and get on with it. But what other men would do didn't help him. He wasn't that sort of fellow, never had been.

Christ. He wanted a willing wife. A passionate wife. Was that too much to ask?

She said she could not trust him. He hadn't pointed out that trust went both ways and so did the ability to inflict hurt. He could have promised Viola that he would never go to any woman's bed but hers, but he wasn't going to make that promise unless he could trust her not to spurn him when she was angry. He would not be the victim of any woman's sexual blackmail, and that was what she had done to him, even if she could not see it. How could they ever get past that?

He thought of Dylan Moore's suggestion to him that he and Viola become friends. It seemed an insane idea, but then, Moore was rather mad, always had been.

John sighed and sat back, looking at the little glass pots of jam on the table. Blackberry and apricot. Hammond Park.

Those days had been shoved to the back of his mind long ago and had lingered there for years like other hazy, half-forgotten dreams of his youth. Yet now they called to him, beckoning him back to a time when he had been content, even happy. He'd made Viola happy, too. He was certain of it. There had to be a way to bring all of that back. He was no longer content to believe it had been lost forever.

Become friends.

John sat up straight in his chair, staring at the jam pots. Perhaps Moore was on to something. He and Viola had been friends once. That was what they'd had back then, that summer in Scotland and that autumn in Northumberland. They had been lovers, too, and fought and scrapped like lovers, but they had laughed and had fun, and he'd been more pleased with his choice of a wife than he could have ever imagined. Then it had all gone wrong.

He wished—God, he wished—they could be like that again, and that he was having breakfast in bed with her right now, kissing blackberry jam off her face. Just now that seemed a dismally remote possibility.

"The morning post, my lord."

Surprised, he looked up as Pershing set a stack of correspondence by his plate. It was usually John's secretary who brought his letters. "Where's Stone today?" he asked the butler.

"Mr. Stone has the measles. Upon the advice of his brother-in-law, who is a physician, he has removed himself to his sister's home in Clapham until he is no longer infectious to others. Mr. Stone said he bitterly regrets that he will be unable to be of service to your lordship for the next ten days."

"Send him a note, and assure him I prefer an absent secretary to a sick household. Tell him to stay in Clapham until he is fully recovered."

"Yes, my lord." The butler withdrew.

John glanced through his letters, sorting them as he went.

An invitation to both Lord and Lady Hammond to dine at the home of Lady Snowden. The Countess of Snowden was clearly more optimistic this morning about the state of his marriage than he was. A note from Tattersall's confirming that the new mare he'd purchased two weeks earlier had been delivered to his estate in Northumberland. He'd bought the horse for Viola. It was a spirited four-year-old thoroughbred with breathtaking speed, but given the current state of things, he didn't think he'd be racing horses on the downs with his wife until this particular mare was tottering into her grave. Since the note needed no reply, he tossed it into the fire that burned in the grate nearby, and continued working his way through the stack of correspondence. A report from his steward on things at Hammond Park. A bill from his tailor, and another from his boot maker, both for the costume he was wearing to Viola's charity ball, a ball to which he had still not received an invitation from his wife. Another letter from Emma Rawlins.

He paused over the folded, sealed square of delicately perfumed paper. He had to admire the lady's persistence. How many letters was this now? A dozen, at least. The first few he had read—an apology for her possessiveness, then a reproof for his cool reply, then a scathing condemnation of his inattention. After those, he had ignored the rest, not bothering to read them or reply. He heard she had sold the cottage he'd given her and was living in France. Hoping she remained there, he tossed her latest letter into the fire unopened.

Keeping only the report from his steward, which he could read in the carriage on his way to Grosvenor Square, and the invitation, which he would ask Viola about before replying, he left the breakfast table. Instructing Pershing to place the bills on Stone's desk for the secretary to pay when he returned, John went upstairs to bathe and shave.

As his valet assisted him with his morning routine, John tried to anticipate what Viola's next move was likely to be. His wife could be as unpredictable as the weather, but if he had to guess, he thought it most likely that she would refuse to see him and force him to go to the House of Lords to get her back. But when he arrived at Grosvenor Square that afternoon, he found that she was not refusing to see him, nor agreeing to see him. Instead, she had left town.

"Where?" he asked, looking into the pretty, violet eyes of the Duchess of Tremore, who had been the one to impart this news.

The duchess did not answer for a moment. Instead, she stirred her tea, her head tilted in consideration as she studied him from behind her gold-rimmed spectacles. "Before I decide to answer that, I would like to ask you a question, Hammond."

"Certainly."

"If Viola refuses to return to you, is it really your intention to petition the House to force her back?"

He smiled a little. "Duchess, I sometimes think even the House of Lords could not make my wife do what she does not want to do," he said, trying to make light of it.

The duchess did not seem satisfied by that. Instead, she continued to look at him with all her placid equanimity. He drew a deep breath and let it out slowly, trying to think of how to answer her when he did not know what the answer was. He gave his sister-in-law the most direct, honest reply he could. "I refuse to accept the possibility that she will not return to me," he answered. "I reject it utterly and completely."

"And how long will you reject it?"

He set his jaw. "Until I make her see sense and reject it, too."

"That may be a long time." She tapped the tiny silver spoon against the side of her cup and set it on the rim of the saucer beneath it.

He could not argue with that. Tight-lipped, he nodded. "Yes."

"Love is not the basis of your determination to win Viola back."

Was that an accusation? A condemnation?

Before he could decide, she took a sip of tea and spoke again. "Viola is at Enderby."

The duchess's sudden capitulation surprised him, and though he tried not to show it, she noticed. "You did not expect that, did you?"

"No, Duchess. I did not."

"In instigating a search for your wife, you would have inquired at Enderby first, and the servants would have told you she was there. They are paid by you, after all."

"Is that the only reason you told me?"

Those pretty lavender-blue eyes widened. "What other reason could there be?"

"There has to be one. You risk your husband's wrath by even sitting down to tea with me."

"True." She did not seem worried about that, and he suspected that this serene and mild-mannered lady held the duke's haughty heart in the palm of her hand. Such was the inexplicable nature of love. "If you hurt Viola again, Tremore will most likely challenge you to a duel. He would kill you quite cheerfully, believe me."

"And you?" he asked, genuinely curious. "Do you share his animus for me?"

"No," she said. "I don't."

He forced a laugh. "I cannot think why not."

"No?" There was compassion in her face as she

looked at him, and that made him shift uncomfortably in his chair. "I know how desperation feels, Hammond. Unlike my husband and my sister-in-law, I have been without money and means, and it was the most terrifying moment of my life. I would have done anything—anything, mind you—to rid myself of that terror. If fortune had not put the Duke of Tremore and a ship passage to England in my path, I might easily have been forced to marry for money." She paused. "Or worse."

"I am glad that did not happen," he said, and meant it wholeheartedly.

"You have another ally besides myself, you know." She smiled a little. "My son has taken quite a liking to you, I understand."

He smiled back at her, remembering Nicolas and Mr. Poppin. "Heard about that, did you?"

"From Beckham."

"He is a fine boy, Duchess." As he said the words, John felt envy begin to burn his insides, the same envy that had seared him while he stared out the window of this very room and watched the Tremore family walk in the park. His smile faded and he turned his head away from the compassionate eyes of his sister-in-law. "A very fine boy."

"Thank you." She stood up. "I hope you are sincere in your desire for a real marriage and a family, Hammond. If not, God help you."

John rose as well. "Because your husband will challenge me to a duel?"

"No," she answered at once. "Because I will save Anthony the trouble and fire a pistol shot into you myself. For blind stupidity, if nothing else."

"I believe you mean that," he murmured, noting the sudden hardness in her face.

"I do mean it." She held out her hand to him.

"Then you may put your mind at ease, Duchess," he said, and bent over her hand to kiss it. Straightening, he went on, "Because I am sincere. Obstinate as well, I grant you. Cynical, certainly. A bad husband, perhaps. But also sincere."

"I hope so, for your sake and for Viola's."

He departed, not knowing quite why he had the duchess's good opinion, but grateful for it. He went home to Bloomsbury Square, but made no move to pack for Enderby.

He was not about to take anything for granted. Viola had clearly decided not to fight a legal battle with him, but she was not ready to give in. The night before in Tremore's library made that perfectly clear. In light of that, he knew his best move was to give his wife a bit of room to breathe. His absence, he thought wryly, might make her heart grow fonder—for a change.

John allowed a week to pass. Then, accompanied by his valet and a pair of footmen, he went to Enderby, arriving there an hour before dinner. His arrival caused a bit of fluster, for the master of Enderby hadn't put in an appearance on this estate in years and had sent no word ahead that he would be arriving. He inquired of Hawthorne, Enderby's current butler, where Viola might be.

"I believe Lady Hammond is taking a nap, my lord. Shall I show you to the drawing room while I inquire?"

"Expect me to sit like a visitor and cool my heels in my drawing room, Hawthorne?" he asked softly, smiling.

The butler flushed a deep red, pained by his inadvertent blunder. "No, my lord," he said stiffly.

"Good." John saw no need to embarrass the fellow further. "Have my things sent up to my room, will you? And show my valet, Stephens, the way of things here at Enderby. Introduce him about, show him the laundry rooms, give him the meal times and such. You know what to do, of course."

Looking profoundly relieved not to be dressed down by a master he had never met, Hawthorne nodded. "Yes, my lord."

John turned away and started up the wide, curving staircase, one hand on the wrought-iron rail. Though Enderby was one of his estates, it had become Viola's primary residence over the years, and since their complete separation two years before, her only residence. He spent most of the year at Hammond Park, and he couldn't remember the last time he'd been here—four years at least. But he'd spent a lot of his childhood here, and after

Cambridge, this had been his home up until his father's death. He remembered exactly where the bedchambers were.

Viola had done a great deal to the house, he noticed as he mounted the stairs. It was as feminine as a house could be, all pastels and flowers. His father would turn in his grave if he knew, John thought, and he tried to take some comfort in that.

He stopped at the door of Viola's room, opened it, then stepped inside without making a sound. He saw that she was indeed taking a nap. He came into the room and shut the door behind him.

The sound caused her to stir, and she made a murmur in her sleep but did not waken. She turned onto her side, facing him, and loose tendrils of hair fell over her face. She looked all tawny and golden, like a sleepy lioness.

He gave a cough, and she stirred again. Slowly, she opened her eyes.

"Comfortable?" he asked.

"You!" She was off the bed in an instant, fully awake.

He reminded himself that he'd pushed her too hard too fast that night a week ago. A light, offhand approach was best. "I was going to curl up with you and kiss you awake, but you woke up too soon." He shook his head in disappointment. "A devilishly good plan spoiled."

Her eyes narrowed. If she were a lioness, he'd

have claw marks. As it was, she settled for a fierce scowl. "What are you doing here?"

He tried to look apologetic. "It is my house."

That did not seem to cut any ice with Viola. She pointed to the door behind him. "Get out of my room."

He did the opposite. Stepping away from the closed door, he looked about him, pretending a great deal of interest in the furnishings. "Is this your room? Oh, but what am I thinking? It's been painted pink. Of course it's your room."

He started across to the door leading into his own bedchamber, then stopped and looked at her. "You did not paint my room pink, did you?"

"I wish I had thought of it."

John let out his breath on a sigh of relief that was only half feigned. "Enjoy your nap, darling. I shall see you at dinner. Are we keeping country hours or town hours? Never mind, I shall inquire of Hawthorne. Would you like to play chess after dessert, or would you prefer piquet?"

She began shaking her head. "Oh, no. Oh, no. You are not staying."

He pretended to be puzzled. "Did you want to return to town and stay at Bloomsbury Square? Personally, I'd rather we stay here for the remainder of the season. So much less gossip."

She put her face in her hands. "God hates me. He must, to set you upon me in this manner."

He made a sound of mock distress as he opened the door to his own room. "You make me sound like the plagues of Egypt."

She lifted her head. "How apt a description of you!" she cried as she followed him and started pushing him through the doorway. "I could not have chosen better. Will you please leave?"

Deciding not to push his luck, he allowed her to propel him through the doorway. "I'm going," he said, and turned around to look at her. "What did you choose for dinner? Nothing too awful, I hope."

She smiled sweetly. "Hemlock."

"Ah, my favorite."

The door slammed in his face. He lingered there, waiting.

After a moment he heard what he'd been waiting for on the other side of the closed door. "Insufferable man!"

With a chuckle, he pulled the bell for Stephens and began to change for dinner.

Chapter 13

⌒◯◯⌒

Sure John would follow her to Enderby, Viola had spent the first few days here on tenterhooks, looking out the front windows of the villa every few minutes, fully expecting to see his carriage. But after a week had passed with no sign of him, she had come to think perhaps he had finally given up on reconciling, and that was when the unthinkable had happened.

She began to miss him.

Especially at night, sitting by the fire as she remembered those passionate moments in the library at Grosvenor Square. She'd even begun to dream about him, about his kiss and his touch, an aggravating development, and one that if he ever learned of it, would be excessively mortifying.

At dinner that evening she kept her head lowered, studying him in quick, surreptitious glances as he sat at the head of the long dining table. Odd to see him there. Odd to have him in this house she had come to regard as her own. But it wasn't hers, of course. As he had reminded her earlier, it was his. And he was the master of it.

What do you want, Viola?

His question echoed through her mind. A few weeks ago her answer had been simple and succinct: go away. Now, she didn't know what the answer should be. Her reprieve was at an end, but that wasn't what kept her silent while he tried to make conversation. It was her own confusion. And frustration. He couldn't even make her the simple promise of fidelity. She was angry with herself because she knew if he made that promise, she was prepared to believe it, and that probably made her twice a fool. Thinking of that evening in the library made her feel more muddled than ever.

And scared. She didn't want to be hurt. She didn't want to believe him, find happiness with him again, only to sit across a tea table from yet another one of his mistresses next season.

What do you want, Viola?

She still wanted what she had always wanted: love and devotion and children. John was only prepared to give her one of those. That was not enough, and she could not understand why he thought her expectation of fidelity unreasonable. It wasn't unreasonable at all, damn him, especially when he demanded it of her.

Suddenly, John put his fork down with a clink. "This just isn't going to work."

She looked up from her apple tart. "What isn't going to work?"

"Spending my meals talking to myself."

"I don't feel much like talking."

"I can see that. What's wrong, Viola?"

Her bite of apple tart was sawdust in her mouth and she took a swallow of water to wash it down. "Where—" She broke off, cleared her throat, glanced at the servants hovering nearby, then back at her plate, unable to look at him. "I understand Stephens had your bed made up."

"Did you have a different location in mind for me to sleep?" he asked bluntly.

"John!" Her dreams of the past two days came rushing back with a vengeance and she blushed, casting a pointed glance at Hawthorne and the two footmen, who were standing by the sideboard.

He looked at her down the long length of the dining table for several seconds. "Hawthorne?"

The butler stepped forward. "Yes, my lord?"

"Take the footmen and leave us. I'll call you if you're needed again."

The butler bowed and withdrew, the footmen behind him. She watched them go in dismay. "We aren't finished eating. Why did you dismiss them?"

"Because I wanted to talk without you using them as an excuse not to do so, of course."

"You want to talk?" That sounded completely unbelievable. "You?"

He leaned forward in his chair and took a sip of wine. "I've been thinking about what you said the other night. You said you don't want a cold sham of a marriage. The sort most people have, where we have a child or two, then go our separate ways. That's what my parents had, and I don't want it that way, either. I think there is only one way to prevent it. We have to become friends."

"What?" This was becoming more astonishing by the moment.

He nodded. "Yes. It is clear that we have spent over eight years at cross purposes, with no real knowledge of each other. You don't trust me, and I admit, you have good reason. I am suggesting the way to remedy that is for us to become friends."

"I have never heard anything more absurd," she scoffed. The idea of being friends with John sounded as likely as pigs sprouting wings. "You and I friends? Where did you get such a notion?"

"Dylan."

"Dylan?"

"Believe it or not, yes. He suggested it. He likes us both, he said, and he is getting a bit tired of the two of us being so at odds. He would love to be able to invite both of us to dinner at the same time, so he's hoping we make peace. He thinks if we become friends with each other, everything will work out between us."

She couldn't help regarding that with skepticism. "I never knew Dylan was such an optimistic fellow," she said dryly.

"He is a father now. He has to be optimistic."

"Now that he is happily settled and is a father, he can't go on scandalous escapades with you."

"It wouldn't matter, because I don't do that sort of thing anyway. Not anymore."

"Please don't try to tell me that you've seen the error of your ways and won't go slumming in Temple Bar any longer, because I shan't believe you."

"I wouldn't say never, but I haven't done it lately. I haven't wanted to for a long time. Despite the urging of my wilder friends, I have been spending most of my free nights at my club. In case you hadn't noticed, I am not much of a subject for gossip this season."

That was true, but she couldn't help wondering how long it would last.

"It's odd," he went on, "but since Dylan got married, we have become closer friends. We used to be just acquaintances who caroused the brothels together or sat at the same gaming table, but it is different this year. I do occasionally go on a wild spree of drinking with Lord Damon and Sir Robert, I admit, but it's Dylan I see the most of."

"What do you and Dylan do if you don't visit the brothels and the gaming hells?" she asked, genuinely curious.

"Fence, mostly. We meet at Angleo's nearly every day."

"I envy you that," she confessed as she ate her last bite of apple tart and cream. "I always wanted to learn to fence when I was a girl, but I wasn't allowed."

"Why not?"

"Madame Dubreuil's Academy in Paris was the most prestigious in Europe, I'll have you know. Girls learning athletic sport?" She put on a face of shock and horror. "Never!"

He grinned. "What did you do?"

"Carried books on our heads when we probably should have been reading them. You see, it was deemed more important to learn the feminine art of walking gracefully than learning Greek or history or mathematics. I became most accomplished at walking. And at piano and watercolors and embroidering cushions."

"But no fencing?"

"No, alas."

He looked at her and a hint of mischief came into his face. Even from where she sat she could see the laugh lines at the corners of his eyes. "Want to learn?"

She frowned, perplexed. "Learn to fence, you mean?"

"Yes." He stood up and came down the length of the table. He moved behind her chair. "You've finished your dessert. Come on."

"Come on?" she repeated, twisting around to look up at him. "Where?"

"For a fencing lesson." He began pulling her chair out from the table. "You said you wanted to learn."

"When I was a girl! That was a long time ago, John."

"I know at twenty-six you're ready for the grave. But I think we have time to squeeze in a few fencing lessons first." He grasped her arms and pulled her to her feet. "Look at it this way. You hate me, isn't that right?"

"Yes," she said at once.

"Well, then, this is your perfect opportunity to stab me with a sword."

It only took her two seconds to make up her mind. "What are we waiting for?"

"I knew that idea would appeal to you." He tilted his head and kissed her neck, but he slipped away before she had the chance to even chastise him for it. "Is my old fencing gear still in the attic?" he asked as he started out the door.

"I don't know," she answered, following him out of the dining room and down the corridor to the stairs. "Is that where you kept it before?"

"When I was a boy."

They went up to the attic and found that his boyhood practice foils were still there, tucked away in a wooden crate.

He pulled them out, took one and gave the other to her. He stood her in the large, empty space in the center of the attic and faced her. "Do what I do," he told her, and when he lifted his left hand high, slightly behind him, she did the same. He pointed his sword at her with his right hand, and she pointed hers at him.

"Good," he said. "Now watch me."

He stepped forward with one foot, bending his knee, and thrusting the sword in his hand forward. The cushioned tip touched her just under her ribs.

Viola tried to do what he did but encountered a problem almost at once. "I can't do that," she complained. "My skirt gets in the way."

He straightened, grinning at her. "Well, if your skirt is really a problem—"

"No," she said before he could finish his thought.

"But if you just took it off—"

"No! Put that possibility out of your mind."

"That possibility is *never* out of my mind." He turned away. "But if you are going to be prudish about these things, we shall have to think of another solution."

He put down his foil and crossed the room to an old trunk. "There used to be costumes in here when I was a boy," he told her as he opened it. "For Fancy Dress parties and putting on plays and such."

Rummaging through the pile of old clothes, he pulled out a pair of trousers. "Mine," he explained. "When I was about fourteen. They should fit you." He pulled an old white linen shirt out of the trunk and tossed both garments to her.

She caught them in her arms and waited, but he didn't move to turn his back. "John, if you want to be friends, you have to be nice."

"I could be very nice to you," he said, a world of meaning in those words and the way he said them.

"That isn't what I meant! Turn around."

He gave a heavy sigh and obeyed. "I'll be honorable about this," he told her over one shoulder as she removed her lacy shawl collar, "although it is most unfair. My own wife and I can't even have a peek at her petticoats."

"You've peeked at plenty of petticoats," she shot back as she unfastened the buttons down the front of her bodice. "You don't need to see mine."

She slid out of her dress and undergarments and kicked off her slippers, then pulled on the trousers and shirt. "All right," she said, buttoning the shirt. "You can turn around."

He took one look at her in his boyhood clothes and chuckled. "They look much better on you than they ever did on me," he said and walked back to the center of the room.

She rolled up the shirtsleeves and turned up the trousers at the hem, then slid her feet back into her slippers and picked up her foil.

They faced each other, blades pointed as they

had been a few moments before, and this time she was able to step forward, bend her knee, and thrust the blade just as he had demonstrated.

"That is called a lunge," he told her. "Do it again, only this time aim for somewhere on my torso."

She bit her lip, tilted her head to one side, considering. She lowered her gaze.

"Somewhere fair," he said at once.

Viola took a step forward, thrusting with her foil toward his stomach, and as she did so, he brought his blade up to block her move. "That," he told her, "is a parry."

She straightened with a nod. "I see."

"Good." He faced her, sword pointed. "Hate me, do you?"

"Yes."

"All right, then. Here's your chance to express it." He gestured with his blade. "Have at me. Stab away."

She looked at him, at the challenge in his eyes, and she lifted the sword, pointing it at him. She mirrored his stance and thrust again, but her jab was halfhearted, and he evaded her simply by turning sideways.

"Pathetic," he said, shaking his head. "You're not trying."

"I don't want to accidently hurt you."

He gave a shout of laughter. "I'll just bet you don't." He gestured with his blade. "Come on. Try again. It might help if you think of all the reasons why you hate me. Why do you hate me, anyway?"

"Why?" She stared at him. "How can you even ask me that? So many reasons, I can't list them all!"

"Then tell me. Show me."

She made another jab at him, harder this time.

"Better," he said, blocking her move with nothing more than a flick of his wrist. "Keep going. Why do you hate me?"

"You lied to me before we got married, that's why." She struck at him with the foil. He parried her again.

"Very good," he said. "You just might have a knack for this."

"You make an appealing target."

"I thought I would." He beckoned her to continue. "Don't stop now. I want you to get all those resentments out in the open once and for all."

"Is that what this is about?" she asked, lunged again and missed him altogether. "You think this will solve everything?"

"No." He thrust with his blade, but very slowly, giving her plenty of time to defend herself by bringing her foil up as he had showed her. "But it is a start."

They both stepped back.

"So," he said, "I told you I loved you before we got married, and that was a lie, and that's why you hate me?"

"Not only for that. There's Elsie."

"Oh, yes, Elsie." He nodded, sounding so infuriatingly calm that she wanted to throw the sword at him. Instead, she jabbed her foil in his direction, pulled back when he parried her, and without waiting did it again. Their swords clashed together.

"When I found out about her, it devastated me. I couldn't bear to sleep with you anymore. So you walked out on me! I hate you for abandoning me."

"I waited a month, sleeping alone, being driven mad by the fact that you were in the next room and wouldn't let me sleep with you. You wouldn't relent. You just cried a lot."

"You waited a month before you left. How big of you, to wait a whole month." With those words, she felt as if a torrent had been unleashed. Using the sword he had given her, she gave vent to what she felt, taking stabs at him with both the blade and her tongue. "You left without a word. You just packed your things and took off. No good-bye, no note! I was so in love with you, I would have forgiven you for Elsie eventually, but you never gave me the chance. You never even tried to see my side. You broke my heart and didn't care."

She drew back. "Two months later, you showed up here. You wanted to make up. Of all the arrogant, conceited—" She broke off and struck again. Their foils clanged together—once, twice, three times. She pulled back, panting.

"I wasn't just saying that," he told her, shaking

back his hair, "and I wasn't feeling conceited, believe me, especially when you slapped me right across the face and told me to go to the devil."

"But you didn't go to the devil, did you?" She lunged at him, he parried her again. "You went to Jane Morrow. I can only assume you didn't want to make up all that badly."

"If that was what you assumed, you were wrong." He moved onto the offensive, thrusting his blade at her, but slowly, giving her plenty of time to defend herself against the move.

"Was I?" she countered, hitting his foil, almost wishing she'd struck him instead. "You had such a fine way of showing me how much regard you had for our marriage."

"Jane meant nothing to me," he said, and straightened. "Nor I to her."

"So, you devastated me a second time for someone who meant nothing to you. How lovely. I suppose you used her to forget about me?"

"Actually, yes."

She laughed in disbelief. "And Maria Allen? Another balm for your wounded male pride?"

"If you want to put it that way." He took a deep breath and lowered his foil. "You probably won't believe this, but I wanted to reconcile with you then, too. At Brighton."

She stared at him in astonishment. "Brighton? What are you talking about?"

"Two years ago, when I followed you down to

Brighton. Remember? And what did you do? You saw me, gave me one contemptuous look that would have frozen any man's blood, told me to go back to my whores, then turned your back and walked away. You left town before I could even unpack my trunk and ran to your brother."

"My departure from Brighton didn't stop you from finding Maria, did it?"

"No. And yes, I got in a duel over her. You want to know why? Nothing very noble, I admit, but I'll tell you. I was the latest in a long line of Maria's lovers when her husband decided he didn't like being cuckolded anymore. He called me out and we shot each other in the shoulder for the sake of honor. Stupid, I grant you, but true."

"And what happened then, John?" she cried. "I went to Hammond Park. Out of concern for you, though God only knows why! When I got there, you were in bed. Loss of blood, the doctor told me. I asked you if you were going to be all right, and what did you say? You said, 'Sorry to disappoint you, darling, but I'm going to live. Maybe you should get some arsenic.'" She stabbed at him and missed. "I was so afraid you were going to die. And then you said that to me."

"After Maria, what did you want me to say?" he asked. "Something along the lines of, 'Sorry, old thing, messed it all up again, but if you stay, I'll make it up to you.' Is that what I should have said? Would anything have been the right thing to say?"

"Words are not what mattered to me! It's the things you've done that matter. Did you ever once give a thought to what life has been like for me, John? Seeing all your other women and knowing you would rather be with any of them than with me?"

"That is not true. I would rather have been with my wife. The woman who should have been the mother of my children, the woman who should have been in my bed and wasn't there. Who made it clear as crystal she loathed me, would never stop loathing me, and couldn't bear to be anywhere near me."

"Do you think that justifies what you did?"

"I am not trying to justify any of the things I've done. I am trying to *explain* why I did them."

The very calmness of his demeanor, the fact that he was not getting defensive and fighting back only made her hurt even more. She lifted the foil in her hand and struck out, going on the attack. She struck at him again and again. He parried each of her movements with an ease that was almost leisurely, but he also moved backward, allowing her to be the aggressor and drive him across the room.

"I hate you for all those women, and I don't care about your reasons for going to them!" she cried as she lunged at him and lunged again. "I hate you for all those other women you have kissed and touched and made love to, women to whom you gave the things that were supposed to be for me and only me!"

His back hit the wall, and she struck one more time, thrusting her blade right at his heart. He didn't even try to block the move, and took the hit square in his chest. "I hate you, John," she said, and drew back, panting. "For taking my love for you and destroying it. And for making no more than two halfhearted attempts to reconcile. And for coming back now just because you need something from me that no other woman can give you."

Out of breath, she lowered her arm and dropped the foil. It clattered to the floor. The image of him in front of her began to blur. "Most of all, I hate you for making me hurt all over again," she choked, "when I had finally gotten over you."

She turned away, but of course, he wouldn't let her leave. She heard his blade drop to the floor, just before she felt his hands close over her arms. He was not even winded, damn him.

"You said you wanted to understand me better, and that's why I've tried to explain things," he said. "I cannot do more than that about what is in the past. I am not walking away again, and I'm not letting you do that, either. This time, we are going to find a way to live together without annihilating each other. That's why we have to be friends."

She shook her head. "It's impossible."

"Why?"

She pulled against his hold, and he let her go.

She didn't answer him, for it was a waste of breath and she was already exhausted. Instead, she walked down the stairs with him right behind her, and neither of them spoke until they reached the door of her room. She paused there and turned toward him. "Good night, John."

"Why is it impossible, Viola? You always want to talk about things, so talk. Why is it impossible for us to be friends?"

She sighed with frustration. "Because, well, because—" She stopped as he reached up to tuck a loose tendril of her hair behind her ear. She pushed his hand away. "Friends have trust, and I don't trust you."

"I will have to earn your trust, then, won't I?"

He was being so damned reasonable. It was always dangerous when John was reasonable. She licked her lips. "You are doing this to trick me," she accused. "Trick me into bed."

He crossed his fingers. "Is it working?"

"No. It will never work again."

"Then you have nothing to worry about, do you?"

"Not a thing." She turned around and reached for the knob of her bedroom door, wanting desperately to get away. "Because I still hate you."

"No, you don't. Not anymore." He closed his hand over hers to stop her from opening the door. "That night at Grosvenor Square, when I came in out of the rain to see you, you let me stay. That's when I knew you didn't hate me anymore." His hand over her hand, he leaned closer. His body brushed against hers, just barely, but enough that Viola's heart began to pound in her chest as if they were fencing again. He kissed her hair, then her temple, then her cheek. "You don't hate me, and if we become friends, you never will." He pressed his lips to her ear. "See how this works?"

That quiver began in her tummy, the quiver of fear and hurt mixed with the desire, and she felt as if she were drowning in her own confused emotions.

"I am going to make you trust me," he murmured. His hand caressed the back of hers where she gripped the doorknob. "I am going to make you stop being afraid."

She closed her eyes. "I'm not afraid of you."

But she was. Oh, she was.

He knew it, too. "Now who is the liar?" he asked, and kissed her ear, then let go of her hand and stepped back. "Good night, Viola," he said, and started toward his own door a bit farther down the corridor.

She went into her room and shut the door. As Celeste helped her change into nightclothes, she listened to the low murmur of his voice in the room beside hers as he spoke to his valet.

He was right. She didn't hate him anymore. She lost her grip on her hate and her resentment a little bit more every time they talked, feeling more of the old magic every time he smiled, every time he made her laugh, every time he did something nice, every time he kissed her. And without her hate, she had no shield. No weapons. She was out in the open, unprotected and vulnerable.

What had happened to her pride? Viola climbed into bed and hugged her pillow, huddling into a tight ball of misery. Pride, she thought, was all very well, but it made for a lonely life.

If she and John became friends, she would fall for him again, and he knew it. If they were friends, it was only a matter of time before she started to believe him again, believe he was sincere, believe that he cared, believe that he might, one day, love her when he had never loved anybody in his life. If she began to believe in him again, she would slide all the way down, right into his bed, heart in her hands for him to take all over again. And God help her after that because if he walked away again, it would smash her heart into a thousand pieces.

Chapter 14

The following morning, Viola did not come down to breakfast, and John decided to take breakfast to her instead. He went to the kitchens, and upon learning that no food had been sent up to her, loaded two trays with some of her favorites and his and took them to her room.

When he opened the door, he found her sitting up in bed, reading her letters, which had come in the morning post. "What are you doing?" she cried as he entered the room, followed by a pair of maids.

"What does it look like?" he asked, gesturing to one of the maids to put the tea tray on the bedside table. He took the tray of food from the other maid and waved both servants out of the room. "I'm bringing you breakfast in bed."

"You can't do this. You can't invade my privacy this way."

"Silly to tell me I cannot do what I have already done," he said as the door closed behind the maids, leaving them alone. He sat on the edge of her bed, set the tray on her lap, and poured tea for them both. "Besides, it is my house."

She groaned and fell back against the burled walnut headboard. "I give up," she moaned. "You are never going to leave me alone."

"Now you are starting to see sense," he said, and plucked the handful of letters out of her hand. He tossed them onto the floor and picked up the jam pot and a knife. "Blackberry jam, Lady Hammond?"

He glanced at her, and she looked so beautiful in the morning sunlight, with her braid coming loose and a hint of pink in her cheeks, he caught his breath. Her nightgown was a delicate muslin affair, so thin he could see the swell of her breasts above the bedclothes, the pucker of her nipples and the faint outline of her aureoles. That was enough to arouse him in an instant, and he knew she'd better give in soon. Too many chaste breakfasts in bed with her would drive him mad. He forced his gaze up to her face.

She sensed what he was thinking and looked away, the blush in her cheeks deepening. She shifted her hips on the bed, and just that tiny move almost sent him over the edge. She wanted him, she did. God, he hoped she did.

But he didn't intend to make the same mistake twice. If he pushed too hard, too fast, she'd run again. He looked down at the tray of food and focused on that, trying not to remember how she looked without a nightgown. He scooped jam onto the knife, set down the pot and picked up a slice of hot buttered toast. After spreading the jam over the slice, he held it out to her, waiting. She bit her lip, wavering, and stared down at the toast for a long moment before she took it with a sigh.

Gratified, he spread jam on another slice for himself. He picked up his fork and began to eat from the plate of eggs and bacon on his lap, watching her from beneath lowered lids, waiting, hoping for an opportunity.

She took another bite of toast, and John thanked God for blackberry jam. He set down his fork and inched a little closer to her on the bed. She went still, holding her toast poised in midair, staring at him, her hazel eyes wide.

He moved even closer. "You have jam on your face."

She looked away. "Don't."

"Don't what?" he murmured. "Don't try to make you want me?" He reached out and touched the bit of jam at the corner of her mouth, then ran his fingers back and forth across her lips, smearing it. The jam was sticky, her mouth so soft. "Sorry," he said, his voice a bit unsteady, "but I can't help myself. I want you, and I want you to want me back. I want that so badly, in fact, I'm going a bit mad. That's why I've been standing out in rainstorms and going shopping. That's why I'm trying to talk about things." He took a deep breath. "And that's why I leased a house with a pink drawing room. Even back then, even when things between us were as bad as they could get, I still had a little scrap of hope that one day you'd live with me again."

Her lower lip quivered against his fingertip. "I don't believe you."

"You used to want me, Viola," he said, stroking her mouth. "Every day for breakfast. Don't you remember? And it was fun, wasn't it?"

"Yes, it was." Her lips brushed against his fingers as she spoke. She reached up, her hand closing around his wrist, but she did not push him away or turn her face aside. "It was fun for a while."

He gently pulled his hand from her grasp and slid it to the back of her neck. The sticky jam on his fingers caught the strands of her hair. He leaned in and pulled her toward him at the same time, making them meet halfway. "You know when things went wrong with us?" he asked, pausing with his face only two inches from hers. "They went wrong when it wasn't fun anymore. When we didn't do our favorite things, and I couldn't make you laugh."

"There are some things fun and laughter can't fix, John."

"I know." He looked at her jam-smeared mouth. Desire was coursing through him with such force, he didn't know how much longer he could contain it. "That's what kissing is for."

"Is it all that simple for you?" she asked. "That easy?"

"Yes. I think you just make things complicated." He had to kiss her. Just once, then he'd let her go. His hand tightened on her neck and he pulled her that last inch closer. His lips touched the corner of her mouth, tasting jam on her skin, and the pleasure was so intense, the longing so great, it took everything he had not to shove the tray out of the way and move on top of her. He sat utterly still, fighting the aching need in his body, holding back, waiting, breathing in deeply of violet warmth as he tasted blackberry jam on Viola's mouth.

She turned her face away, breaking the kiss.

He knew he had to let her go. Now, while he still could. She wasn't ready yet, and he didn't want to send her running away again. He let his hand fall from her neck and leaned back, striving to ignore the agony of being fully aroused with no relief in sight. He picked up his fork and resumed eating eggs and bacon.

She did the same, not looking at him, but at the plate in her lap.

They were almost finished eating before John felt able to put on a casual air and attempt ordinary conversation. "So, are you going to show me what you've done to the place?" he asked. "I mean the outside, mind you," he went on, and gestured to their surroundings with a slice of bacon. "Not this feminine floral fantasy you've made of the inside."

"After that comment, you can take your own walk around," she told him around a mouthful of toast. "By yourself."

"But if I'm by myself, I can't trap you anywhere and steal more kisses," he pointed out, and popped the bacon into his mouth, thinking that stealing any more kisses from her today without some clothes coming off would probably destroy him.

She ate her last bite of toast and jam. "Exactly."

"You love my kisses, and you know it," he said lightly, and stood up. Taking the tray, he turned and set it on a nearby table. "I'll have you swooning over me by dinnertime. Get dressed. I'll wait for you downstairs."

"I have never swooned over you," she pointed out as she brushed crumbs from her nightgown. "Never."

He bent over her, placing one hand on each side of her hips. The mattress dipped with his weight as he leaned close. "Not yet, but the day is long," he said, and kissed her quick before she could stop him. He straightened and turned away, heading for the door. "The night is even longer."

"Lovely," she groaned, sounding as if she were the one about to endure a day of torture. "That's just lovely."

* * *

Viola gave him a tour of the villa, showing him some of the things she had done. He liked the box-wood maze she'd put in the gardens, was highly indignant that she'd torn down the ramshackle boathouse by the river, and he loved the new stables she'd had built the previous year. He also expressed his approval for the new granary.

"You've done an excellent job here," he told her, and stopped beside the millpond, looking out over the water. "You've made some very fine improvements. Everything looks shipshape and Bristol fashion."

"Thank you."

Something caught his attention and he paused. Viola watched as he crossed to the wooden quay that stood out over the millpond. Beside the quay, a rowboat bobbed in the water. "The oars are in the bottom," he said. "Let's take it out. We can go across the pond and down the stream."

Viola felt her insides clench with apprehension, and she searched for an excuse. "It's a bit too chilly to go out on the water."

"Chilly? Not a bit. It's a lovely afternoon. Besides, we're not going swimming." He pulled off his coat and tossed it aside.

"I don't want to go rowing."

"I'll do the work," he said. "You just have to sit in the stern and look beautiful while I pull the oars, gaze at you, and recite some Shelley."

She watched as he pulled off his cravat, unbuttoned the three buttons of his shirt, and took off his waistcoat. He knelt on the quay, leaning over the boat to retrieve the oars, and her fear increased. "No, John," she said. "I don't want to go."

"It's the least you can do after you tore down my boathouse. Be a sport, Viola. It'll be fun."

She wiped her sweaty palms on her skirt. "John, I am not getting in that boat!"

The sharp rise of her voice caught his attention. He glanced at her over his shoulder. "Why not? Do you get sick in a boat?"

She pressed a hand to her tummy and felt as if she were going to be sick, sick with fear. Wordlessly, she shook her head.

He watched her for a moment, then set down the oars and crossed the quay back to her. "What's wrong?"

"I can't swim!"

He laughed. "Is that all?"

"All?" She was truly panicking now. "What if the boat tips over? I could drown."

"You're not going to drown." He stopped laughing and reached out to cup her cheek in his hand. "I am a very good swimmer."

She shook her head. "No."

"The pond is shallow, and the stream is very slow and meandering. Besides, nothing will happen to you if the boat tips over because I'll be there." He leaned down and kissed her. "You just have to trust me," he said, and grabbed her hand. "Come on. I won't let anything happen to you. I promise."

"I'm sure I'm going to hate this," she moaned as he led her to the rowboat.

One foot planted on the planks, he put his other foot in the boat and pulled it right up against the wooden quay. "I've got it steady," he told her. "Just get in."

She took a deep breath, grabbed a handful of her skirt to keep it out of the way, and stepped gingerly into the boat, holding onto his hand for dear life. She eased herself down in the stern of the rowboat, and when he let go of her hand, she gripped the wooden sides, hoping she didn't mortify herself by throwing up.

He sat down in the boat, untied the rope to free it from its moorings, and grabbed the oars. Holding them with one hand, he shoved the boat away from the quay, then locked the oars into the stops, glanced behind him, and began rowing her across the pond.

"You have to tell me whenever we are coming to a bend in the stream," he told her as he pulled the oars with smooth strokes, gliding the boat through the water at a rapid clip. "I'll use the oars to steer."

"You're coming up on the mouth of the stream now," she answered, looking past his shoulder. "To your left."

He glanced behind him, guiding the boat as he

rowed, maneuvering it onto the stream that meandered off into the thicket of weeping willows and birches. When they came to a long, straight stretch, he turned to look at her.

"Are you all right?" he asked. "Not feeling sick or nervous anymore?"

She lied. "No."

"You see? First fencing, now boats. Pretty soon I'll be giving you swimming lessons."

She looked at him in horror. "No, you won't."

"Yes, I will." He pulled on the oars. "Naked," he added. "By moonlight."

Heat washed over her. She looked past him, chin in the air, pretending to look for bends in the stream, pretending she wasn't blushing all the way down to her toes. "You have a vivid imagination."

"Yes," he agreed with fervor. She knew he was still looking at her, and she knew what he was imagining. "Yes, I do."

The stream was slow and he rowed easily against the mild current. His body was powerful and his motions smooth and fluid. It was almost hypnotic to watch him, and as the boat journeyed along the stream, she had to keep reminding herself to watch where they were going. "You row very well," she said.

"This isn't rowing," he said. "When it's two oars like this, it's sculling. Rowing is with one oar."

"Well then, you scull very well. Row well, too, I imagine."

"I should. I've had enough practice. I did both at Harrow and Cambridge." He leaned back with another pull of the oars. "I was lead oar for our team in the boat races on the Cam every May Week all four years I was at Cambridge."

"Did you win?"

"Usually." He began to laugh. "Percy was our coxswain, and a good one, too. He was so methodical, he could set the pace better than anybody."

"You must miss him."

The laughter faded from his face and he stopped rowing. The boat stopped moving forward and began to drift, but he didn't seem to notice. He leaned on his oars, bringing the tips out of the water. She waited, thinking he might talk about his cousin, but he didn't. Instead, he turned his head, staring at the bank of the stream and the woods beyond, lost in thought.

"John, what are you thinking about?"

"I miss him so much, it hurts." He shook his head as if to clear his mind, then started rowing again. "Let's talk about something pleasant. We're supposed to be having fun today. We might as well put my university education to work. What poet would you like to hear? Pick a romantic one, then I can be torrid and passionate and make you want me."

She wondered if he had done this before, taken a woman out in a boat and recited passionate poetry. She took a deep breath and tamped down the flare of horrid jealousy. "John, you don't have to recite poetry to me."

"No fairer face than hers I see, none other is so dear. Precious moments of my life are these, whenever she is near."

The carelessly uttered lines were unfamiliar, but the look in his eyes was one she knew well. She had already seen it twice today, over toast in her room and just a moment before when he talked about swimming lessons. Each time, it got easier to believe it might mean more than simple desire. She swallowed hard and looked away. "I don't recognize that verse."

"I'd be very surprised if you did." His voice was wry. "Since I just made it up."

Startled, she returned her gaze to his face. "What, just now?"

He nodded. "I used to write poetry all the time."

"I never knew that. I mean, I know about the limericks you and Dylan are always coming up with, but I didn't know you wrote poetry."

"I never knew you didn't know how to swim." His lashes lowered. "Speaking of which, we should start those swimming lessons very soon. The millpond here is shallow enough for you to stand in. Perfect place. We could start tonight."

"And I think we should go back to the house. It must be nigh on three o'clock by now, and I want to bathe and change before dinner. We're keeping country hours," she reminded him, "so dinner is at five."

He tilted his head, looking at her. "Do we have a bathtub big enough for two?"

"No, we do not."

He began to laugh at the firm primness of her voice, but he didn't say anything more about it. He glanced behind him and used one oar to turn the boat around.

He rowed with the current, and neither of them spoke. Her mind kept repeating the lines of that bit of poetry he'd made up. Her head kept telling her he wasn't sincere. Her heart didn't want to listen.

"Since you didn't seem suitably impressed by my last poem about you, I have another one for you," he said, breaking the silence. He stopped and lifted the oars out of the water, and in the still water of the pond, the boat stopped moving. "A limerick."

She saw that teasing gleam in his eyes. "A limerick about me?"

"There's a woman I know from Hampshire, with a smile that beguiles a man sure. Her gold hair is a prize, like mud are her eyes, and her kiss is a pleasure for damn sure."

"What?" She straightened on the plank seat, feeling a bit indignant, despite the part about her kiss being a pleasure. "My eyes are not the color of mud!"

"They are the exact same color." He pointed to

the nearby bank of the millpond. "Like that. Greenish-brown. Not that there's anything wrong with that," he added as she made a huff of vexation. "Very English, I think. And rather poetic."

"Poetic?" She folded her arms. "Poets are supposed to compare women's eyes to stars and sky and things like that. If comparing my eyes to greenish-brown mud is part of your plan to seduce me, it is not working."

The tease went out of his eyes. He pulled the oars out of the stops and dropped them into the bottom of the boat with a thud. He moved toward her, and she caught her breath at the sudden intensity in his countenance. He slid to his knees in front of her and put a hand on each side of her hips, curling his fingers around the back edge of the plank seat.

He leaned forward and brushed his lips lightly, briefly, against hers. "How about this?" he asked. "Is this working?"

She began to quiver inside. "No," she said, and pressed her lips together against the caress of his.

"Viola, be fair," he murmured against her mouth. "I know I said your eyes were like pond mud, but I also said your gold hair was a prize. And your kiss was a pleasure." He nipped at her lips. "So give me some of that pleasure right now and kiss me."

She turned her face aside. "I'm not going to kiss you," she said, and spoiled her pretense of hurt feelings by laughing. "No, no, you ruined your chance with that part about the mud."

He began to laugh with her, a low, deep chuckle in his throat. "But English pond mud is very pretty," he said, and kissed her cheek. "I like it."

His hands slid beneath her, and with a suddenness that startled her, he hauled her forward onto his knees. Not expecting the move, she twisted in his hold with a shriek of laughter, sending the boat rocking. "John, stop it!" she cried, struggling as he turned her sideways on his lap. The boat rocked again, tipped too far, and overturned, sending both of them tumbling into the pond.

Viola felt water rush over her head, smothering her laughter. She flailed her arms in sudden panic, disoriented and unable to see anything in the murky depths. But then John's hands were on her arms, hauling her up to a standing position. "I've got you," he said, wrapping his arms around her. "I've got you."

She sucked in gulps of air and clutched at the wet folds of his shirt, panic receding as she realized John was holding her tight against him, her feet were on the bottom of the pond, and the water was only up to her armpits.

"Are you all right?" he asked, and pulled back to look at her. He pushed soaking wet hair out of her face. "Hmm?"

"I'm all right." She rubbed her arms. "Cold, but all right."

John bent at the knees and picked her up in his arms, wet clothes and all. "Some reward I get for composing poetry about you," he told her in mock injury as he carried her toward the bank. "A dunk in cold water and no kiss to show for it."

"Serves you right," she told him as he set her on her feet by the edge of the water. She turned away as he went back to retrieve the boat. "Eyes like mud, indeed!" she added over her shoulder for his benefit, but she couldn't help smiling as she grasped sodden handfuls of skirt in her hands and climbed the bank toward the grassy knoll above.

Chapter 15

⌒◯◯⌒

After their dunking in the murky water of the pond, it was necessary for both John and Viola to bathe and change before dinner. The kitchen maids brought hot water up to the bathing room and filled the copper bathtub. Viola took the first bath, and as Celeste washed and towel-dried her hair, all she could think of was the look in John's eyes when he'd recited those lines of poetry about her. Had he meant it?

The question ran through her mind over and over as Celeste helped her dry off and wrapped her in a robe of heavy rose-colored silk. She walked into the dressing room that adjoined the bath, and Celeste followed. The maid began pulling out gowns for her to choose from, but Viola's mind was not on changing for dinner.

Was he sincere? With all the other women he'd had, how could she ever believe she meant more to him than any other? And how could she be sure it would last? Viola could hear servants bringing fresh hot water into the bathing room for John, and she imagined him stepping naked into that bathtub. She remembered full well what his body looked like, and her memories and her imagination began to tease and torment her now, just as her dreams had been doing night after night.

He'd said there was none so dear as her. He'd said no fairer face than hers. Did he ever mean any of the things he said? She tried to remind herself that words weren't enough. That his desire didn't mean anything. But it was hard to care about that when all she could do was remember the desire she felt when he kissed her and touched her.

It was good with us, once. Remember?

She remembered.

Viola pressed her fingers to her forehead, so muddled and upside down she couldn't think.

"My lady?" Celeste asked. "Are you unwell?"

She lowered her hand. "I'm perfectly well, thank you, Celeste."

The woman who had been her maid since she was fifteen gave her a smile of relief and held up two gowns. "Ivory or ice-blue?"

"Blue," Viola said without caring, and her maid left the dressing room with the blue gown in her hands. Viola remained behind. On the other side of the door to the bathing room, she heard John's voice as he talked with Stephens. She didn't know what he was saying to his valet because in her mind she was hearing what he'd said that morning over breakfast.

I want you, and I want you to want me back. I want that so badly, in fact, I'm going a bit mad . . . even when things between us were as bad as they could ever be, I still had a little scrap of hope that one day you'd live with me again.

Suddenly, everything seemed crystal clear, and all her mixed-up emotions fused into one simple decision. She took a deep breath, marched into her bedchamber and walked to where her maid was laying the blue silk gown out on the bed.

"Celeste," she said, pausing beside the maid, "go send someone to tell the kitchens dinner is going to be delayed at least a couple of hours."

Her maid gave her a puzzled look, but she nodded. "Yes, my lady."

"And go find something to do until I send for you. If I send for you at all. I might not."

Comprehension dawned in the older woman's face, comprehension and complete astonishment. But the maid bobbed a curtsy and departed, leaving Viola alone in her bedchamber.

She walked to her dressing table and picked up a comb. She untangled the damp strands of her hair, but she didn't braid them back. Instead, she left them loose, put down the comb and walked back through the dressing room.

He was still in the bath—she could hear the splash of water and his voice as he spoke with his valet. Hand on the knob, she paused long enough to take a deep breath, then opened the door.

He was leaning back in the tub, his arms resting on the copper sides, and Stephens was standing nearby with a towel in his hands. Both men looked up in surprise as she came in.

Ignoring the valet, she looked at her husband. "Did you mean it?" she asked without ceremony. "What you said?"

He glanced at Stephens and gave a quick nod. The valet dropped the towel onto a padded bench by the tub and departed at once through the door into the corridor, closing it behind him.

Viola hooked the fingers of one hand around the fingers of the other, waiting. "Did you?"

John leaned back in the tub, smiling faintly as he looked at her. "Did I mean what?" he asked, sounding innocent, the hot look in his eyes making him anything but. "About your eyes being the color of mud?"

She shifted her weight from one foot to the other, suddenly shy and flustered, wondering if she was about to make a horrible mistake. "No," she whispered, and her fear began to return. Her heart started thudding in her chest, so loud she was sure he could hear it all the way across the room as she stood there in an agony of uncertainty. "The other poem. About the 'none so dear' and 'precious moments' and all that. And . . . and what you said this morning about hoping we'd live together again one day. Did you mean it, or was it all just words you think I wanted to hear?"

He didn't answer, and her moment of bravado deserted her. "Never mind," she muttered, and turned around, starting back toward the safety of her own dressing room. A splash was her only warning before he was out of the bathtub, and she had only taken two steps before his arm was around her waist, hauling her back against him.

"I meant it," he said, his voice low and thick. He pressed his lips to the side of her neck. "I meant it, Viola."

His body was wet, his mouth was hot, and the feel of both disintegrated any resistance left in her. Like a dam breaking, the hunger she had been holding back for years was unleashed in an instant. With a cry, she turned and wrapped her arms around his neck. She caught his mouth with hers and kissed him, a hungry, open-mouthed kiss borne of being so long without him, of being alone and hurting. She clung to him now, kissing him with all the passion she had denied to him and to herself.

He made a sound against her mouth, surprise perhaps, but then his arms wrapped around her and he deepened the kiss, his tongue entering her mouth, his hands cupping her buttocks. Everything in the world faded to insignificance. Everything but John.

His mouth tasted her in hot, deep kisses and quick little nibbles of her lips as he guided her backward through the door into her dressing room and on into her bedchamber beyond.

Inside her room, he moved and guided her body as if they were engaged in a dance. When her back hit the wall beside her bed, he reached for the sash of her robe. He untied it and yanked the edges apart, then pulled the garment back and slid it off her shoulders and down her arms. It caught on her hips, and she leaned forward away from the wall. The robe fell and landed in a soft pool at her heels.

The air of her room was cool, but when John's hands touched her naked skin, warmth surged through her like fire. He cupped her breasts, embraced them with his hands, shaped them in his palms. His fingertips closed around her erect nipples, pinching them ever so gently as he pressed kisses to her cheeks and her chin, her forehead and her lips.

She put her hands on his broad shoulders. His skin was still slick and wet from the bathwater, but hot, like fire in her hands. She moved her hands over him and watched her fingers touch him. She remembered this—the hard muscular wall of his chest and the rippled muscles of his abdomen beneath her fingers. John's body, his hard strength as beautiful now as it had been nine years ago. She flattened her hands on his flat stomach, but before she could move any lower, he took her hands and pulled them wide, away from him.

"Shhh," he said as she made a sound of protest.

"But I want to touch you."

"Later." He kissed her to silence any further argument and pulled at her hands, spreading her arms wide, pressing the backs of her wrists against the wall. Then he bent his head and took one of her nipples into his mouth. He pulled and suckled, first one nipple then the other, as he held her imprisoned against the wall.

Viola's whole body tingled as he teased and toyed with her breasts, and she moaned, wanting more. When he grazed her nipple between his teeth, her body jerked and she gave a soft, keening wail of agonized pleasure. She felt the liquid heat forming down low, between her thighs. She stirred, pulling against his hold, her hips moving, wanting still more. She arched her hips toward him, but his body was out of reach. "John, touch me."

His mouth left her nipple, kissed the soft swell above it. "I'm already touching you."

"Don't tease me now," she implored. "Touch me."

"Where?"

"You know where."

"No, I don't." He resumed suckling her.

She moaned, straining against his hold. "You do know, you do."

He straightened, his hand playing with her breast. "Tell me. I like it when you tell me. Remember?"

She remembered. Shameful excitement flooded through her and she buried her hot face against his shoulder, shaking her head. He wanted too much, too soon. He brushed his fingers against the apex of her thighs. "Is that where?" he asked tenderly.

She nodded against his shoulder, and he slid one finger between her legs, to caress the wet, soft place where she ached the most. She moaned into his shoulder. "I love that, John, I love that."

"I know, Viola." He kissed her mouth and said, "But there's something I know you love even more."

He knelt in front of her, and she knew what he was going to do. She began to shiver as he trailed kisses down her tummy, over her abdomen, and lower still. His fingertips followed his mouth, moving in light caresses around her navel. He smiled, touching the tip of one finger to the brown, violin-shaped birthmark on her thigh. "I remember that birthmark," he murmured. "I've been having some damned erotic dreams about it lately." He pressed his lips to it, then kissed her again a bit higher, his lips brushing the soft bush of her hair. She jerked against him, crying out with the carnal pleasure of that kiss, and his hands grasped her hips, holding her there, pressed against the wall.

He licked her gently, first down, then up again, his tongue moving along the crease of her sex, tasting her, sending sensations of heat pulsing through her whole body. She shivered, gasping with each soft lash of his tongue, and her hands tightened on his shoulders in convulsive little squeezes.

"John, oh, John," she panted, her hips working against his hold. She wanted to move, unable to stand such sweet imprisonment as this.

His tongue flicked over the special place he knew gave her the greatest pleasure, caressing it in quick, feather light strokes, and just as she thought she would go mad, he relaxed his grip and she was able to move her hips against his mouth to gain her peak. She climaxed in waves against his mouth, rippling waves of ecstasy that seemed to go on and on and on, even as he slowed the caresses of his tongue to brief light kisses. He took one last taste of her, then stopped and stood up.

All the strength drained out of her, and she fell forward against him, panting, her arms wrapping around his waist, her body still pulsing with the force of her orgasms.

He pressed his hips against her, and she felt his arousal, hot and hard against her tummy. She took him in her hand, her fingers not able to completely surround his shaft, and she stroked him, her hand exploring the shape, a shape still so familiar.

He stopped her. "I want to be inside you," he said with sudden urgency. He grasped both her hands in his and pulled them both down onto the bed. Then he rolled her onto her back and his knee moved between her thighs, urging her legs to part.

"Open for me," he groaned, settling his body over her, resting his weight on his forearms. "Now, Viola, now."

His turn to be desperate, she thought, taking delight and satisfaction in his plea. His penis pressed urgently against the folds of her opening, demanding entrance, and she spread her legs wide, welcoming him.

He entered her, and she sucked in her breath sharply. Yes, she remembered this. This was John, thick and hot and so hard, pushing into her. This was John, who kissed and nibbled her neck, her throat and her shoulder, making her shiver even now as he rocked his hips, stretching her to accommodate his size, penetrating her more deeply with each stroke.

Yes, she remembered this, the hot sweetness of him inside her. When the head of his penis touched her deep within, at that exquisite place even more pleasurable than the one he had tasted moments ago, she remembered that, too, and she cried out. "Yes, John, yes!"

Frantic with longing for that last and best explosion, she matched his hard thrusts with her own, and her pleading words all began running together in a panting, disjointed series of syllables. "Faster-oh-oh-please-oh-please-yes-oh-yes-oh-please!"

Weight on his forearms, he obeyed her frantic command, pushing hard and quick, over and over, until he sent her to climax again, his shoulders and arms shaking with the strain of holding back his own.

"Come, John, come," she pleaded, "take it, take it." When he came fully into her again, she squeezed his buttocks hard and all her inner muscles clenched in tight convulsions around his shaft.

He gave a hoarse cry smothered against her hair and slid his arms beneath her, crushing her against him as if he couldn't get her close enough, thrusting as deep as he could. He shuddered violently as his own pleasure was at last unleashed, and his body went rigid as the warmth of his climax poured from him into her.

He collapsed on top of her, breathing hard against the pillow. His hand came up to stroke her cheek. "Viola," he groaned. "Oh, God, Viola." He sucked in deep breaths of air, pressing kisses against her hair and her ear and her temple. "Meant it," he told her in a hoarse, fierce whisper. "Meant every damn word."

She smiled, caressing his back, running her fingers over the strong, lean lines of muscle and sinew, relishing the familiar, heavy weight of her husband's body. *John*, she thought, holding him tight and deep within her, *welcome home*.

Chapter 16

❦

"**J**ohn?"

He woke at the sound of her voice, and it was only then that he realized he had fallen asleep. He inhaled the scent of violets, and it aroused him in an instant, bringing him fully awake as he remembered the passionate lovemaking of a short time ago. His arms tightened around her and he pressed closer to her, his chest against the soft, smooth skin of her back. He nuzzled her neck, kissed her bare shoulder. "Hmm?"

"It's dinnertime." Viola stirred in his hold. "I'm hungry."

"So am I," he said with feeling, trailing one hand along her naked hip.

She began to laugh and pushed his hand away. "For *food*. I want my dinner."

"Can't we frolic first?" He spread one hand across her tummy, cupped her breast with the other. "Then have food?"

"Frolic requires sustenance," she pointed out, but even as she said it, she began to yield, arching her body against his, her hips pressing his groin.

Gently, he nipped her shoulder and toyed with her breast. He brushed his fingers along her tummy, feeling her muscles quiver at the light touch. "Still ticklish, I see."

"John!" She wriggled in his hold, laughing.

He slid his hand between her legs. When he did, her laughter changed to a moan of pure pleasure.

She was already moist, and he began to caress her. "Food or frolic? Which do you want first?"

"Food."

"Really?" He stroked her slowly, gently, teasing. "I think you want this more. I know I do."

He could see her profile in the dim light of late afternoon that peeped between a gap in the draperies. He saw her bite her lip, shake her head. "Uh-uh," she denied, even as she began to move in rhythm with the touch of his fingers. "Food."

"Frolic first." He pushed the tip of his finger into her, then pulled back, spreading her moisture in light circles, then stroking again. "Come on, Viola," he coaxed. "Give in."

She shook her head again, panting now.

John pushed his cock between her thighs, but he did not enter her. He groaned even as he continued to tease her. She began to shiver with each upward stroke of his fingers, and began to make the soft, whimpering sounds that told him she was close to climax.

"If you really want food," he went on, his own breath coming faster, "I could stop now, and we could go have dinner. Hmm? You want me to stop?"

"No, no. Don't stop, John. Don't stop."

"Sure?"

She nodded, frantic. "Sure."

"Want me more than food, do you?"

"Yes, yes," she gasped. "Yes."

He entered her, pushing deep into her from behind as he stroked her in front. She came almost at once, crying out as she tightened around him in the tiny convulsions of feminine bliss that sent him to climax as well.

Afterward, he caressed her hip as the muscles inside her slowly stopped clenching him and she was sated. Even then he did not move. He liked this, holding her this way, with himself deep within her. He always had.

"John?"

Her voice was almost plaintive.

"Hmm?"

"Now can we have dinner?"

He gave a shout of laughter and rolled onto his back. "I should hope so," he said in an injured voice. "If you keep demanding these strenuous demonstrations of my affection, you're going to have to feed me once in a while."

She hit him with a pillow.

During dinner, Viola tried not to stare at her husband, but her gaze kept straying to him seated at the other end of the long dining table. It was still strange to see him there, but it felt good, somehow. It felt right.

He looked up and caught her gaze. His brows drew together in puzzlement. "You are staring at me quite intently," he said, smiling. "Why?"

"I am trying to get used to seeing you in that chair."

John took a sip of wine. "Is it a good sight, Viola?" he asked. "Or not so good?"

He wasn't teasing. "Good," she admitted. "Strange, but good. Although," she added, her voice taking on a hint of mock severity, "you really need to appreciate the schedule of things here at Enderby and not come down so late to dinner."

"I am terribly sorry." He smiled, and she caught her breath. He could still make her heart race when he smiled. "I was unavoidably detained."

"Dessert, my lord." Hawthorne placed a glass bowl in front of him, and a footmen did the same for her. Viola picked up her spoon and took a bite of trifle.

"Take it away."

John's voice, the emotionless words, had her looking up. His face was as expressionless as his voice, and the very flatness of it was so startling, she set down her spoon. It was as if she were looking not at her husband's face, but at a mask of it.

Hawthorne removed the dessert he had just placed on the table. "Would you like something else, my lord?"

"Just the port."

The butler stepped back and set John's dessert on the sideboard. He brought a flagon of port and a glass, poured out the wine, and once again withdrew.

As if sensing her scrutiny, he shifted uneasily in his chair. "I don't eat trifle," he said without looking at her.

"I had forgotten how much you dislike it."

"Odd, what? Jam, sponge cake, custard. What is there about it to dislike? It must be that I have an absurd desire to be different from everyone else in Britain."

He smiled again, that brilliant, heart-stopping smile, but this time it did not reach his eyes. This was more than just dislike. There was something oddly painful in that smile that hurt her, too. An emptiness. Viola set her serviette beside her plate. "Hawthorne," she said, signaling the butler forward again. "Take mine away as well, please. I don't want it. And bring me a glass of madeira."

"You didn't have to do that," John said as the

servant stepped back with her uneaten dessert.

"I think I did. It bothers you to even look at it."

He didn't answer, but he didn't have to. She knew it bothered him a great deal. "Why?" she asked.

He turned his face away.

"Would it be so hard, John?" she asked. "To tell me?"

When he still said nothing, she shoved aside her disappointment and rose to her feet. "The sun is setting," she said. "You always liked to walk at sunset. I may have forgotten about the trifle, but I remember that." She took her glass of madeira from where Hawthorne had just placed it on the table. "Shall we take our wine and go for a walk in the garden?"

He picked up his port and they went outside into the cool air of the May evening. By unspoken agreement they started down a graveled path flanked by herbaceous borders, toward the folly that overlooked the river. As they walked, she inhaled the sweet scent of stocks and half-opened roses, and memories rose up, bittersweet, of their courting days, when John would have her and her brother to dine here at Enderby, how he would try to hold her hand if Anthony wasn't looking. She was in residence here most of the year, but she hadn't walked this path since those days. Without John it hadn't been the same.

"Remember when you used to have dinner parties here?" she asked. "Before we were married?

We always took this walk afterward."

He reached for her hand, holding it fast when she tried to pull away. He laced their fingers together. "I remember, Viola."

They walked up the steps of the folly, a round, open structure of limestone columns, capped by a copper dome long ago turned to verdigris. They climbed over the three-foot stone wall at the back of the folly and sat down on it like they used to do. Hand in hand, they stared out over Kew Gardens on the opposite side of the Thames and watched as the boats pulled into docks along the river, their work done for the day.

Neither of them spoke as twilight settled in. He did not seem inclined to talk. She didn't know why he found it so hard to reveal himself. She didn't understand what held him back.

But in her bed that night, in the hot sweet dark, there was nothing held back. There was nothing baffling about the way he touched her and kissed her. The way he made love to her. Viola savored it with all the hunger of the eight years she had been without him, but as much as he could pleasure her, it wasn't enough.

There were things that stood between them now as much as they ever had. Without love, what did she have to hold him? She was afraid that whatever she had, whatever she did, would never be enough to make him tell her why he didn't like trifle and why his boyhood was a nightmare. She was afraid that she would never find the key to his heart. Most of all, she was afraid he would never save all his smiles, all his kisses, all his caresses, and all his poetry for her and her alone.

Viola loved making love in the morning, but when John woke up, any notion he had of pleasing his wife in that respect was banished almost at once. He managed to get one, only one, kiss before the first interruption.

A scratch on the door was the only warning before the door opened and Tate came marching in with a bundle of letters in her hand. "The morning post, my lady," she said, and looked up. When she saw the mistress of the house sitting on top of her husband, naked, with the sheets only partly covering them, she flushed a deep scarlet. "Oh!" she gasped, and promptly dropped the letters on the floor. "I'm so terribly sorry!"

She fumbled for the doorknob and backed out of the room, closing the door behind her.

"Did you see her face?" Viola whispered. "Good heavens. What a shock we've given her. I'm sure she thinks we're most improper to be making love in daylight. And me without my nightgown on."

John rolled on top of her, feeling the cool air of the room on his back and the warmth of her body beneath him. "Forget about Tate. Where were we?"

"Hmm, let me think." Her eyes half closed, she tilted her head back. "I think you were kissing me."

"Ah, that was it." He bent his head and tasted her mouth. "I wish I had some blackberry jam."

As if in answer to this request, another scratch was heard on the door and a maid came in, rattling dishes. "Early tea, my lady. Oh!"

"Lord, have mercy," John muttered, and the maid hastily deposited the tray on a table, then vanished, pulling the door shut.

He heard some voices murmuring in the corridor and a few shocked giggles, no doubt commenting on the fact that no man ever slept all night in his wife's room. John waited until the sounds died away just to be sure another maid wasn't about to come in with coal for the grate, then resumed his pleasurable explorations of his wife's luscious body.

"Don't you want any tea?" she asked, pushing him back to give him a smile that was downright wicked.

"Unless it's something I can kiss off of you, forget it," he said, and slid his leg between both of hers.

The door from the corridor into his bedchamber opened. "My lord?" Stephens called as if looking for him. "Mr. Stone is downstairs, waiting to see you."

"Stephens," he shouted through the open doorway to his room, "get out of here!"

"Yes, my lord."

John heard the door close, but his valet proved to be one interruption too many. The moment was lost.

"Remind me to have a little talk with our staff about the morning routine," John muttered, and rolled onto his back, giving it up.

Viola laughed and got out of bed. Swinging her loose hair back over her shoulders, she picked up her nightdress and robe and put them on. "Maybe you are just too greedy," she said as she tied the sash of her robe.

"Greedy, am I?" He jumped up and came after her. She gave a shriek of laughter and dodged out of reach, but he caught her around the waist and hauled her back. "You are the one who almost starved me last night, you couldn't get enough of me."

"What? Oh, how outrageous!" She pushed at him.

He kissed her neck. "Admit it."

"I shan't! You are too conceited as it is." She pulled out of his hold and tugged the bell pull for her maid. "Besides, your secretary is waiting for you, and I have to go back to town today, so we'd best stop lazing our day away and get on with things."

"Why do we have to go to London?"

"I have a ball to attend. My charity ball for the hospitals."

He groaned. "Do we have to go? I hate these Fancy Dress affairs."

"My charities are very important to me. Besides, I missed it last year. I cannot miss it twice. And I don't know why you're complaining anyway," she added. "You can't go."

"Why not?"

She grinned, sure she had the upper hand for once. "I never sent you an invitation."

"Doesn't matter," he said, and grinned right back at her. "I finagled one from Lady Deane ages ago." He kissed her and started for his own room. "No wonder you're so bad at chess," he said, shaking his head.

He closed the door, and from the other side he heard her say, "I can't believe I married such an impossible man!"

His secretary was waiting for him in the study.

"Glad to see you've recovered from the measles, Stone," he said, and circled the desk. A long time, he thought, since he had used this desk. It felt good to stand behind it.

"Thank you, my lord." The secretary opened his dispatch case. "You have quite a bit of correspondence to answer."

"I'm sure I do with you lazing away in Clapham

for the past week and a half at my expense."

Stone had worked for him long enough to recognize that he was teasing, but the poor fellow, alas, had no sense of humor. He did not change expression. "My apologies, my lord."

John sighed and gave it up. "Anything important?"

Instead of replying, Stone turned the opened case around so John could see the contents. It was full. Completely full of small, folded, sealed sheets of pink paper. Emma.

John stared at the letters and all his amusement faded. A mild irritation took its place. "Good God," he muttered, "How many are there?"

"Fifty-nine, sir. All addressed from Calais."

"All in the past ten days?" He picked up a handful, wondering what manner of woman did something like this. He strove to think back to the woman who had been his mistress through the autumn and winter, and he could remember only vague things, unimportant things. Red hair. Green eyes. A sweet sort of charm easily enjoyed and quickly forgotten. "What does she hope to gain by such a barrage of correspondence? More money?"

Stone did not answer, since he knew the question was rhetorical. He simply waited for instructions.

"Stone, I want you to—"

The opening of the door interrupted him.

"John, when do you want to leave for town?" Viola stopped in the doorway, her gaze fixed on the bundle of pink letters in his hand. Her face went pale and her eyes went wide, and John could read her thoughts at that moment as if they were written above her head.

"Viola—" he began.

"I'm sorry," she said. "I did not mean to interrupt you. Forgive me." She pressed a hand to her mouth, turned around and walked away.

"Viola!" he called after her.

She stopped, then continued on without a backward glance until she turned and disappeared from view.

John dropped the handful of letters back into the case. "Burn these damn things," he said, loud enough for Viola to hear him as she walked away. "Better yet, send them all back to Mrs. Rawlins with a letter telling her I'm not paying her a farthing more and never to contact me again. Understood?"

Without waiting for an answer, he went after Viola. He found her on the terrace, staring out at the river that curved and glittered in the distance. She must have heard the tap of his boot heels on the flagstones, but she did not turn around and look at him as he approached her.

"Those are love letters, aren't they?" she said, then made a chiding sound. "What am I saying?

Of course they are. Pink paper, and I could smell the perfume on them from the doorway."

"The woman writes to me," he told her. "I do not write to her."

"I see." She nodded, but continued to stare out at the river without turning around.

The very fact that she was so calm impelled him to speak. "I am not with Emma. I ended it months ago."

"You don't have to explain."

"Damned right I don't. There's nothing to explain. It is over."

She wrapped her arms around herself and turned her head slightly in his direction. "From the amount of correspondence she sends you, it seems Mrs. Rawlins does not realize that fact."

"She should. I made it clear. I paid off her contract. I set her aside months before Percy died. You are the only woman I have been with since then."

She turned and looked at him. "I believe you," she said, but there was a cool, polished hardness in her face that hurt him.

Don't, he thought. *Don't do this.*

"Is Emma Rawlins in love with you?"

"Love?" His voice was harsh, contemptuous of such a notion. She winced, and he gentled his voice at once. "She was a mistress, Viola. She was paid. Love has nothing to do with such arrangements. Don't you see that?"

"I think it is Mrs. Rawlins who does not see that," Viola said, and turned again to look out at the view. John stared at his wife's rigid back for a long moment, but he did not know what she wanted him to say. He did not know what she wanted him to do. With an oath, he turned and walked away.

Chapter 17

Once again the charity ball for London hospitals proved to be a raging success. Thousands of pounds were raised, for over the past few years the ball had become one of the most popular events of the season, and anyone who attended had to pay the exorbitant subscription fee.

Viola was gratified by the success, for London hospitals were among her favorite charities, but the event itself proved to be a difficult, exhausting business. John attended with her, something that had never happened before, and speculation about their presence together began to circulate the ballroom within minutes of their arrival.

The general conclusion would probably be that Lord and Lady Hammond had, indeed, reconciled. This morning they might have been right about that, but this evening, Viola was not so sure.

The carriage ride from Chiswick had been silent. John had made no attempts at conversation, and neither had she. The letters from Emma Rawlins were probably on their way back to France by now, but they stood between John and herself as if they had been piled up on the carriage floor. John did not understand why, she knew. He didn't understand that even a mistress who was paid could fall desperately in love.

At the ball, they danced one quadrille together, then separated to mingle with other guests. After a few hours of circulating through the crowd with a smile pasted on her face as she encountered some of the women from Lady Deane's guest list, Viola's head began to ache and she sought out a quiet corner of the ballroom.

She leaned back against the wall, sipping her glass of punch as her gaze roamed over the crowd. She remembered that day over a month ago when she had been going over her guest list for the ball with Tate and how John had warned her about the spitefulness of Lady Deane. Not presenting her guest list to the baroness in person had been a social snub that Viola knew she was paying for now, because among the knights and nobles, the princesses and jesters, the bewigged judges and Greek muses, were all of John's former mistresses, except Emma Rawlins. Lady Deane had been very busy. And very spiteful, indeed.

Viola sought out their faces. Anne Pomeroy, so polished and elegant. Peggy Darwin, laughing and pretty. Jane Morrow, blond and hazel-eyed like herself, a demirep on the fringes of society, still a good enough courtesan to afford the subscription fee for this ball. Dark-haired and doe-eyed Maria Allen. Her reconciliation with her husband had not succeeded, and she was Lord Dewhurst's mistress now. Maybe she thought her husband fighting in a duel was romantic. Elizabeth Blunt, another beautiful and promiscuous countess with whom Viola had been forced to drink tea and play cards over the years. Even Elsie Gallant was here, and the years had not been kind to her, for the vivacious, lovely face that had made her a popular demirep now marked what she was—an aging courtesan.

Viola studied them one by one and was surprised to find that she felt no rage of jealousy. She felt strangely distant, oddly detached, with a hint of pity for these women.

He hadn't loved any of them, but how had they felt? She remembered the brief hint of tenderness in Peggy Darwin's face that day in the draper's shop when she had looked at John, confirming what she had known for years, what John refused to see. The countess had been in love with him once. Wasn't now, perhaps, but she had been. Viola thought of the pile of pink letters in Mr. Stone's dispatch case. Poor Emma Rawlins.

And what of herself? She was his wife. Yet, if she'd had no dowry, if she hadn't been born a lady, if she hadn't married him, she would still have fallen in love with John Hammond, for he made falling in love with him so easy. Without even realizing it. It was in his smile and his charm and his ability to make a woman laugh. It was because he remembered what food a woman liked and what activities she enjoyed and how she liked to be touched. But his heart was never engaged. How could she ever hold his heart if he never gave it away?

Viola pressed a hand to her forehead. Her head ached. Her heart ached. Her monthly was coming, she could feel it, but she knew that wasn't why she felt tired, lonely, and so terribly depressed. She could not stop thinking about how desperate and hurting a woman had to be to send a man stacks of letters when he hadn't ever cared tuppence for her. She understood Emma Rawlins's desperate love for a man who did not love her back. How odd to feel empathy for your husband's former mistress, she thought.

She and John left the ball early and went back to Chiswick that night. She slept by herself, using her impending courses as an excuse. He seemed to accept it, and she was glad because she did not want him to see her when she laid down in bed and wept. She did it silently into the pillow so he would not hear.

She was pulling away. He could feel it. John laid in bed, staring at the ceiling in the dark, and tried to tell himself it was her courses—he knew such things had an affect on a woman's disposition. He'd learned long ago that steering clear was the best move a man could make in such circumstances.

He tried to tell himself her monthly illness was the reason she'd been so strange about Emma's letters, but he knew that wasn't it. She was pulling away from him.

The ball tonight hadn't helped matters. Damn Lady Deane's malicious nature. But even as he damned her, he knew his own culpability there.

John rubbed his hands over his face and asked himself the same question he'd asked himself countless times over the years. What did Viola want from him? What could he do or say that would make things right? There had to be a way.

The years ran across his mind like the pages of a storybook, but the things that he kept coming back to were those early days, especially Hammond Park. He thought of riding on the downs and making Viola laugh. She'd been happy at Hammond Park. He knew that much.

With sudden clarity, he knew what he had to do. He had to take her home—to their home, where she belonged. Sleeping in that big mahogany bed with him, getting trounced by him at chess in their library there, riding that spirited mare he'd bought her. He imagined her racing ahead of him, tossing off her hat and laughing, and that was when he was finally able to fall asleep.

Viola made no objection to leaving London, but during the trip to Northumberland, she said little. Though he got an occasional smile or laugh out of her, she was restrained and distant. He knew she probably had some discomfort from her courses, and the six-day journey could not have helped ease that. But he remembered full well how long her monthly lasted, yet by the time they reached Hammond Park on the seventh day, her restrained manner still enveloped her like a shield to keep him away.

Nonetheless, John had no intention of allowing any closed bedroom doors this time around. That night, when he went to the master bedchamber, he had every intention of making it clear that they would be sharing one bed.

She was there when he came in, sitting at the dressing table in her nightgown, brushing her hair. She stopped a moment as he entered the room, then resumed her task.

He went into the dressing room and saw the cot had been made up, but he had no intention of using it. Not tonight, not any night, not ever again. He stripped off his clothes, walked out of the dressing room, and moved to stand behind her chair.

She stopped, the brush poised against her long

hair. She looked at his reflection in the mirror, her face framed against the backdrop of his naked chest.

He leaned down and slid his arms around her. He kissed her neck. She set down the brush, wrapped her hands around his wrists and pushed his arms away.

He straightened, and knew he had to know what he was dealing with. "Are we going to have a fight tonight?" he asked quietly.

"Why do you ask? Because I am not in a mood to make love with you?"

These were the moments when women were truly baffling. "Well, something is wrong, and I do not know what it is."

"It's just—" She broke off and turned around, looking up at him in the lamplight with an odd sadness in her face that twisted something in his guts.

"Are you still angry about Emma's letters?" he asked.

"I'm not angry, John. I was never angry."

"What is this strange mood, then? Are you still—" He broke off, making a vague motion toward her abdomen, hoping it was as simple and temporary as that, knowing full well it wasn't.

Her cheeks got pink. "No."

He made another guess. "Are you upset that we left London before the season was over?"

"Heavens, no."

John gave up. "Then what is it?"

She lifted a hand helplessly. "I feel so sorry for that woman."

"What woman? Emma?" He was too amazed not to ask the next question. "Why?"

"Oh, John, really!" Exasperation came into her face and she turned her back to him. "She has feelings for you," she said over her shoulder. "Desperate feelings. She must, or she would not be sending you stacks of letters and humiliating herself in that way."

He'd asked a stupid question, he should have known he wouldn't like the answer. He put his hands on her shoulders and pressed his forehead to the top of her head with a sigh. "What would you suggest I do about that?"

"I don't know." she admitted. She shrugged as if she wanted him to remove his hands.

He didn't. He straightened and met her eyes in the mirror. "I may be dense, Viola, but I still do not understand the problem."

"I know how she feels, John," she whispered. "There. Now you know the problem."

His hands tightened on her shoulders. "It isn't the same thing."

"It is exactly the same. Do men really think that mistresses do not have feelings? That they do not fall in love? Yes," she said when he made an exclamation of impatience, "love. I tried to tell you this before, after we saw Peggy Darwin in the draper's shop. She was in love with you once, too. I always knew that. Why do you think it hurt so much to see her looking at you?"

"I was never in love with Peggy Darwin."

"I am not talking about your feelings. I am talking about hers. And Emma Rawlins's. And mine. Oh, John, do you not see? Women fall in love with you. It's in the way you smile and the things you say. It's in everything you do."

That was absurd. He looked away. "I cannot believe that women would think that a few smiles are worth falling in love with."

"You are an unbelievably handsome man, and you have so much magnetism, so much charm. You flirt with women, you remember things, you pay attention. Women are putty in your hands." She paused, then said softly, "I was."

"Viola, you have never been putty in my hands," he assured her. "If that were true," he said, trying to make light of it, "I'd have half a dozen sons by now."

She slid off the seat, stepped away from him and climbed into bed. "I want to go to sleep."

He looked back over his shoulder at the cot that had been made up for him in the dressing room. He leaned against the carved footboard of the bed, gripping its edge in his hands, and looked at her again.

"Tell me one thing," he said, and took a deep breath, feeling as if he were about to jump over a cliff. The carving on the footboard was pressing so hard into his hands that it hurt. "Do you want me to sleep in the dressing room?"

She looked away. "I—" She broke off and bit her lip.

"Yes or no."

"I don't want to make love, John. I'm not saying that because I'm angry at you," she added. "Truly. It's just that I am not . . . I am not inclined to it tonight."

Just holding and touching her for those few brief moments a short time ago had been enough to arouse him. It was going to be torture to just lie in bed with her and hold her, but if that was how it had to be, he'd endure it. However many nights he had to, with every intention of persuading her differently every chance he got.

He looked into her eyes and did something he swore he would never do with Viola again. He lied. "If you don't want to make love, then I don't, either."

She lowered her gaze, and looked so damn lovely in that huge bed, his bed, with her pristine white nightgown and her angelic hair. If he could only hear her lusty laugh, he'd think he had died and gone—unbelievable as it might be—to heaven.

"Where am I sleeping, Viola?"

She looked at him, and it seemed an eternity before she pulled back the bedclothes. Relief flooded through him, relief so great it took all he had not to show it. He slid into the bed beside her, and when she turned away, he wrapped his arms around her, held her fast, buried his face against her hair.

"John," she reproved, but she did not shove his arms away this time. He went still and laid there in the dark, holding her body pressed to his. He was deliberately torturing himself, he knew, but he did it anyway.

He'd brought Viola to Hammond Park thinking that would solve everything. He deserved this agony for such a cocky assumption. When it came to his wife, nothing was ever as easy as that.

He was gone when she woke up. Viola sat up in bed, pushing her hair out of her eyes. Sunlight peeped between the drapery panels at the windows, and she looked around her.

So strange to be here again. Strange, and yet familiar. She leaned back against the headboard, smiling a little at the maroon-red walls. John had reminded her not long ago how they had argued about that so long ago. She had forgotten, but he had remembered.

There was a scratch on the door, and a maid came in with a tray. "Morning, my lady," the girl said, smiling shyly. "I'm Hill. Second housemaid. Mrs. Miller had me bring your breakfast up. She said you always like to have your breakfast in bed."

"Miller is still here?"

"Oh, yes. Will be until she's too old to stir the puddings, she says."

Viola laughed. "I remember Miller's Christmas pudding. She prepared it in September and she made everyone in the house come to the kitchens and give it a stir before she put it away in the buttery."

"She still does that, my lady. Every year. Even the master has to come stir the Christmas pudding. He never minds, though."

"Where is my husband this morning?"

"He's with Mr. Whitmore, the steward."

"I see." Viola felt a hint of disappointment as the maid placed the tray across her lap, but she knew he had an estate to run, and she understood from having managed things at Enderby that it was a great deal of work, especially since he had been away for the season. She knew she couldn't expect John to have breakfast up here with her every morning. Even back in the early days he hadn't always been able to do that.

"Mind if I draw the curtains, my lady?"

"No, I don't mind."

Bright sunlight flooded the room as Hill pulled back the draperies. Viola set the tray aside and got up, then walked to the windows. "What a lovely day."

"Yes. Not raining for a change. The master said to tell you that if you decide to go walking before he gets back, you can't go near the stables. He wants to show those to you himself."

Viola smiled, her disappointment about breakfast vanishing in an instant. He wanted to show her the horses. "Thank you, Hill. Send my maid in, would you? And tell Miss Tate that I'll want to see her in an hour down in the drawing room."

"I will." The girl smiled back at her, gave a curtsy and started for the door. "It's good to have you here, my lady. Everyone's glad you've come home."

"I'm glad, too," she said, and meant it.

It was a mare, the prettiest chestnut mare she'd seen in a long time. "John!" she cried, laughing with delight as the groom brought the horse to her. "Where did you get her? Tattersall's?"

"About a month ago. Like her?"

"Like her?" She rubbed the mare's nose with her palm. "She's a beauty!" She turned and flung her arms around her husband's neck and kissed him. "Thank you!" she cried, and returned her attention to the mare. "Come on, let's take her out!"

She grasped the reins, John lifted her up, and she swung onto the sidesaddle. When he had mounted his gelding, they set out together. He took her around the estate and the farms, showing her some of the improvements he had made to the estate over the years, and there were many. After that they headed for the downs, their favorite place—the rolling hills of open pastureland that stretched for miles on Hammond property.

She did what he remembered. As they galloped across the downs, she tugged at her riding hat, pulled it off and tossed it into the air, shaking back her loose hair and letting it fly behind her.

Beside her, John began to laugh. "I love that," he called to her.

She smiled back at him. "I know."

They stopped at one of the cliffs at the edge of the downs to rest the horses, and sat on the turf, looking out over the tenant farms that stretched out below them.

"It looks much improved, John. I remember that it was a bit shabby when I came here the first time."

"It was in far better condition by the time I brought you here than it was before we got married. Before we were wed, it was a horror."

Viola frowned, thinking it out. "Was that why we stayed in Scotland for so long?"

"Yes. I used your dowry to make things halfway decent for your arrival. I also borrowed a huge sum from your brother to pay off other debts and fix the drains here. Only after that was done did I bring you here."

"You've done an excellent job, then. Everything seems very prosperous now."

"It is, and that is because of your money as well as the income from the rents." He looked over at her and reached out to take her hand in his. "I wanted you to see what I've done with your income, Viola."

She lifted their joined hands to her lips, kissing his. "Thank you."

He looked down over the valley below and gave a short laugh. "The odd thing is, before I came into the title, I hated this place. I never came here."

She stared at him, not sure she'd heard him right. "But it's your home. It's what you've spent the last nine years salvaging. You hate it?"

"I don't hate it now. I did when I was a boy. It was the coldest house you can imagine. Especially after . . . " He paused, then shook his head and spoke again. "I saw my mother only half a dozen times a year, whenever she could be bothered to come home from whichever lover she was living with. I barely remember her. My father didn't care. He had plenty of lovers of his own, unless he was too drunk to visit them. Whenever Father was in residence, watching him pass out before the dessert was a common occurrence at our table. When I was a boy, the only thing bearable about this place was leaving it. I always went to Percy's home during the summer holidays."

Viola didn't speak. It was rare for John to speak of things like this, and she didn't want to spoil the moment by interrupting. She just held his hand and listened.

"Getting sent off to school was the best thing that happened to me," he told her. "Percy and I went to Harrow, and I seldom saw either of my parents after that. When my mother died, I came down from Cambridge for the funeral, stayed two hours, and left again. I had no desire to be here, and until my father died, I did not come back."

He turned his head and looked at her. "You've said you didn't know me, and you wanted to. I've never told you things about me because I didn't want you to know what an irresponsible scapegrace I truly was. Your brother was dead right about me, and I thought—" He coughed, looking a little embarrassed. "I knew you disagreed with him and thought I was quite a wonderful fellow. I didn't want you to ever know how untrue that really was."

He squeezed her hand hard. "When I was at Cambridge, I was so damnably wild. I almost got sent down half a dozen times. I spent every shilling of my quarterly allowance and then some. I got into debt. I gambled, deep stakes. I drank."

He lifted her hand, kissed it, let it go. "And then there were the women," he said. "I had mistresses from the time I was fifteen, and I gave them the most lavish gifts you can imagine. What did I care? I'd be a viscount one day. I spent so much money, and I never gave a thought to where it came from. I didn't know, and I didn't want to know. In other words, I was just like my father, a man I despised."

It pained her that he talked so disparagingly about himself, and yet she knew there was a great deal of truth in it. If she was ever going to understand him, she had to accept that.

"Because I'd been away from here for so long," he went on, "I had no idea what sorry shape Hammond Park had gotten into, and to be honest, it never occurred to me to inquire. After Cambridge, I lived at Enderby. Then I went on a Grand Tour. Wherever I was, my father still sent me my quarterly allowance, and I still spent every shilling of it. Then he died of typhoid and I came back to England."

He reached out, sweeping his arm across the view of the tenant farms in the valley below. "All of that was mine, and what a pathetic legacy it was. Until I got here, I didn't know that if drains don't get repaired, the standing water can cause typhoid outbreaks. My father was not the only one who died. There were dozens of others. As I toured the place, I was shocked by the state of things. Not only the drains, but everything else. My father had bankrupted it. The tenants were in misery, the animals were sick, the fields were unplanted, and the creditors were about to take everything that wasn't entailed."

Anthony had tried to tell her the state of Hammond's finances and what she was getting, but she had refused to listen to her brother's warnings. She listened now. "That must have been quite a shock to you," she said gently.

He pointed down to one of the thatched cottages below. "There was a girl of twelve who lived there. Nan was her name. Her mother had just died, I was told. I was looking over the place, and she stood there in the doorway of that cottage—so ramshackle it was in those days—and she had her baby sister on her hip. She was dirty and thin, and she had on this ragged dress. She asked if I was the new lord, and when I said yes, she gave me this look. She ran her gaze up and down my elegant suit and white linen, then she looked into my eyes, and I saw such contempt in hers that I was shocked. I shall never forget that look in her eyes as long as I live. And what she said. To this day, it haunts me."

"What did she say?"

"She said, 'Acorns don't fall far, do they?' and turned her back on me and went inside. That was like a kick in the stomach, and something changed inside me. I knew I had to do something about all this. It was my responsibility. I was the lord."

"That's when you decided to marry a girl with money."

He looked at her with defiant eyes, unashamed. "Yes. And I was scared enough and desperate enough that I lied to that girl to win her. I lied to her and I manipulated her with every wile I could think of, and I let her fall in love with the man she thought I was. I'd do it again, Viola. I don't regret it." He grabbed her by the shoulders and kissed her mouth, a hard kiss, as defiant as the fire in his eyes. He pushed her down into the soft grass and rolled her backward, down into a dip in the turf where they could not be seen from the valley below. He leaned over her and slid one arm behind her head. "I'll never regret it."

She looked up at her handsome husband, into his proud face. "I don't regret it, either."

"You don't?"

"No, John," she said, and meant it. "I don't know quite when I realized it, but I don't regret marrying you. Maybe I realized it that day in the boat when you made up that poem about me." She smiled and reached up to toy with a lock of his dark brown hair in her fingers. "You always have been a silver-tongued devil."

His lashes lowered a fraction and he smiled back at her. His hand spread over her hip. "Does this mean I get to steal some kisses today?"

She pursed her lips, pretending to think about it. "That depends. Are you going to make up with me first?"

"No."

"No?" she repeated, and let her hand fall. "What do you mean, no?"

"I am not going to make up." Even as he said it, he grasped a handful of her broadcloth riding habit and began pulling the skirt upward. "I did it last time. This time, it's your turn to do the making up."

He was so outrageous sometimes. "We're supposed to take turns now?"

He nodded, sliding her skirt up her leg. With a huff of pretended vexation, she made a half-hearted effort to jerk her skirt back down, but he managed to maneuver his hand beneath the layers of broadcloth and undergarments. "I'm getting tired of being the only one who ever does this making up business," he said, caressing her calf above the top of her boot.

"That's because you're always the one doing something wrong."

"The conceit of the woman!" He slid his palm along her calf, moving in lazy upward circles to her thigh. "Torture me all night by lying there right next to me without even trying to kiss and make up, and you say you've done nothing wrong?"

"One whole night," she murmured, and closed her eyes, breathing in deeply as that aching warmth started through her, the ache of desire he could always bring with his hands. She was giving in. She'd known she would all along. "How you must have been suffering."

"More than you can imagine. And was a deuced good sport about it, too." He moved his hand higher, rubbed his fingers across the top of her thigh right where her birthmark was. "Come on, Viola. Say you're sorry for torturing me so cruelly."

She closed her eyes and shook her head. She began to laugh. "I'm not sorry."

John's hand moved between her thighs, and any thought of laughing went out of her head. She moved beneath him with a soft moan, and his fingers brushed the curls between her legs, just enough to torment her. "Say you want to make up."

She arched upward into his hand, excitement rising as he began to caress her in that exquisite place. "I'm not saying it," she gasped, her hips moving faster with the strokes of his hand.

"Say it," he demanded, caressing her over and over, until her arousal climbed to a fever pitch.

"No, no. I shan't."

"Fine." He pulled his hand away and rolled onto his back away from her.

"Oh, you are such a tease!" she cried, laughing. She sat up and leaned over him. "You are the one who should be sorry for tormenting me in this wicked way." She paused, and ran her hand over his chest and down his flat abdomen. "I shall exact my revenge."

She laid her hand over his groin, felt his erection. He drew in a sharp breath as she began to unbutton his trousers, and he groaned when she took him in her hand.

She made it last. He'd taught her how a long

time ago, and she remembered. She wrapped her hand around him and stroked him until his hips began to thrust upward, then she relaxed her grip, rubbing her finger lightly along the underside of his penis, up and down, just the way she knew tormented him. She brought her mouth close enough that he would feel her breath on his shaft, then she kissed the tip. His hand touched her hair, wanting to keep her there for more of that pleasure, but she sat up, too quick for him.

"All right," he said, his breath coming hard and fast, "You win. You win. I'll say it first. Let's make up."

She straddled him, opened over him, took him inside her. She felt him thrust upward, deep into her, again and again. She watched his face in the sunlight as he came, and she felt the joy of it as if it were her pleasure when he cried out her name.

Afterward, she leaned down and kissed him. "Tricked you. Made you say it first."

"So you did." He opened his eyes and smiled that heart-stopping smile. He pushed her hair back to caress her face. "I hope to hell you're planning to trick me again tonight."

Chapter 18

$\sim\!\!\sim\!\!\circ\!\!\rangle\!\!\circ\!\!\sim\!\!\sim$

John lost no time in making it clear to the staff at Hammond Park that when the breakfast tray was brought, a simple scratch on the door to announce the fact would be enough, and to place the tray in the corridor. Until the breakfast tray was back outside the door and empty, there were to be no servants coming into the master's room unless the house was on fire. As the days of June went by, he and Viola had breakfast in bed together nearly every morning.

He trounced her at chess every time they played, but let her win at piquet to make up for it. He got his wish and taught her to swim. Naked, by moonlight.

They gave a fete and all the country families came. They had dinner parties for the local gentry. They raced on the downs and he got to see her hair fly back behind her every time. He spent a lot of money on new riding hats for her. He didn't care.

June gave way to July. Slowly, the emptiness inside John—the emptiness he had never known existed until that night in the rain in Grosvenor Square—began to give way to the contentment he so badly wanted, that he had missed for so long. The cold war of the years gone by seemed far away, and he began to forget that there had ever been a time when Viola wasn't sleeping beside him.

They fought often. Usually because she would insist on talking about things, and he avoided it as often as possible. They always made up, and he liked that part. A lot. No matter how many times they fought, there was no sleeping on a cot in the dressing room.

He loved to tease her because she always fell for it. When she asked him if they could have Dylan, Grace, Anthony, and Daphne come for a house party, he played it for all it was worth.

"No."

She looked at him over the breakfast tray, wide-eyed and pretty with her hair loose, surrounded by snowy white sheets and pillows. "Why not?"

"Your brother hates me."

"He doesn't hate you."

John munched on a slice of bacon. "He would happily cut off my head if he could get away with it."

"Dylan will be here to keep things civil."

"Hah! Dylan never keeps things civil. He just sits back and enjoys the fray and laughs."

"Grace, then. And Daphne." She pushed the

tray aside and moved closer to him. "Daphne likes you. She's been on your side for ages. Even when I still thought you were a scoundrel, she defended you."

"She did?" That surprised him, but then he remembered his sister-in-law's face that day when Viola had run off to Enderby.

I know how desperation feels, Hammond.

"I have a great deal of respect for Tremore's wife," he said, "but it does not alter the fact that your brother loathes me."

Viola snuggled up to him, kissed his ear. "Maybe it's time the two of you made up."

He turned his head, let her kiss him. Then he leaned back in bed, looking at her through half-closed eyes. "If I agree to this," he drawled, "do I get some kind of reward?"

Her hand fluttered to his bare chest and she pressed her lips together, knowing full well she'd already won and trying not to smile about it, playing the game. "What do you want?"

He told her, and she blushed from head to toe. But ten days later the Duke of Tremore and Mr. Dylan Moore and their wives received invitations to spend the last two weeks of August at Hammond Park.

The warm, lazy days of August drifted by. Every day, John found some way to make her laugh. He made up the most absurd limericks for her, and sometimes he read her poetry he'd written. She began to sense his moods and the nature of them, though it was like prying open live oysters to get him to tell her anything of a personal nature. He usually deflected it with a witty comment or a careless change of subject. She learned not to ask such questions, coming to understand he would tell her things when he was ready to do so, and not before. On those rare occasions when he chose to reveal himself in some sort of personal way, it always took her by surprise. One evening when they were in the library and she was going over menu plans for the impending house party, John finally told her about the trifle.

She was reading through the suggestions of Mrs. Miller, shaking her head. "No, no," she murmured to herself. "This won't do at all." Viola picked up a quill, dipped it in the inkwell, and crossed out one of the cook's suggestions.

"What won't do?" John asked over the top of his newspaper.

"Pâté. Anthony hates pâté. Always has. The very idea of liver makes him green. I won't subject him to it."

John laughed. "I'd love to see Tremore turn green."

"Stop it, John." She shot him a warning look. "This party is partly so that the two of you can reconcile, remember? I should so like it if the two of you became friends."

"I know, I know." He gave the sigh of a suffering husband. "No liver, then. What other delights am I going to be deprived of during your brother's visit?"

"There won't be any trifle, if you were worried about that," she said gently.

"Better not be, or I shall give Miller the sack. She knows better."

Viola wanted to ask about it but knew he would not tell her. She resumed going over the menu. She crossed off mutton, which she despised, and replaced it with beef fillets. She added a selection of chocolates to be ordered because Daphne liked chocolates. She was contemplating the wine selections when John spoke.

"It was because my sister died." His voice was so low, she barely heard his words.

"Your sister?" She looked over at him, surprised by a comment that seemed to come out of nowhere. Her husband wasn't looking at her. Instead, he was staring down at his newspaper.

"The trifle," he said. "It was because of my sister, Kate. I was seven, and I was in the nursery upstairs, eating my dinner when I found out. My nanny was the one who told me. My mother could not be bothered to leave her lover in Paris, and my father was at his mistress's home in Yorkshire. It's odd, you know," he added, his voice so terribly soft that the sound of it hurt her heart.

She walked over to his chair, knelt beside it, put her hand on his knee. "What is odd?"

"How things come back to you and tear you up even if they happened years ago. I don't remember anything else about that day, but I remember what dessert I had. I was sitting there staring at that damned bowl, and the only thing I was thinking when my nanny was breaking the news to me was that trifle was Kate's favorite thing in the world, and she wasn't going to get to eat it anymore."

One hand balled into a fist, crumpling the newspaper. "Even now, I miss my sister," he said through clenched teeth, as if the words were being torn out of him. He let go of the paper and rubbed the heels of his hands over his eyes, a savage, furtive movement with his face turned away from her.

"Kate made everything bearable, you see. It's been twenty-eight years since then, and I know it sounds stupid, but every time I see trifle, the red jam and the yellow custard and the white cream, I am seven years old again, and my parents are hundreds of miles away, and my sister is dead, and I have that awful, sick feeling in my guts." He did not look at her. Instead, he straightened in his chair, smoothed out the newspaper and pretended to resume reading it as if nothing had happened.

She looked at his stiff, proud profile, and she

thought of why she had fallen in love with him when she was seventeen. For his smile and his wit, for his way of making her laugh. But she wasn't seventeen anymore, and when she looked at him now, she saw none of those things that had mattered to her so long ago. And at that moment, because they were not there, Viola fell in love with John Hammond all over again.

She knew there were no words she could say that would be of any use, so she said none. Instead, she reached over and pulled the newspaper gently away from him. "Come with me," she said, and took one of his hands in hers.

"Where are we going?"

"Just let me be in charge of things for a change, will you?" She pulled him to his feet and led him upstairs. She lit the lamp in their room and began to undress him. She removed his evening coat and his cravat and tossed them aside. She unbuttoned his waistcoat, his braces and his shirt, and pulled them off one by one. He stood there silent as she undressed him. There was no smile on his lips. His handsome face was grave as he watched her hands roam over his body. He was rigidly still, his muscles hard and tense beneath the light caress of her fingers.

She ran her hands over his naked torso—his wide shoulders and chest, along his abdomen. She sank to her knees and unbuttoned his trousers. He was flagrantly aroused as she took him in her hand.

She kissed the head of his penis, and he breathed in deeply, sinking his hand into the knot of her hair. Head thrown back, he groaned as she parted her lips and took him in her mouth. She stroked him in her palm and sucked him with her mouth. With her free hand, she gently cupped his testes.

He made a rough sound and stopped her. He caught her hands and shoved them away. Gripping her shoulders, he pulled her to her feet. He kissed her hard and his hands began tugging at her skirts, pulling them up, quick and desperate, out of control.

Tossing up yards of silk and muslin, he wadded her skirts between them, then he gripped her buttocks in his hands and lifted her. "Wrap your legs around me," he ordered, and when she did, he impaled her against him as he pressed her back against the wall.

"Oh God, oh God," he groaned, and thrust into her hard—once, twice. Then he came, tremors running through his body as he climaxed.

He held her there, pressed to the wall, gulping in air. Then, slowly, he lowered her to her feet. He caught her in a frantic hold, tight against him, kissing her hair. "Viola," he whispered. "My wife. My wife."

Chapter 19

Despite John's doubts about having her brother come for a visit, Viola was looking forward to it. She knew Anthony would be polite, if only for her sake and the sake of good manners, and once he saw how contented she was, he would begin to forgive and forget. Daphne, of course, would be able to encourage that happy outcome. And Dylan and Grace would also be of great assistance in bringing about a truce, for they were friends to both sides. By the end of the fortnight visit, Anthony and John would each be regarding the other man as a brother. At least, that was how Viola hoped things would go.

Despite her hopes, things did not start out well. The first few days were awkward beyond belief. She knew that both her husband and her brother were trying to be civil, but John's attempts at light-hearted humor did not amuse Anthony, and her brother's resentment of John's past behavior was palpable. That made for long silences at dinner, broken only by the occasional comment from Dylan and the skillful use of small talk by Daphne, Grace, and herself. The trickiest part of the evening, however, was always when the men remained in the dining room for port and brandy after dinner while the ladies retired to the drawing room. Custom usually dictated this practice to last about half an hour. However, less than half that amount of time was usually all that elapsed before the men were joining them. Until the fifth night of the visit. That night, everything changed.

Fifteen minutes went by, then half an hour, then an hour, then more. "What do you suppose they are doing down there?" Viola asked the other two women, trying not to be nervous. "Are they getting along or killing each other?"

Suddenly, male laughter erupted from downstairs, and Viola grasped Daphne's arm. "Listen," she ordered as another round of hearty male amusement was heard.

"They are laughing," Viola said, stunned. She glanced from Daphne to Grace and back again. "Anthony and John are together, and they are laughing."

"Probably because they are drunk," Grace said serenely, taking a sip of her madeira. There was a hint of amusement in her green eyes as she looked at Viola. "Dylan said this stupid feud between his two best friends had gone on long enough. He said he was going to get them both drunk tonight and put an end to it once and for all."

"Getting them drunk?" Daphne repeated. "That's his solution? What if they kill each other instead?"

"I asked him the same question." Grace smiled, tucked back a loose strand of her blond hair, and took another sip of her wine. "Dylan said that wouldn't happen. John is especially witty when he's drunk, and Anthony is always much more amiable because he forgets to be ducal and haughty."

Another round of male laughter echoed up from the dining room, and Viola rose to her feet. "I cannot stand it," she said. "My curiosity is eating away at me. I have to find out what they are laughing about down there. Come on."

The other two women willingly accompanied her out of the drawing room and down the stairs. They huddled together outside the dining room and listened. It only took a moment to discover what all the laughing was about. The three men were composing limericks. Naughty ones.

"There once was a bawd from Cheshire," Dylan began as Viola peeked around the edge of the door to have a look at them.

"There once was a bawd from Cheshire," Dylan said again, then stopped. "What rhymes with Cheshire?" he asked as he poured himself a brandy from the half-empty bottle in front of him.

"Stupid question, Moore," John said at once, and took a sip of his port. "Pleasure, of course. What else?"

"Measure," Anthony suggested, and uttered a cry of triumph. "I've got it," he said, and leaned forward in his chair, lifting his glass of port. "There once was a bawd from Cheshire, with talents well beyond measure. A face like a lime, pickled with time, but God, could she give a man pleasure."

The other two men burst out laughing, and Viola shook her head in amazement. Her brother was composing naughty limericks with John and Dylan.

"Deuce take it, Tremore," John said, "you've a talent for this. We must do another one. There once was a girl from Norfolk . . ."

Viola pulled back from the doorway and whispered, "And to think men are the ones who rule the world."

"Frightening, isn't it?" Grace whispered back.

The three women nodded agreement on that point and tiptoed back up the stairs. Once they were back in the drawing room, Daphne fell into a chair, laughing merrily, and said, "Viola, I think we can be sure of two things. First, that my husband and yours are going to get along much better in future. And second, when they wake up tomorrow, all three of them will be very cranky."

Viola smiled, thinking that a very small price to pay for domestic peace.

Though Daphne's prediction about how the men would feel the following morning came true, the outcome of that evening was a successful one. By the time her guests had been at Hammond Park a little over a week, John and Anthony were discussing business ventures together, fishing for trout, and agreeing on some issues of politics. Dylan, Viola noticed, often took an outrageously opposing view, and she realized it was deliberate, for it always forced Anthony and John to stand together against him on a topic. Dylan had always been a devilishly clever fellow.

On the eighth day of the visit, they took tea at the home of Lord and Lady Steyne, and this further cemented good relations, for Earl Steyne was good friends with John and was well-respected by Anthony.

The following morning, all six of them went riding before breakfast, and Anthony was so impressed with his sister's beautiful mare, he insisted that if they bred her, he wanted a foal. Yes, Viola thought watching her brother and her husband discussing horses as they walked back to the house, the visit was going famously.

"Hammond, your gardens are lovely," Daphne commented as the six of them mounted the wide front steps and crossed the portico toward the front doors of the house. "I now have many new ideas for our gardens at Tremore Hall," she told her husband.

"My wife has become quite passionate about English gardens," Anthony told the men. "And why? She likes to walk in them in the rain. She says an English garden in the rain smells like heaven."

Before anyone could comment about that, the sound of carriage wheels crunching on the gravel was heard, and all of them paused on the portico, turning as an unmarked carriage pulled into the drive and came to a stop.

The footman jumped off the dummy board. He opened the door, unfolded the steps, and a slender woman in green descended from the vehicle. She lifted her head and saw them.

It was Emma Rawlins.

Viola could scarcely believe it. The woman glanced at her, and though her eyes widened in surprise, she turned her attention to John at once.

"My lord," she said, halting at the bottom of the steps, "you and I have business to discuss."

Business? It was brass indeed for a former mistress to come to a man's home. And to speak thus, in front of his wife and his guests was unthinkable, but Emma did not seem to care about the propriety of it.

"We've no business, madam," John said evenly, his face expressionless. "I thought I had made that clear."

"Clear?" Her voice rose shrilly. "How could you make anything clear when you have not written to me? Nor have you answered my letters."

"I answered the first three. After that I saw no point."

"You did not even read them. You sent them back." She reached into the pockets of her skirt and pulled out handfuls of paper—folded pink sheets just like those Viola had seen that day at Enderby. She threw them in his face. "You are the cruelest man I have ever known!"

"Control yourself, Mrs. Rawlins," he said in a low voice as letters fluttered all around him to the ground. "We are not alone."

"Control myself?" she cried. "Why should I?" She cast a glance in Viola's direction. "Because your wife is here? Because you have guests? Because it might humiliate you?" Her face twisted with terrible pain and she began to weep. "It is I who have been humiliated, my lord. Not you!"

As if her strength had suddenly given way, she fell into a heap at his feet. "I loved you," she said, sagging against the stone steps. "God, how I loved you. I gave you everything, John. Everything. How could you do this to me?"

Viola stared at the woman in horror, watching Emma's shoulders shake with the force of her crying, watching her fingers curling in spasms against the cool gray flagstones near his boots.

She glanced around, but all the people on the portico, including the servants who had come out of the house at the sound of the carriage, were watching the woman as if paralyzed, staring at Emma as if they were witnessing some horrible accident. No one moved.

"You loved me, too," Emma moaned. "I know you did. You must have. The things you said. All the special things you did because I liked them. The yellow roses you sent because you knew they were my favorites, and the tea from Ceylon you gave me because I once said I liked it. You did love me. You did."

Viola looked into her husband's face. He was staring down at the woman sprawled at his feet, hands behind his back, tight-lipped and silent. His face was white, his body utterly still. His countenance was blank, with no emotion in it, no affection, no compassion, nothing.

"What did I do to drive you away?" Emma lifted her face, looking at him in bewilderment, tears streaking her cheeks. "What did I do wrong?"

John made a wordless sound, and reached out a hand toward the bent head in front of him as if in pity, then changed his mind and pressed his fist to his mouth.

"I wrote you," she went on, heedless of all the other people watching, "sheets and sheets. And your secretary sent them back to me with a letter from him to never write you again." She let out a faint, bitter wail, so like a wounded animal that Viola was startled. The woman's body slumped forward, red curls falling over her face. "Your secretary. After everything we had, what we once meant to each other, you couldn't even be bothered to write such a letter to me in your own hand?"

Viola stared down at the weeping woman on the stone steps. She pressed her fingers to her mouth, her heart aching with pity, and she could not bear it. She started forward, then stopped, knowing that as John's wife it would be cruel beyond belief for her to attempt to give comfort or assistance to this woman. She turned to Daphne and Grace.

Daphne caught her pleading glance. As if coming out of a daze, she moved, turning to touch Grace's shoulder. The two of them stepped forward in unison, descending the steps on either side of the wretched woman. Together, they made an attempt to lift her to her feet.

Emma's head snapped up, the bright red lights in her hair glinting like fire in the morning sun. She slapped away the hands that tried to assist her and jumped up on her own. She stumbled backward down the steps but stayed on her feet, staring at John. "I hate you!" she cried, hands balling into fists. "I loved you, and all my love was wasted. And for what? I'll show you the results of loving you."

Whirling around, she ran for her coach as if to depart. Flinging open the door, she reached inside and pulled a bundle from the coach. It was only when she turned around again that Viola could see what it was. It was a baby.

"Look at him!" Emma demanded, holding the child with its face toward John. "Look at your son. What do you think I wrote in all those letters I sent you? The letters you couldn't even be bothered to read. I told you that I was with child. And yes, he is yours, John. You shall pay the support for him, per the terms of our contract."

She gave the tiny baby a shake as if it were a lifeless doll, and that snapped Viola out of shock and into action. She walked down the steps and over to the woman. As gently as she could, she took the baby from her. Emma, green eyes glittering with tears of pain and devastation, barely noticed. Her gaze was fixed on John, demanding he do right by her.

The baby was crying. Viola cradled him in her arms, patting his bottom and making little soothing sounds. She turned to look at her husband again and found he was not looking at Emma. Instead, he was looking at her. His face might have been carved out of stone.

Viola felt cold suddenly, cold in the sultry August air, and she wondered how any man could be the cause of such a heartbreaking display, watch it play out before him, and say nothing to the miserable woman, not even a kind word. She stared back at her husband, waiting in expectation for him to do something.

A muscle worked in his jaw, his lips parted, but he did not speak. Instead, he turned on his heel and strode toward the house.

"I hate you, John!" Emma shouted after him. "I hate you, and I will hate you until the day I die!" She turned, grabbed a leather traveling case from the carriage and turned, throwing it at Viola's feet. Then, without retrieving the baby, she climbed up into her carriage, slammed the door, and thumped sharply on the roof with her fist. The footman jumped on the back of the carriage, and her driver pulled away. The carriage rolled out of the graveled drive and down the lane toward Falstone.

Daphne, Grace, Dylan, and Anthony all went into the house, but Viola did not follow them. Instead, she turned and walked in the opposite direction. She circled around the side of the house, spied a stone bench by kitchen gardens, and sat down. She held the tiny baby close and kissed his cheek, listening to his heart-wrenching sobs and feeling his tears on her face. "Hell," she said, and started crying herself.

John strode straight through the house and out the back. He walked through the gardens, past the stables and into the woods. He had no conscious direction, no conscious thought. Outrage smothered him, but it could not smother the sound of Emma Rawlins's wrenching sobs. They seemed to reverberate all around him—from the trees and the sky and the ground beneath his feet as he walked.

He tried to tell himself that his outrage was justified for Emma's gall in coming to his house and for the horrible scene to which she had subjected Viola. Outrage at fate for giving him a son who could never be the heir he needed. Outrage at the whole baffling idea that a mistress would fall in love. The tea, the roses, harmless things, so innocuous. How could any woman think that those things and cold, hard sterling for bedroom services amounted to love?

Viola's voice echoed through his mind, overtaking Emma's wretched sobbing.

Oh, John, do you not see? Women fall in love with you. It's in the way you smile and the things you say. The way you pay attention to what we tell you and how you remember what we like.

Ludicrous, he'd thought at the time. Viola being overly sentimental and kindhearted about a woman she should by all rights despise. Emma Rawlins in love with him was silly, absurd. Yet, only moments ago, Emma Rawlins had debased herself at his feet.

Not so silly after all.

He hadn't known, he told himself. He'd never dreamt the woman had such passionate feelings for him. And a baby with her had never entered his head. Why should it have? He had used the proper protections. Could he be sure the child was his? What business did a mistress have falling in love with a man anyway?

Even as he heard his own attempts at self-defense and justification, they nauseated him. Loathing followed on nausea's heels, loathing for himself and his thoughtless, callous behavior.

That was really the cause of his anger. Not poor Emma, who had been pregnant and hiding from the shame of it in France, writing him all those letters, no doubt terribly frightened at what would happen to her if he continued to ignore her. Nor was he angry at fate. Whether it was fornication or lovemaking, whether it was with or without the protection of French letters, children were the eventual, inevitable result, as hard as that was for a man to remember when a woman was in his arms and his wits were slipping. No, all his outrage was directed at himself.

John stopped walking and leaned his back against a tree. Nothing has changed, he realized with despair. After all that he had done these past nine years to become a responsible man, to do his duty by his estates and his family name, to be a good caretaker of his wife's income and his own, yet in his private life, he was still as careless and thoughtless of the feelings of others as he had been as a youth. And as heedless of the consequences of his actions.

He sank down to the ground and put his head in his hands, Emma's pathetic wail of sorrow ringing in his ears. Her emotional display might have been pitiful, but it was he who deserved the blame for it. He and he alone.

No, mistresses were not supposed to fall in love, but it was clear that sometimes they did. Viola had tried to tell him, had tried to explain, had tried to make him understand. He had refused to listen, refused to believe it. But he was now faced with the undeniable truth and the wretched results. He was now face-to-face with something he'd been running from his whole life: the weaknesses in his own character.

Viola had married him because she had loved him, she had trusted him, and he had lied to her. It had seemed harmless enough at the time, even kind. He hadn't realized just what a deep and lasting wound he would inflict with something he'd thought so innocuous.

Do you love me? she'd asked him, her beautiful hazel eyes wide, so hopeful, so painfully vulnerable.

Of course I do, he'd answered, lightly, laughing, giving her a kiss and a careless smile and the answer she wanted because it had been the easy thing to do. The convenient thing. The only thing that would get him what he needed. Had his father been in his place, his father would have lied just as he had done. Without blinking an eye.

For the first time, John understood what he was. A heartbreaker. He'd held Viola's heart in his hands nine years ago, and with thoughtless disregard, he had broken it. He hadn't known what he'd been toying with.

Peggy Darwin had loved him, too. She'd said it once, laughing, with a pain in her eyes when he hadn't said it back. Yes, she'd been married, but to a man who did not love her. She'd been starved for affection, and he'd willingly provided it. And he had ended it without a second thought.

Four years had passed since then, but that day in the draper's shop a few months back, Peggy had still looked at him with a hint of what had been in her eyes when she'd said she loved him, a hint of what was in Emma's face today, a hint of what Viola had felt for him when she had married him.

Viola. That hurt most of all. No bandages for her wounds, no way to mend her heart or laugh it all away. She would hate him now as much as she ever had, loathing him as much as he loathed himself. How could she not?

John rubbed his hands over his face. He couldn't bear to think about Viola right now. One thing at a time. He had a baby son, and he had to figure out what to do about that first.

There'd be no walking away. He knew that

much. He'd told Viola that: no more walking away. He'd meant it about her and their marriage, but he knew it applied to every single thing in his life.

John stood up and went back toward the house, making for the stables. He had a groom saddle his horse, and he rode to Falstone.

Her tears were dry by the time Anthony found her in the garden. He sat down beside her on the stone bench. He studied her and the baby in her arms for a long moment, then said, "I could kill him, but somehow, I don't think you want me to do that, do you?"

"No." Viola smiled a little and looked at him. "But thank you for offering. Very noble and brotherly of you."

"If it's any comfort to you, he did break with the Rawlins woman before the season even began. I know that much."

"I know it, too." She paused. "I love him, you know. I have always loved him. Even when I hated him."

Anthony put an arm around her shoulders. "Would you like me to take you away from here?"

Viola had been contemplating that very thing for over an hour. She thought of her husband, the charming man who could make everyday life such a delight, and she tried to reconcile that man with the one who had stood stone-faced a few moments ago while a heartbroken woman lay sobbing at his feet. With sudden clarity, she understood what it meant when her husband bore that hard, implacable expression. It was the face of a man in agony who wanted to make everything right and did not know how.

Viola stood up. "No, Anthony," she answered her brother's question, "I am not going anywhere. What I would like is for everyone to go home. Hammond and I need to work this out ourselves."

He rose to his feet. "Are you sure?"

Viola looked down at the baby in her arms. This was her husband's son. His affair with Emma Rawlins was in the past, ended before he had ever come back to her, and she was not going to condemn him for things in the past. The past could never be undone, and it was the future that mattered.

She knew her husband well enough to know that he would do right by his son now that he knew about him. By the fact that Emma had left the child behind, it was clear the woman did not want it. The baby was staying right here, Viola decided, and so was she.

That meant she was a mother now. She had things to do. The nursery had to be cleaned. A nanny and a wet nurse would have to be hired. Viola held the baby tight, kissed him, and made him a silent promise. The woman who had borne him might not want him, but she did. And she was going to love him and be the best mother to him that she could be.

She looked up at her brother. "I'm sure," she said quietly.

Chapter 20

Emma was staying at the Black Swan. John presented his card to the innkeeper's wife and waited in the parlor while she took it up to Emma's room. Ten minutes later Emma came down. Inside the parlor of the inn, she shut the door and leaned back against it.

"The baby is yours," she said at once. "Are you going to deny it?"

Her face was pale, still blotchy with tears. Her resentment was palpable, her pain obvious, her love for him undeniable.

"No," he answered. "I believe you." He looked down at his hat in his hands, drew a deep breath and looked at her again. "I'm sorry, Emma," he said simply. "I am so sorry."

She moved across the room and sat down on the settee. He sat beside her. Head bent, she stared at her hands. "Do you think saying you are sorry is going to make everything all right?"

"No." He set his hat aside. "But I have been told of late that although I talk a lot of nonsense, I am not a man who is good at talking about things that matter. An apology matters, I think. I owe you that, and so much more."

He saw a tear fall on her hand.

No walking away.

He pulled out a handkerchief and handed it to her. "I did not know about the baby."

"If you had read any of my letters, you would have known."

"I read the first few. Why did you not tell me straight away?"

She sniffed, dabbed the linen to her eyes. Without looking at him, she mumbled, "At first, I didn't want to believe it myself. I kept ignoring it, hoping it wasn't true. Weak of me not to face the truth."

"I understand." Indeed, he did.

"By the time I saw you at Kettering's ball, I knew I had to face up to things, and I wanted so badly to talk with you, to get you alone to tell you, but you were with your wife."

The last word was said with venom, which he chose to ignore. He supposed it was understandable from her point of view. "Go on," he said.

"I came to your house in Bloomsbury Square, but you were not at home. At least, your butler told me so."

In that, at least, he was blameless. "If you came

to see me, Emma, I knew nothing of it. I must truly not have been home at the time."

She twisted the handkerchief in her hands. "By then I was starting to show, and I knew I had to leave town. I couldn't bear the gossip, and I took what money I had left from your settlement and went to France. I have a cousin who lives there. I have been living with her and writing to you from Calais."

"Why did you not send a second to tell me?"

"Who would I send?" She looked at him, green eyes wide and helpless. "Except for my one cousin, who is a widow like myself, my family disowned me long ago. It was because I married Rawlins. Such a scoundrel he was, and he left me nothing when he died."

She fell silent, crying quietly into his handkerchief.

That was how women became mistresses. Desperation. God, he knew all about that. He also knew women always loved a scoundrel. It was one of the most baffling things about their sex, but it was an irrefutable fact. He was living proof.

He'd never asked her one thing about her life before he'd met her, not about her circumstances, her finances, nor anything else. His concerns had been wholly selfish ones, and the shame of the man he had been would haunt him for the rest of his days. His cross to bear, and one he heartily deserved, but he would never be that man again.

No going back.

"What is my son's name, Emma?"

"James."

His father's Christian name. Now that was an irony. "What do you want to do about the baby?" he asked.

"I can't keep him, John," she said, her voice rising with her despair. "I can't. He is a bastard. People will talk about it, say things about me and about him. Horrid things. I couldn't bear it. I'm not very good at being a mistress, I'm afraid."

"You're not hard enough for it, Em," he said gently. "I should have seen that. What are you going to do?"

"I am going to America. I intend to make a new life, and I can't take the baby with me. The post coach goes in a few hours, and I must be on it. The next ship for New York sails out of Liverpool in two days, and I have passage." She sniffed. "Terribly selfish of me."

"No, it's not. It's perfectly understandable." He took a deep breath, chose his words with care. "If you cannot keep him, then I should like to. Keep him and raise him."

"What?" She looked at him askance. "You want to raise him in your own house? A bastard son?"

"Yes."

Emma's eyes welled up with tears again, and she turned her face away, pressing his balled-up handkerchief to her nose. She didn't say it, but he knew she was wishing that he wasn't married to someone else, that they could raise the baby—their son—together.

After a moment, she spoke. "What . . . what do we have to do? Are there papers to sign, or something? I do not have much time."

"My attorney is just down the High Street. Let's go see him and have it done right now. You can get on that ship and go make that new life."

"Yes, yes," she agreed eagerly, her relief obvious. "Let's go now."

An hour later, papers were in his pocket that made James his son. Emma willingly gave up all rights and claims to the boy and agreed to a cash settlement in exchange. His attorney raised an eyebrow at the amount of the settlement, but John knew it would never be enough. As they were standing by the post coach, he said, "Emma?"

She paused in the act of stepping into the vehicle and turned to look at him.

"If you ever need anything, money or credit, anything of that kind, write to me." He started to smile, then stopped. "I'll read it, I swear."

She began to weep again and turned away. She stepped in the post coach and looked at him through the window. "Don't tell him about me, John. Not ever."

"Good-bye, Em."

John watched the coach pull away, and he knew

that despite Emma's wishes, he was one day going to tell James about his mother. The boy would ask, and he deserved to know that his mother had been a sweet woman whose only mistake had been falling in love with the wrong man.

He turned and started back to the Black Swan to get his horse. When he reached the inn, he walked toward the stables, then stopped, suddenly rooted to the sidewalk.

A richly appointed carriage stood before the doors of the Wild Boar, a rival inn across the street from the Black Swan. The carriage bore the unmistakable insignia of the Duke of Tremore, and it was loaded with trunks and traveling cases.

Viola was leaving him. Her brother was taking her away. John's heart rejected it utterly, his mind went blank, and his body moved, straight toward the doors of the Wild Boar.

They were having a midday meal at the inn before starting home, and Viola had come with them. Dylan and Anthony had gone to the barkeep to each get a tankard of ale and discuss the state of the roads for travel, and the three women were seated at one of the tables in the crowded dining room.

"How does one go about finding a wet nurse?" she asked the other two women. "I haven't any idea."

"See the local doctor," Daphne answered. "He would know."

"Excellent idea. After we're finished here, I will call on Dr. Morrison."

"Are you certain you wish to take this on, Viola?" Grace asked. "There will be talk. Mean and vicious talk. Taking on a child that is not your own, an illegitimate child, is very difficult."

"You managed it," Viola pointed out, referring to Dylan's eight-year-old daughter, Isabel, whose mother had been a courtesan.

"I know, but Isabel was older, and Dylan wasn't married to me at that time," she answered. "And Dylan isn't a peer. Your situation is a bit different. No other lord's wife would keep her husband's illegitimate child in her own house and raise it. And what if John doesn't want to do it?"

"John will want to keep the baby." She was absolutely sure of that. She didn't know why. Perhaps it was because she remembered the look on his face when he'd been holding baby Nicholas.

Dylan and Anthony joined them just then and sat down, placing their tankards on the table.

"I agree with Viola," Dylan said, entering the conversation as he sat down beside his wife. "Hammond will keep it. He's mad on babies at present."

Anthony made a sound of clear skepticism. "How good a father will he be, is my question."

"There is only one important question involved in any of this," Daphne said. "Viola, does Hammond love you?"

Anthony groaned. "Trust a woman to alway bring love into any discussion."

"Does he?" Daphne repeated, ignoring tha comment.

Viola looked at her sister-in-law with a wobbl smile. "I honestly don't know."

At that moment the door of the Wild Boa opened and the subject of their conversatior walked in. He took one look around and strod straight toward them.

He yanked off his hat and halted at their table facing his wife, ignoring everyone else. He took deep breath, looked into her eyes, and said on word. "No."

"What?" Viola blinked, staring at him. "No what? Are you talking about the baby?"

"No, you're not leaving me. I won't let you."

Viola's lips parted in astonishment as his word slowly sank in. He thought she was leaving him "John—" she began.

"No arguments about this, Viola." He gestured around the table with his hat. "They can all g home, but you're not going anywhere."

She tried again. "I—"

"And we're keeping James."

"What?"

"The baby. We're keeping him, and we'll rais him. You and I. Together. See, I've been thinkin; things over and what to do about it all, and it ha:

to be that way. I know I don't have any right to ask it of you, and it's going to be hard, but we have to do it. He's my responsibility, and I have to take care of him. You know I do. It's only right."

"Yes, of course, but—"

"And Emma's going to America. She doesn't want him, and I do. And you have to help me raise him. He needs a mother, so you can't leave me. You can't." His jaw set. "No running away, Viola. Not for either of us. That's been the problem all along, you know. We've both been running away. Mostly me, I admit, but that's not going to happen anymore. I told you that, remember? I promised I wasn't going to walk away from you, and I'm not. Not ever again. And I'm not letting you walk away, either."

She tried one more time. "John, I am—"

"Damn it, I'm trying to talk to you. Woman, you're the one who always wants me to talk about things. Will you stop interrupting me so I can do so?"

She gave it up.

"God, Viola, sometimes, you drive me insane, you really do. Wanting to talk, and then when I try . . . " He paused, with a sound of thorough exasperation with her. "No one gets under my skin like you. And I don't know why."

Viola fought to keep a smile off her face. A

smile would ruin everything, and this was just getting good.

"I don't know what it is, but no one else can give me one look and shred me to ribbons. No one else can make the heavens open when she smiles at me. No one but you, Viola. I've had a lot of women in my life, God knows, but I've only had one who can make me remember that I have a heart inside my chest instead of an empty hole. And that woman is you."

Any thought of smiling vanished in the wake of that little speech. He was in complete earnest. Nothing clever or amusing about it. It was the most beautiful thing she'd ever heard.

John paused long enough to suck in a breath, then said, "I love that you have eyes like mud and hair like sunlight, and I thank God every day for blackberry jam. I love that mole at the corner of your mouth, and I love the way you laugh. I love fighting with you because I love making up with you. When I made up that poem that day in the boat, I meant every word of it. Every word, Viola. No face so fair and none so dear. And I don't want any other. Ever. For all the precious moments of my life, you're the only one."

He scowled at her, looking handsome and fierce, and so resentful. "Nobody *ever* gets to hear my poetry. Nobody but you. And I may be the stupidest man on God's earth—"

"Hear, hear," muttered Anthony.

John ignored that. "And it may have taken me nine years to figure things out, but now I know what love is. I know because you taught me. I love you. Don't deserve you. Never did, but I love you. I love you more than my life."

He fell silent.

Viola waited a moment, but he did not speak again. She gave a little cough. "Are you finished?" she asked.

He glanced around, and she saw it suddenly dawn on him that the dining room of the inn was filled with people, and that all of them were staring at him. He lifted his chin a notch and straightened his cravat. "Yes."

He turned and strode away, but stopped at the door to look back at her. "I'll be at Hammond Park," he told her, all that proud defiance in his face. "*Our* home. Waiting for *my* wife to come back there where she belongs!"

With that, he opened the door and walked out, slamming it behind him.

The room was as silent as a Quaker meeting. It was Dylan who spoke first. "Well," he said, leaning back in his chair, "I don't believe we need have any further debate on the subject. It's clear your husband is madly in love with you, Viola, because he just made a complete ass of himself."

The nursery was one of the few places at Hammond Park that John never went to. That afternoon, he did. When he entered, one of his maids, Hill, was there, seated in a chair beside a wooden cradle. His cradle once upon a time, he fancied. The summer sun washed over the room, bathing the ivory walls in yellow light.

Hill rose to her feet when he came in and bobbed a curtsy. He walked to her side and looked into the cradle. The baby was asleep in his white nightshirt, a plain one, and there was a linen cap on his head. Dark hair stuck out from beneath it, wispy strands of it over closed eyes with absurdly long dark lashes.

John stared at the infant for a moment, reached down and touched his finger tentatively to the baby's hand, then pulled back. "He's so small."

"He'll grow, my lord." Hill looked at him and smiled. "He's only a month old now, I'd say. Plenty of growing yet to do."

The baby's eyes opened at the sound of their voices. Brown eyes stared up at him. Brandy brown, like his own.

"Hullo, James," he said, and looked at the maid. "I want to hold him, but he seems so fragile."

"No baby's that fragile," she said, smiling with all the indulgence of a woman for male absurdities. "A baby's always ready to be held. It's just with a baby this young, you have to be sure to support his neck."

He pulled off his coat and threw it aside. "Show me."

He watched as the girl lifted the baby out of the crib, noting the position of her hands, one under James's bottom and one securely behind his head. She placed the baby in the crook of his arm, and John sank into the chair beside the crib.

"Am I doing this right?"

"You might have been holding babies all your life, my lord," Hill said, reminding him of that night at Tremore House when Beckham had made a similar comment. He hoped they were right, because he was going to be the best damn father in all England. Right now, however, he felt he was in way over his head.

James closed his eyes and drifted off to sleep again with a little sigh.

Hill sighed, too. "Right sweet that is, if you don't mind my saying so, my lord."

He didn't mind.

She gave a little cough. "If you please, sir, I need to be getting some fresh laundry for him. He'll need changing any time now. Do you want to give him back, and I'll take him with me?"

He shook his head, gazing at his son. "Not a bit of it. I'm not giving him over. Go on to the laundry, Hill. I'll stay here and watch him until you get back."

"Oh, no, sir!" She sounded horrified. "I couldn't leave you. What if he started to cry and fuss? Men hate that."

"I won't hate it." He looked up. "Hill, get that worried frown off your pretty face and go."

He winked at her and smiled, and that made her laugh. He was still a shameless flirt. Probably always would be. Ah, well.

The girl bobbed a curtsy, then left the room, and he was alone with his son.

He touched the baby's cheek. It was the softest thing he'd ever felt in his life. "We'll buy you an estate," he said, thinking out loud. "And railway stocks."

James stirred, making a distressed sound in his sleep.

"What's wrong with railway stocks?" John murmured. "Railways are the way of the future. You watch and see if I'm not right. With an estate and good investments, you'll be a rich man by the time you're out of Cambridge."

His son hit him in the chest with one tiny fist, but did not wake up.

"Cambridge," he repeated for emphasis. "Not Oxford."

Brown eyes blinked open at the firmness of his voice, then closed again. The small mouth opened for a huge, uninterested yawn.

John laughed softly. "Bored by school already, my son? You won't know what boredom is until they throw Latin at you." He smoothed the fine brown hair across the baby's forehead at the eyelet edge of the cap. "They'll be cruel, James. No getting around it. They'll call you a bastard, and I'm sorry about that. But I'll teach you to keep your head up and act like you don't give a damn, because that's what a man has to do, you see."

James stirred again, turning his face to the side, his nose brushing the ruffles of John's shirtfront. He grasped a handful of the ruffles, still asleep.

John looked down, staring at the tiny, perfect fingernails of his son, and something hot and fierce unfolded inside him. A powerful feeling of wonder and awe and love that filled the last crevices of the hole in his soul.

"I'll take care of you," he said in a savage whisper. "Don't worry about a thing. I'll see that you have an income of your own, so you won't ever feel desperate or scared. And I'll be right there to see that you don't squander it on stupid things. No getting into debt. No deep stakes gambling. And about the women . . ."

He considered that for a moment, then sighed, giving in to the inevitable. "I know I'm going to lose if I even try to reason with you on that one." Leaning closer, he pressed a kiss to his son's brow and murmured, "We won't tell Viola. She might get upset about that."

If she comes home.

The thought whispered in his mind like a shiver in a cold room. If Viola didn't come home, what would he do?

That hideous feeling of helplessness returned,

the same thing he'd felt looking at her in the Wild Boar. He could tell she hadn't been all that impressed by his little speech. He couldn't even remember what he said, but it hadn't been witty, and it hadn't been clever, and it sure as hell hadn't been poetic. And there she'd sat, staring at him in complete astonishment, as if he was off his chump for even daring to follow her and talk about love after what had happened.

John knew there was nothing he could do to make her come home. Nothing he could say to undo the past or right his wrongs. Nothing. She wouldn't come back to him. After all, he was the one who had always done the walking away. No surprise if she turned the tables. He deserved it.

But desperate men did desperate things. He knew that better than anybody. Being a desperate man, he prayed. "Come home, Viola," he said, holding his son and praying hard. "Just come home."

Viola pressed her fist to her mouth, listening. Oh, how she loved this man. Always had. Always would.

She moved into the doorway and saw him sitting by the cradle. When she looked at him with the baby in his arms, her heart began to ache with a joy so sweet, she could hardly breathe. All her life she had dreamed romantic dreams of having the honest love of one good man. It wasn't a dream anymore. It was life. And it wasn't the life she'd imagined at all. It wasn't easy, and it wasn't bliss, and it may have been paid for with tears and pain, and every day was a lesson in learning to just get along. But it was real and it was precious and it was hers. From now on she was hanging onto that life and this man with everything she had.

She made a sound from the doorway, soft enough not to wake the baby, and he looked up. When he saw her, he didn't smile. He didn't move. He was as still as an image in a painting by Reynolds, with the sun washing over him and the child in his arms. She walked into the room. "I came to make up," she said.

"You did?"

She nodded. "It was that speech," she said, deciding not to tell him she'd never intended to leave. She'd tell him someday. Maybe. Or maybe not. "It was the most incoherent, rambling, beautiful thing I've ever heard." She knelt by the chair. She put her hand on his knee. "I love you, too, by the way."

He gave a short, disbelieving laugh. "I can't think why."

Viola looked at her husband. Reaching up, she brushed back the unruly hair at his temple and smiled. "Because you keep tricking me." She began to laugh. "You silver-tongued devil."

Epilogue

〰〰

"**I** want to go up." John turned at the end of the long gallery at Hammond Park, chewing on his thumbnail as he came back toward the stairs. "Deuce take it, why can't I go up?"

Anthony poured a glass of port and brought it to him. "Husbands are not allowed," he said for perhaps the twentieth time.

"Stupid," John muttered, "since we're the cause of it all." He raked a hand through his hair. He hated this waiting, this helplessness. He was so scared, he thought he was going to throw up.

His brother-in-law held out the glass. "Have another drink."

"I don't want another drink. How can you be so damned calm about this?"

Anthony sighed and set the port on the table beneath a painting of the tenth Viscount Hammond, John's grandfather. "I know what you're feeling, believe me. And I'm not calm. I'm just doing better at hiding it than you are."

A cry floated to them from the nearby stairs, a cry of intense pain, smothered almost at once by the slam of a door. That cry tore his guts apart. "That's it," he said, and started for the stairs. "I'm going up."

Anthony hauled him back. "You can't."

"Christ," John muttered, and started pacing again. "It's been half the night already. How long does this take?"

"Forever."

Footsteps sounded over their heads, but another hour went by, and no one came. John's fear deepened with each turn he took down the gallery, and he nearly came apart when he heard another cry of pain from his wife echoing down the stairs.

"I'm going up. She needs me." Anthony made a grab for him, but he evaded it and started up the stairs. On the landing, he encountered Daphne coming down.

Nothing in John's life had ever felt like this moment. He stopped. "Viola?"

"She is well," Daphne assured him. "I came down to tell you that because I thought you might be worried."

"Worried?" That was so patently tame a description of how he felt that he almost laughed at her.

She put a hand on his arm. "Come," she said, and started to guide him back down, but he resisted. "John," she said with quiet firmness, "you cannot help. You will only get in the way. Come."

He reluctantly allowed himself to be pulled back down the stairs.

"This sort of thing takes a long time," Daphne told him. "I was in labor for two days."

"God!" Two days of this and he'd go mad.

Daphne patted his back in a soothing motion. "She's doing well, truly."

They returned to the gallery. "Everything is all right," Daphne told Anthony, and went back upstairs.

It was another hour, another eternity, before Daphne came back down again. He was at the far end of the gallery when she called his name. "John?"

He came at a run and was halfway to her before she spoke again. "Now you can go up."

"Is she all right?" he cried, racing past his sister-in-law.

"Yes," she answered, following him as he started up the stairs.

He had to see that for himself. He took the stairs two at a time and entered the bedchamber, racing right past Dr. Morrison. John took one look at his wife, at her pale face and disheveled hair, and he skidded to a halt just inside the door, his heart in his throat.

She looked so tired.

"Viola." He walked over to the side of the bed, and as he did so, he saw the baby in her arms, a red-faced, wailing bit of a thing with an absurdly tiny nose.

"Viola," he said again, because he couldn't think of anything to say but her name. He sank to his knees next to the bed.

Her hand reached out, touched his hair. "What happened to that silver-tongued devil I married?" she murmured with a tired, throaty chuckle.

He shook his head violently, seized her hand in both of his and kissed it. What the hell was a man supposed to say at a time like this? There weren't any words.

"John," she said as he half rose and kissed her cheek, her hair. "I'm all right. The baby's all right."

"Sure?"

She nodded and bit her lip, looking at him. Then she spoke. "We have a girl."

"A girl?" Stunned, he sank back to his knees and looked at the baby again. He stared, watching her as her fierce, angry wails died away into hiccoughs and she nestled into the vee of Viola's open nightgown, seeking her breast. She's hungry, he thought.

A girl.

He leaned closer, studying the baby in the dim lamplight, and it was then that he saw the tiny mole at the corner of her mouth. Joy welled up in his chest like a wave. He began to laugh. A girl.

"She's gorgeous!" he cried. "By God, she is. She looks just like her mother!"

"Oh, stop," Viola said, almost laughing.

"She does." He turned to Daphne, who was standing by the door with the doctor. "Doesn't she?"

Daphne smiled. "I believe you are right."

"Of course I am." He turned back to his wife. "Look," he said, touching the baby's head, smoothing the damp, fine, barely visible blond fuzz that passed for hair. "She's got your hair. And that little mole and, by heaven, she's got that pretty, pretty mouth." He laughed again. "Her eyes are the color of pond mud, I'll wager a thousand pounds on it."

This time Viola did laugh. "We won't know for a while. All babies are born with blue eyes. We'll have to wait and see."

John didn't need to wait. He looked at his beautiful baby girl and he looked at his beautiful wife. Yes, he thought, eyes like pond mud, hair like golden sunlight, and a heart big enough to love even him. And he had a strong, healthy son sleeping upstairs in the nursery. Damn, how did an irresponsible, reckless scapegrace like him ever get so lucky?

Don't miss the heat in these sizzling new August releases from Avon Romance!

Love According to Lily by Julianne MacLean

An Avon Romantic Treasure

Lady Lily Langdon is ready to take matters of passion into her own hands. With lessons in flirtation from her American sister-in-law, Duchess Sophia, Lily means to seduce the object of her affection: the Earl of Whitby, a man who up to now has only seen Lily as a troublesome girl. He'll soon find that though she is still troublesome, she is no longer just a girl . . .

How to Marry a Millionaire Vampire by Kerrelyn Sparks

An Avon Contemporary Romance

Welcome to the dangerous—and hilarious—world of modern day vampires. There are vampire cable channels, a celebrity magazine called Live! With the Undead, and just like the living, vampires have dental emergencies. That's how dentist Shanna Whelan, a human female, meets the smolderingly undead Roman Draganesti, and finds her life turning absolutely, well, batty . . .

Daring the Duke by Anne Mallory

An Avon Romance

She once lived a secret life. He, a reluctant duke, once pursued that secret to the ends of the earth. Could he know her identity—and if he does can she trust the aid he offers? And what will happen to their growing passion when he discovers her final secret—the one that proves how powerfully they are connected?

Courting Claudia by Robyn DeHart

An Avon Romance

After a lifetime of chafing under her father's high expectations, Claudia Prattley is determined to please him by marrying the man of his choosing, but a dashing rogue is bent on foiling her plans. That rogue is Derrick Middleton, and he's so drawn to Claudia's enchanting combination of passion and trust that he knows he must take a chance on winning her love.

Avon Romantic Treasures